For Chuck Cahoy, my Lobster of Eternity

# PART I
## *Not New York*

# 1

THE BILLINGS ZOO has no animals.

Fewer than twenty-four hours ago, I was standing in Gray's Papaya on Seventy-Second Street and Amsterdam Avenue in New York City, watching passersby ignore someone who was having what appeared to be an epileptic seizure while eating a chili dog. Taxicabs whirred by, mere mustard stains on the frankfurter that is the Upper West Side. Hordes of humans hustling in every direction, screaming, shouting, howling.

Now, I am in a place so quiet that I can still hear the noises of Manhattan in the back of my skull, like they are working their way out, slowly. And I am at a zoo where I may actually be the wildest life.

I'm here because after we landed and got our rental car for the summer, my mother suggested she take me for "a treat." We cruised past multiple Arby's and shops that sell discount mattresses and a Wonder Bread thrift store, whatever that is. She dropped me here, at the zoo, and told me she'd pick me up in a couple hours, after she got us settled in at my dad's house. She said that the zoo might be a place to "locate and center myself" before seeing him for the first time in fourteen years.

My mom, a therapist slash school counselor, "hears" that I feel like she's ripped me out of my normal summer, but "what she wants to say to me" is that I need to stop moping. And what better place to drop off a mopey seventeen-year-old boy in a strange new city than at the zoo? Had she just asked me where I wanted to go, I would have been like, *I don't know, a coffee shop. A movie theater.* Any place a guy in his summer before senior year might want to hang. But whatever. My mom is down with the kids and how they all just want to stare at monkeys all day.

I do, in fact, feel a little ripped out of my normal summer — such as it is. But it's possible that I'm milking it a bit. I mean, I was going to be working at a Pinkberry on the Upper West Side, which is the best frozen yogurt place in the city, tied with every other frozen yogurt place in the city, as they are all exactly the same. I won't actually miss that. So "ripped" may be a little strong.

The zoo is apparently called ZooMontana, as it is the greatest of all the Montana zoos. At the gate, I buy a ticket from an old, tired-looking bald man and walk in. I wind through the trees along roped-off gravel trails. There are some nice trees. But what becomes painfully apparent is that there are basically no animals.

Perhaps because there are no animals, there are also no people at the zoo. Well, a few people. The bald ticket taker. And I come across a wedding procession at one point, with an overly chipper, pregnant bride in an off-white gown, and a goateed dude in a polyester suit by her side, his greasy mullet glistening in the sun.

Matrimony at a zoo with no animals. Wedding bliss fail.

I finally do find one lonely, depressed Siberian tiger. Here he is in the Siberia of America, lazing on the ground, staring into space, a look of what that guy Kierkegaard would call existential despair in his eyes. (Thanks, philosophy class!) I can barely blame him. I am that tiger. Relocated against my will for the summer to the northern tundra of my country, with nothing to do, nothing to look at, nothing but nothing.

So after I decide that sitting and staring at a depressed tiger isn't all it's cracked up to be, I walk back toward the entrance to the gift shop (plastic eagle sculptures and red-tailed squirrel magnets) to fritter away my final ninety-five minutes here (but who's counting).

A ridiculously beautiful girl is organizing the greeting card display. In terms of attractiveness, she is in the 99.9th percentile of zoo employees. Her skin is black, almost purple black, and her jeans are dark blue and super tight. Her voluminous hair covers her ears almost entirely. She has sinewy arm muscles like the gymnastics girls back at my high school in the Bronx, and she wears a turquoise tank top that shows off her curves just right. Her face is wow. Soft, clear skin, uberhigh cheekbones that seem to pull her cheeks upward like a slingshot.

I can't take my eyes off her. I do not believe in God, but in this instance, I wonder if there's some deity to thank for the miracle of a dazzling girl in an otherwise deserted zoo. And I decide it's very important to get a closer look at the greeting cards.

As I get within about five feet of her, she turns slightly toward me. I instinctively lower my head and turn away, as if I'm now perusing the almost empty shelf of stuffed animals, which consists of two pink frogs. I want so much to be the kind of guy who knows what to say in this situation. Unfortunately, I'm about 3,000 percent better in my brain than out of it. I've tried it before, verbalizing my thoughts to other people. It rarely works well.

She faces me completely now.

"Under what circumstance would you buy a greeting card in which a bear is dancing through a field of sunflowers?" she asks.

She's taken a half step toward me, and I am now close enough to smell a light trace of her sweat. I try to pretend this has no effect on me. She shows me the card. On it, a cartoon bear pirouettes through a pretty field. Somehow, I manage to say actual words.

"Are you trying to figure out what section to put it in?" I ask.

Her eyebrows are arched like boomerangs in a way that suggests mischief. "Yep."

"Is there a sympathy section?"

She raises her left eyebrow even higher. "Why?"

"I would put it there. Maybe someone whose bear just got shot might get some comfort from imagining the bear dancing through a field of flowers."

She purses her lips and nods. "I guess I'll have to make a sympathy section."

"Glad I could help," I say, unable to take my eyes off her. And the crazy thing is, she's still looking at me too. Is Billings like a magical parallel universe where I am a guy to whom hot girls voluntarily speak? She is waiting for me to say something, and I worry that I might say all the wrong things, and then I think, *Screw it, why worry about saying the wrong thing when you surely will anyway? Just do it.* So I do.

"So what is there to see here?" I ask.

She puts the card back. In the birthday section, I notice. "What do you want to see?"

I gulp. "Well, animals, for starters. No offense, but this is not quite the Bronx Zoo."

She looks me over. Up, down, up. "Not from around here," she says. "Lucky."

I smile, relieved she isn't a huge Billings fan. "Just off the plane like two hours ago."

"And you came to the zoo . . ."

"My mom . . ." I say, like it's obvious what comes next. Then I realize that's not a sentence that works without finishing the thought. "I'm one of those few, fortunate, proud New Yorkers who gets to spend the summer in Billings."

"Well, today's your lucky day. Want a tour?"

"You do tours?"

Her smile starts with her eyes. They open a bit wider, and then her face animates, as if her eyes are part of a pulley system that controls her upper lips, which rise, allowing me to see her perfect, glistening teeth. "Do I do tours? Five bucks will get you the best darn tootin'-est zoo tour you ever done dreamed of," she says in a cowboy accent.

I grab my wallet, pull out a five, and hand it to her. "Did you just say 'tootin'-est'?"

She slowly nods. "I sher did," she says, her voice authoritative. She stuffs the five in her pocket and leads me outside. The sun is out and it's warm, like bread just out of the oven at a bakery, and the trees are every shade of green possible. In my first walk, I hadn't actually looked at a lot of the nature stuff. Just like how I was still hearing the noises of New York City, I think the sights were still inside my eyes too. Where I live, life is mostly concrete and brick. We have a park — two, actually, near our apartment — but even when you're so deep in one of those parks that you can't see out, it's hard to forget that the world is skyscrapers and boutiques, bodegas and subway tracks. In a way, those things feel more real to me than this scenery.

We take a footbridge over a creek, and while we walk, she tells me the zoo's history. Apparently it was built in 1922 as a refuge for wildlife dislocated by the 1921 caldera eruption in Washington State. Volunteers from all over the West hauled as many animals as they could to Billings.

"Wow," I say. I've heard about calderas, which are like extreme volcanos, but I hadn't realized there had actually been one in the U.S.

"If it seems empty, you have to understand," she says. "The zoo has a policy of not taking in any other animals. So these are all the descendants of those first arrivals all those years ago. It keeps the place pure."

At the red-tailed squirrel habitat, she explains that the squirrels used to live in the redwood forests of California. "They're amazing creatures. Did you know they only mate during a full moon?"

"Really?"

"That's right," she says.

We pass a sign that reads WOLF WOODS, and she puts her hands on the mesh enclosure.

"There are four wolves left. There were many more at one time, but one of the wolves was a psychopath."

I laugh, figuring she is making a joke. She doesn't laugh back. I catch sight of one of the wolves. He's white with steely eyes, and he's staring at me. I feel a shiver run through my veins.

"A psychopath?"

"Well, what would you call it? Wolves were showing up dead. Disemboweled. They couldn't figure out who had done it, so they brought in a wolf detective. She got right to solving the case. We only lost three more after that, and once she found the killer, they hung him."

I look out at the area. A wolf detective! I've never heard of that. And then I look back at her. "Wait. They hung a wolf?"

She sucks her lips in, rolls her eyes up, and stares at the sky. "Too much?"

"You made that all up, didn't you?" I ask.

She tilts her head. "I may have."

"Cool," I say.

"Is it?"

I think, *Yeah*. It's the kind of thing that the improv comedy group at my high school does. I joined this year, because of a girl, of course, and that didn't work out, of course. But I really like improv. I like coming up with stuff no one's ever come up with before. "It's totally cool," I say.

It feels like she is exploring my face with her eyes. "Interesting," she says.

I scratch my ear. "Do they know you make stuff up on your tours?"

"I have no idea."

"Do you even work here?"

"I do not."

I laugh. "Wow."

"You want your money back?" She takes the crumpled five out of her pocket.

I wave her off. "Nah. It was totally worth it. More than worth it. Why do you do that?"

She shrugs and stuffs the money back into her pocket. "Why does anyone do anything? Why do red-tailed squirrels only mate during a full moon?"

"They don't, do they?"

She shrugs again. "Beats the shit out of me."

I grin. "I like that. That's like something I would do."

"Well, you know," she says, demurely kicking up her back foot in a way that doesn't match her personality at all. I can tell it's meant to be funny, and it is.

"I'm Carson Smith," I say.

"Aisha," she says back. "Aisha Stinson."

"You made all that shit up? The wolf detective?"

"Most definitely. *Especially* the part about the wolf detective."

We start walking again. "So is that a detective who deals with wolf crimes, or a wolf who is a detective? And if it's the latter, is it exclusively focused on wolf crimes?"

Aisha seems to ponder this. "It can be all of the above."

# 2

AISHA KEEPS THE tour going, making up stories about all the different animals, which is challenging because we see almost none. I join in and tell her that the red panda (which we also do not see) is the actual daughter of the panda used as the model for the Panda Express logo. She tells me that the bighorn sheep got their name because they are the most well-hung of all the sheep, and I wonder how to get from a conversation about large sheep dicks to asking her if she wants to hang out sometime. Like not at the zoo, maybe.

When we reach the Siberian tiger's cage (he is in therapy and on two antidepressants, she explains), I ask her why such a beautiful tiger is all alone.

"His father kicked him out of the house for being gay," she says. "He did it in the name of the Jesus. The Jesus said, 'You straighten out, mister, and go mack on the lady tigers, or you'll be sleeping at the zoo.' "

"Ah yes. The Jesus," I say. "He's kind of a judgmental prick, isn't he?"

She laughs. "That's the one. Which is funny, 'cause those stories in that book his dad wrote make him sound maybe a little crazy at times, but not judgmental at all."

I haven't actually read the Bible, so I can't say much about it. "Yeah, I always thought he was kind of a hippie guy, what with the

Jesus sandals and the scraggly Jesus beard and the 'love your neighbors' thing."

" 'Round these parts," Aisha says in that bad cowboy accent, "Jesus kills them hippies."

I haven't had a conversation this long with another person in about forever. My mom and I, for instance, just took a five-hour plane ride, and we said maybe twenty words to each other. I love her and all, but she just has weird . . . ways of showing love and support, maybe. Which is why I've been dropped off at a zoo, by myself. Things don't surprise me anymore. I just go with it, because she pretty much lets me do whatever the hell I want.

So anyway, Mom and I don't do a lot of talking. Most of my conversations happen in my own mind at school too. I'm not a freak or anything, but I don't have a lot of friends with whom I can let my brain really hang out, pardon the disgusting image. Here at ZooMontana with Aisha, my brain is out, and so is hers, and I don't want it to end.

So then, of course, we both go quiet and walk in silence, while I try frantically to find something to keep it all going.

"There are, like, no animals in this zoo," I finally say.

"I know. Ain't it the worst?"

"We should free them. Free all the animals."

"Ha. Just to be real for a moment, we should definitely *not* do that. That's about the worst possible idea, because all the animals would wind up dead."

"Huh. Is that more misinformation?"

"No. That there is real information. Don't ever free animals from the zoo. It would get real, fast."

At the bald eagle habitat, I explain that I don't think it is really fair for ZooMontana to claim it "has" birds. I mean, unless it's an enclosed dome — which it does not appear to be — it can't very well claim ownership of anything that happens to fly above it. "ZooMontana is a home to birds in much the same way that the backyard of my dad's house is a bird sanctuary."

She grins. "I'm giving you my number," she says. "We need to do this again."

Score. "Well, maybe not this exactly."

"No. Exactly this," she says.

I feel like I've won the lottery. How do you just happen across an awesome girl on your first day in Billings? What are the odds? Is everyone here like Aisha? I've only seen a handful of people so far, but I doubt it. "I wanna meet your friends," I say, and then I feel a little embarrassed that I've been too forward.

"Me too," she says, rolling her eyes.

We walk on. I wonder if that's true. If, somehow, Aisha is friendless. It makes sense, in a way. I worry sometimes that our world actually values a lack of intelligence. Like we are considered normal if we spend our time thinking about what one of the Kardashians wears to a party, and we are considered strange if we wonder whether a bee's parents grieve if said bee dives into the Central Park Reservoir and never makes it back to the hive. One of these lines of thought makes me want to carve my eyes out, and I can assure you it has nothing to do with bees.

"So can you be trusted?" Aisha asks me out of the blue as we pass through a particularly densely wooded area.

"Why do I need to be trusted?" I say, and her shoulders rise slightly toward her ears. "I mean, yeah. Sure."

She looks me over, then clasps my hand and leads me off the path to the right. Her grip is strong, but her fingers are slightly clammy and cold. She walks me through a path of trees, and then, as she passes a particularly thick elm, she turns toward it and we stop. A red knapsack leans against a rolled-up blue sleeping bag at the foot of the tree. Both are hidden from view unless you venture down this particular row of trees.

I look at Aisha and she smiles and bites her lower lip. "I sometimes sleep here," she says.

"What?"

"Sometimes."

"Why?"

She looks into my eyes, and I look back, and in the slight crease of her forehead I see pain. Fear. It shocks me, and she sees me see it, and then a veil goes up. The whites of her eyes go cold.

"Never mind," she says. "I shouldn't have said anything. Forget I said it. Please."

"Tell me," I say, because now I'm worried. But she is already walking back toward the path. I'm thinking, *If I told her about my dad and why I'm here, would she tell me her thing?*

"My dad," I say, and she turns around and waits for me to say something else.

My head spins. I am not so good at serious talks.

"Is an alien," I say.

The joke floats up and around us like a bad smell. It's strange. It's not funny. And I can't take it back.

"Sorry, I'm weird. Tell me why you sleep here," I say.

She pauses, and for a moment I think perhaps my weirdness

was enough to get her to talk. Then she says, "Another time. Long story."

"I like long stories," I say.

"Did I tell you about the mainland sika deer?" she asks.

I want to press, but I am afraid if I do, I'll freak her out. "Tell me," I say as we start walking, and she proceeds to explain how these particular deer are known for never obeying the DEER CROSSING signs and just crossing roads wherever the hell they want to.

"Tragic," I say. "So can I have your number?"

She stops walking and tilts her head to the side. She thinks about this for longer than I'm comfortable.

"Give me yours," she finally says. "I'll call you."

Defeated, deflated, and aware that I will never hear from her again, I recite my number and she seemingly enters it into her phone. Probably just faking it. And it especially sucks because in an hour I've fallen a little in love with Aisha Stinson, mysterious zoo sleeper. I need to hear more of her weird thoughts. I have to make her laugh.

We keep walking until we have completed the circle. When I see the gift shop, my heart sinks. What started so magically has ended so poorly, and I'm not sure why.

We stand in front of a large, empty field. She turns to face me and sticks her arms out like a legitimate tour guide might. "And this, my friend, is the end of our tour. Behold, the" — and she turns around to glance at a sign behind her — "Optimist Club's Children's Play Area."

I laugh, though my heart is not in it anymore. "Yeah, the Optimist Club," I say. "They probably see the zoo as half-full."

Her smile gives me just the faintest bit of hope that I might hear from her. Just maybe. But probably not.

**3**

ON THE DRIVE back to my dad's place, my mom tells me that he doesn't look well, that the house is a bit of a mess, and that she could use my help cleaning all of it up. I nod and nod, mostly still thinking about Aisha.

She pulls off a main road and up a steep gravel driveway, and she drops me off once again. This time it's because she needs to get groceries.

"The back door is open," she says. "Your dad mostly sticks to his room, so don't be surprised if he doesn't come out to greet you. It's not — personal."

I shrug and undo my seat belt. "Okay."

"He means well."

"Fine."

"Also, don't be shocked if the place looks a bit underappreciated."

"Does that mean it's more than a bit of a mess?"

She shakes her head for a full five seconds and sucks in her cheeks. "It means your father . . ." she says. She runs her hand through her auburn hair. "My suggestion is to get yourself settled and locate yourself a bit. Pay him a visit in his room."

My mom is all about self-locating. It's one of the infuriating things she always says. "Sure," I say, totally unsure.

I get out of the car, and she pulls away. I pause at the back door and take a look around. I know we are only three minutes or so from what passes as downtown, but it feels rural here. The house has a big backyard full of weeds and a separate garage, outside of which sits an old blue pickup truck. Looming huge behind the garage is a massive rock formation that my mom called the Rim. I walk around to the front yard. The house is dark green, a single story, dwarfed by the yellow two-story house next door and a huge pine tree that pretty much hides the house from the street. A rusty rocking chair sits alone on a dilapidated front porch covered in pine needles.

I walk around back and go in the back door, which opens into a mudroom. There are stairs down to the basement, or, if you turn left, you enter a white-walled kitchen, which looks like something you'd see on Nick at Nite. Yellow window curtains with green stalks of corn on them. A squat white refrigerator with a metal latch that opens it and a yellow Frigidaire logo front and center. Faded blue Formica countertops.

I know I've been here before, back when I was three and Grandma lived here. But I don't remember it at all. My dad moved in to his family's home when my grandma Phyllis got sick seven years ago. After she died, he stayed, and he's been here ever since. The place does look a bit "underappreciated," to use my mom's word.

I decide to check out the basement. When Mom told me I'd have the basement here to myself, I warmed up to the idea of having an entire floor of a house just for me. It was actually one of the only things I was looking forward to.

That's before I walk down the rickety stairs and sniff. The air is dank. Like bitter seaweed. Like how I imagine a dry lake would smell. The walls are concrete, and the room feels ten degrees colder than it was upstairs. My mother has set up an air mattress for me on the carpeted floor. In the far corner of the room, next to the door to a bathroom with a little shower, a mess of storage boxes are piled high. They look like they've been there since the dawn of time. I walk over to a dark corner and find a billiard table, the kind with mesh pockets to catch the balls. The felt on the table is peeling off in places. Under it is a plastic garbage bag. I peer in, and it's filled with empty whiskey bottles. It *is* nice to have my own space, but it's . . . I don't know. Like a remote bunker where people store their afterthoughts.

When I can't stall anymore, I head upstairs and check out the rest of the house. The living room has a charcoal-colored, scratchy flannel couch and love seat, naked white walls, and, where a television might be, a big old radio. *Way to update this place, Dad.* I check out the green-carpeted guest room, where my mother's unpacked suitcase sits empty on the made bed. And then I see the closed door across the hall, and I know it's my dad's room.

I stare at the door until it looks and feels a million miles away. Then I close my eyes, breathe deeply, and take the short, long walk down the hall.

I knock. After a few moments, I hear him lumbering slowly toward me.

My dad opens the door, and my impression when I see his face for the first time in fourteen years is that he looks like me if I were put through a meat grinder. His face is raw yet colorless. His hair is ratty. He's bloated yet skinny. I have to look away, because seeing my dad look so sick is way more intense than I even expected it to be, and I feel bile rise into my throat.

"Carson," he says, his voice not exactly as I remember it from

16

our annual birthday phone conversations. Softer yet rustier. "Death warmed over. I know."

He opens his arms and I stand there, frozen. He looks so pathetic, a scrawny death triangle with his arms out to the side and slightly pointed down. A Christmas tree the following April. Finally, I stutter-step over to him and we do a side hug. My chin juts into his bony shoulder. He smells like a mixture of baby powder and pee.

"Good to see you," I say to his shoulder blade.

"You look wonderful," he says, though he can't see me either. "Your mom did a good job with you."

*How do you know?* I want to ask. *Can you somehow tell just by side-hugging me?*

He lets me go and motions me into his room. His bed is a beaten-up gray pullout couch, and it faces a small, old, chubby television with two silver antennae in the shape of a V on top of it. There are no bedside tables, nothing else in the room, except a few old photos on the far wall and, in one dark corner, a maroon chair with holes in the fabric. It feels like the room itself needs antidepressants. He's lived here alone for seven years, and this is where he sleeps? Not even in a real bed?

I ease into the maroon chair as he sits on the corner of his bed, facing me. The chair farts. "Wow, nice place you have here," I say.

He laughs. "Bullshit. It's awful, I know. Needs a woman's touch."

"No," I say, "seriously. You should rent it out as a bed and breakfast."

He laughs again, and I crack a smile. My face heats up. It's funny how you can hate someone and wish them dead, and at the same time you just want to curl up in their lap like a baby. Is that deranged? I mean, I'm seventeen. That's a little deranged, probably.

"I may do that. You have my sense of humor," Dad says.

"Well, take it back," I answer. "No one likes it."

We laugh together for the first time, and the room lightens up a little, which is necessary because it was about to commit suicide. But then there is no follow-up joke. We sit across from each other and stare.

What do you say to your dad whom you haven't seen in fourteen years? On the phone, our typical conversation went like this:

*"Happy birthday, Carson."*

*"Thanks."*

*"How are you?"*

*"Fine."*

*"How's school?"*

*"Fine."*

*"Okay then. We'll talk again soon, okay?"*

*"Okay."*

I'd get off the phone, and Mom would say to me, "You know, it's okay to be angry with your father," and I'd say, "Sure." And she'd say, "What I want you to hear me say is that it's okay to own those feelings." And I'd say back, "Great idea."

I don't know if I was angry at my dad so much as *done* with him. When someone disappears from your life when you're three, you don't really appreciate his yearly reappearances.

And now he'd reappeared, only this time in the flesh. And maybe Mom would like me to *own* certain feelings, and *locate* them like we're playing a game of feelings hide-and-seek. But frankly, I'm not that sure I want to play. Or maybe I do. I don't even know anymore.

"So," he says.

"So," I say back. "What's going on?"

"Well, I'm dying. So that's something," he says, and even though we do probably share the same sense of humor, him just blurting this out makes me feel like I'm choking. I lean back on the raggedy recliner for support.

"Sorry," he says, seeing that his words have had an impact on me. "Why am I such an asshole?"

I shake my head. Part of me wants to say, *You're not an asshole*, but I can't say those — or any — words. I count to twenty-five, and then to eighty-four by sevens. It brings me back. One of the good things about having a mom who doesn't do a lot of mom-ing is that you learn to take care of yourself.

"So Billings is a city," I say to change the subject.

"Yes," he says. "It's a city in Montana."

"You live here. I used to live here."

He coughs into his hands. "Yes, I do. You did."

*Why did you stay here?* I want to say. This place has such bad family memories for him. His dad disappeared when he was my age; his mom had cancer for seven years and then died. And even though we left because he wouldn't stop drinking, I guess I still don't understand *why* he couldn't stop drinking and leave himself behind too. Come with us to New York and start a new life.

"Mom said you stopped working."

"Yup."

"I don't even know what you did for work."

"I was a bartender."

"Terrific," I say. He shrugs, and I can tell there's a part of him that is also looking at this situation and realizing how insane it all is. That he is just as horrified as I am that he allowed himself to become a drunk and then went to work as a bartender. When I was a baby, he was a carpenter. *What happened to that?* I wonder.

"People do different things," he says, his voice defensive. "Not everyone's a school psychologist. Your mom did well for herself."

I cross my legs, and then I uncross them, as if there's some weird inborn part of me that wants to make sure my dad knows I'm manly. His eyes keep wandering around the room. There's not much to look at. A blue-green vase on the floor to the left of his bed, some sort of food basket next to his feet, the old photos on the wall. And yet he doesn't spend much time looking at me. It's like he can't.

"What's with the food basket?" I ask, pointing.

"The warden," he says.

"Huh?"

"Pastor John Logan," he says. "Lives next door. My mom's — your grandma's — best friend. Your granddad's too, I guess. Hasn't left me alone for half a second since your grandma died. Doesn't take hints too well. As long as I've lived here, he brings me my mail, like I can't do it myself. And now that I'm sick, he keeps bringin' me tuna fish. I fuckin' hate tuna fish. Wish he'd mind his own business and let me die in peace."

I wince.

He smiles a bit and picks at his scalp with his thumb and forefinger. "Sorry. Gotta work on my tact. Not used to visitors, I guess. I just . . . The guy's a relic. My dad — your granddad — he was a piece of shit. I don't need the pastor man coming around here feeling sorry for me. My father left over thirty years ago. I'm over it. Piece of shit. Gone. Good riddance."

We have more awkward silence.

"I'm not sure what I'll do here this summer," I finally say. "I mean, I'm here to help — I mean, visit, obviously."

"Well, sure," he says. "But you have to do other things. Maybe you could run a lemonade stand? Five cents a glass?"

I know he's joking, but I'm not in the mood to laugh. "Probably," I say. "I'll probably just do that."

I stand to look at the pictures on his wall. One is a shot of a large, curly-haired woman with a round-faced boy standing in front of her, squinting at the sun. That must be my dad and my grandmother. Another, amber-tinted in that way that old photographs sometimes are, is a portrait of my grandmother posing with a man who must be my grandfather. I look closer, and I realize it definitely is, since he looks like me — long-faced, with the same high cheekbones, dark eyes, and lanky build. In another one, my dad, maybe ten, stands in front of my grandmother, who is flanked by my grandfather and another chubby, freckle-cheeked guy my granddad's age. The two men have hands on my dad's shoulders, and he has a goofy smile on his face. I close my eyes, trying to figure out how you get from there to here, to this sad room, all alone.

I turn back to Dad to ask him a question, and that's when I see it, behind the blue-green vase on the floor. A glass with brown liquid in it. I look at my father, who sees me see it. He stares at his feet like a kindergarten kid caught chewing gum.

I pick up the glass and sniff it. It smells like paint varnish. I stand in front of him, waiting for him to look up at me. He doesn't.

"Somebody must have left this here. Like your last visitor," I say.

He nods.

What I should say is, *Because obviously you were not just drinking this, since you have cirrhosis of the liver, right? And people with cirrhosis can't drink alcohol.* Instead, I say, "What's the world coming to, all these inconsiderate people not cleaning up after themselves."

He chews on a fingernail. I want to continue, *You know Mom and me, we came here to take care of you, right? We flew here? We rented a car? I forfeited my summer?* But as I stand above him and watch him chew his cuticle, I can tell that even if I said it, he wouldn't be able to, as my mother would say, *hear* it.

His voice is barely above a hoarse whisper. "People are the worst."

I turn away and take the glass out of his room and into the kitchen, where I pour the contents down the drain. "They really are," I yell back to him. "You better tell those friends to stop coming around here."

He coughs, and I see he's followed me out. I feel my throat tense up. He's short of breath from the ten-step walk from his bedroom.

"I'm a drunk, Carson."

"Shocking," I say, and I start opening his cabinets to see if he has more bottles. The first cabinet has Corn Pops and about twenty boxes of instant Jell-O. The next one has ramen noodle soups, a twelve-pack. I go through a few more and I don't see any alcohol. I wonder if my mom did a sweep while I was at the zoo.

I open the cabinets under the sink, and behind the dishwasher detergent and garbage bags, something catches my eye. Two bottles. I push the garbage bags out of the way and pull out a Johnnie Walker and a Jack Daniel's. I stand up, turn around toward him, and hoist them forward like evidence. My jaw is so tight that it's hard to breathe.

He sways a bit on his feet like he's not too stable. "I'm a drunk. So was my dad. Hey, maybe you'll be one too someday." He stares at the ceiling.

I exhale deeply. I want to say so many things to him. I want to say, *You know, I didn't really expect it would be like in the movies and you'd be all sorry for not being in my life and barely ever calling. But I did kind of think that maybe, just maybe, you'd try a little harder. Because you're right. You're going to die. And this is it, Dad. This is your last chance. And it's my last chance too. So maybe think about that — how you can be a little less of a total fucking asshole, okay?*

But that's not something I can say. I am physically unable to say it. I close my eyes and count to 217 by sevens. My head is pounding like something is trying to get out of there, a brain mouse trying to find its way out of a maze. I lift the bottles over my head and swing them back and forth like I'm a six-year-old trying to be cute, but it's fucking ugly.

"Need these for my lemonade stand," I say.

His eyes glance my way and then over to the bare refrigerator door. It's like he wants to object, but he knows not to. "Take 'em," he says, as if he doesn't care.

I wait for him to look at me again, and when it becomes painfully obvious that he'd rather study a closed Frigidaire than his son, when it begins to feel a little like I'm going to vomit up my heart, I exhale loudly. He turns around and hobbles back to his sickroom.

"I'm sorry, by the way," he says. It's hard to believe how small he is. He's like a speck of dirt walking away. A talking wisp. "Really. I'm the worst father in the world. I truly get that."

"They should have an award," I call toward him. The words get caught in my dry throat.

He closes the door softly behind him. I stand there in the kitchen for a long time, the bottles still in my hands. *Is that what happens to a guy without a father? He drinks and becomes that? Is that going to happen to me?*

After a while, my mother comes through the back door and into the kitchen with groceries. "How'd your visit with your father go, honey?" she asks when she sees me standing there.

Normally I like to make sure I don't say anything to upset my mother, but my voice is quaking and I can't quell my sarcasm. "Fantastic," I say, exhibiting the two bottles. "It was like one of those holiday movies. We sat around the table and ate a turkey, and then we toasted marshmallows."

She puts the groceries down on the counter, then walks over to where I'm standing. She places her hand lightly on my shoulder. We are not a huggy people. "Are those your father's?" she asks.

*Top ten stupid questions of all time*, I think. But I don't say that. I nod.

She nods back, then removes her hand from my shoulder, then puts it back. "I truly hear underneath the sarcasm that you're feeling pain, Carson. And I want you to know that I feel a lot of sadness as I think about how hard that must be for you."

"Yep, thanks," I say, fighting the impulse to scream, *I'M RIGHT HERE, MOM! STOP TRYING TO LOCATE ME! STOP ANALYZING ME!*

As I pour the contents of the bottles down the sink and she loads groceries into the cabinets and refrigerator, an image crosses my mind. It's a mom and a young son, and the mom is, like, holding the son so close that he can't breathe. She's suffocating him. I watch the boy struggle to break free from his mom's embrace.

And I think, *What's the opposite of suffocation?*

I WAKE UP the next morning with the need to get the hell out of the house. Instead of wandering upstairs and scrounging for some breakfast, I find a pair of shorts, a T-shirt, and sneakers.

"Out for a run," I say as I sweep past my mother, who is sitting alone in the kitchen, working on one of her many lists.

"Have fun," she says without looking up.

I'm not much of a runner. I never do it at home. I think some people do it because it gives them the time to think, but in my life, I have a surplus of time to think.

I stand under the pine tree in our front yard and stretch my legs a few times, then I jog across Rimrock Road and down Michigan Street. I turn right, and in the wide street ahead of me, there is absolutely no movement. I cannot recall ever seeing such stillness before.

I run and run and run. I skip over weeds peeking through the cracks in the concrete. I pass fenced-in yards with old swing sets. The sun feels crisp on the back of my head, and I start to enjoy the burn I feel in my lungs. When I come to a T, I decide to turn left, even though I don't know how long I'll be able to go before I get tired. I don't feel tired yet, and it's probably been, what, a mile? Two? In the city, every twenty streets is a mile, pretty much. Here I have no clue.

I'm running. Voluntarily. And nobody knows it but me.

There are a lot of things people don't know about me. There are a lot of things I never tell anyone. In my school, kids don't tend to text or talk about real things. I mean, we talk about school stuff, or we talk about sports stuff, or we talk about stuff stuff, but nobody is really up for, you know, a text that says, *So yesterday my alcoholic dad . . .* It would be like, *wtf, smh. Yolo.*

You only live once. Doesn't that suck?

I have a few friends I'll probably text this summer, but so far we haven't been in touch. It's fine. We aren't that close. I'm not that close to anyone, and I'm fine with it.

And Mom. I love her and all, but the way she brings her work home with her and talks to me like a patient makes me feel like I'm visiting another planet. And I'm afraid of what it would do to her if I said half the things I think.

So people don't know a lot of what goes on in my head.

One time last year, Kendra Salazar — one of the kids with whom I semi-hang out — convinced me to go to something called "gentle yoga" at this studio on Amsterdam Avenue. I went because Kendra is nice and pretty in a quirky way, and she described gentle yoga as basically napping in unusual positions. "You get these soft blocks, and you put one under your legs," she said, "and you just, I don't know. You just be."

So I tried it, and it was about the most unpleasant hour of my life. Here is sixty seconds of Carson Smith's brain on gentle yoga: *Am I doing this right? Why is my breathing so loud? Why does the instructor keep telling us to breathe? If I forget to make myself breathe, will I die? What if I had a heart attack right now and I died and no one knew because I didn't make a noise and then they didn't*

27

*find out and I was dead on the floor of the yoga studio and they had to do this big cover-up so no one thought gentle yoga was dangerous but it is? Kendra ran her hand through her hair earlier when she saw me. Does she like me? Why? What would she do if she knew the real me, the real Carson? Am I good or am I bad? What if I'm bad? Do people go to heaven if they are bad? Is there a heaven? What would that even be like? And are we that stupid that we think that there's some God up there who is keeping track of our rights and wrongs like Santa Claus and making a list and checking it twice? But what if there is? It would totally suck to be this guy who thinks there's no God and be all cocky about it all your life and then you die on the floor of a yoga studio one day and poof! You go up to heaven and they're like, so, um, Mr. Smith, sorry to let you know this, but you know those televangelists you thought were so stupid? They were right, and while yes, you were mostly kind and good, you didn't believe in God enough, so I'm going to click this lever. . . . No! No! Bam! Dude, you're in hell. Hell is gentle yoga and quieting your brain for sixty seconds. God, I want some fried chicken right now. Give me fried chicken! Or give me death! Right here on the floor of gentle yoga!*

So yeah, I'm not really the Zen guy I could be, I guess.

My legs start to get a little tired, so I turn right, back toward Rimrock Road. It's a bit of an uphill climb, and I feel it in my lungs. Then I'm in the home stretch. I see Michigan Street, and I pump my arms to make up for my ready-to-give-out legs. I'm just a block away, and then I'm crossing the street and at the finish line of our house and I don't know how far I've run but I know it feels incredible, the ache in my quads, the burn in my throat. This is running Carson, the new Carson, the —

Falling Carson.

My left foot flops into a crevice I don't see, and I topple forward. My knee scrapes hard against the street, leaving a trickle of blood that looks like it could have come from a raw steak.

"Are you okay, son?"

I look up. A man with white hair is standing above me, and in my bleary state I think, *God*? But when he lowers his right hand to me and I see a wedding ring, I realize it probably isn't God.

He helps lift me to my feet, and once I'm standing, I reach down and feel my raw knee. It's wet — very.

"I'm fine," I say. "Just hanging out on the ground like usual."

When he laughs, his freckled cheeks rise, and I think back to yesterday in my dad's room, the photo of the guy posing with my dad and grandparents. "That may be your story, but I'm not buying it. Sure looked like a fall to me. Was sitting right out there." He points to the front porch of the house next door to ours.

"Pastor guy neighbor," I say, my mouth extremely dry.

He nods. "I thought you might be Matthew and Renee's boy," he says, as a smile spreads across his very round face like marmalade on toast. "The last time I saw you, you were yay high." He puts his hand low against his leg.

"I think I saw your picture yesterday," I say. "On my dad's wall. It was the first time I ever saw a picture of my grandfather."

He nods in that way that adults nod to let you know that the general topic is sad. "Come on, let's get you cleaned up."

"It's fine," I say. "I'll just —"

But it's too late. He old-man hobbles toward his house, so I shrug and follow him.

His house smells like mothballs and pinecones. Like old people and comfort. He places a towel on the beige couch and sits me down, and then he hands me a glass of ice water that disappears in one gulp. He brings me a refill. I inhale the second glass of water, still trying to catch my breath.

He walks away and comes back with a first aid kit. He dabs some alcohol on my knee, which stings so badly I have to close my eyes. When I open them, he's covered the cut with ointment, and he is placing a bandage over it.

"Thank you," I say. "Really. Thanks. I better get going."

He looks up at me. "Sit. Stay a while. I could use the company." He sticks a chubby, lily-white hand in my face. "John. John Logan."

I don't really want to stay. I mean, he seems like a perfectly nice guy, but he's at least fifty years older than me, and there's this whole drama with my dad that I don't want to get any closer to. But his hand is there, so I shake it.

"Carson," I say, and then I remember that he's known my name ever since I was "yay high."

"Your mother told me she was concerned you wouldn't find things to do this summer. I told her I'd be happy if you took care of my lawn, and she said you wouldn't know the first thing about what to do with it."

My first thought is that I'm a little surprised she mentioned me at all. The second is that in terms of lawns, she's right. I have no idea what lawn care consists of, in the same way I don't know exactly how eggs happen. The honest-to-God truth is I have no idea how many holes a chicken has, how some eggs have chickens in them and some not. I think growing up in the city makes you not question some of these basic things. "If you need any computer stuff done, maybe I could help," I say.

He smiles. "I haven't quite caught up with the computers," he says.

It gets quiet, and again I am struck by how silent Montana is. You stop talking, and instead of a general buzz you get nothing.

"So what was my grandfather like?" I ask to fill the quiet.

He crosses his legs. "Good man," he says. "He was funny. Very, very funny."

"Nice," I say. And then I flash on what my dad said yesterday, that his dad was an alcoholic too. *Yeah, good man*, I think.

He nods. "I worked with him for many years."

"What kind of work?"

"He was a choir director."

"Um, okay. Where?"

"At my church."

"Do you think maybe he's still —" I can't finish the sentence, because there's really no right way to ask the question. *Alive? Out there?*

He seems to get that. "I truly don't know. A tragedy, really. For all of us."

I nod, because obviously it has been hard. I mean, I vaguely remember Grandma Phyllis. She wore dangly turquoise earrings, and when we went to her house she always had those soft white mint candies with the pink stripes. I got a stomachache eating them once, and I've never liked them since. My mom has told me stories about her over the years, and it's pretty clear she was an unhappy lady. And my dad, well. Forget about it. "I'm sure," I say.

The pastor nods. "He was my closest friend."

I worry that he might be about to get emotional, so I look away, and I say, "He sounds great." A pause.

"So you work at a church?"

"You could come down, if you want. Rimrock United Methodist. It's just down the road. I've been the pastor there for forty-one years."

*So I'm Methodist,* I think, and the thought means absolutely nothing to me. I know it's a brand of Christianity, but that's about it. "I will," I say, lying. I stand up. "This was really nice of you. Thanks a lot."

"I hope you'll stop by for a chat once in a while. You seem like a very nice young man."

"I will do that," I say, lying again. "Absolutely."

He looks at me like he's waiting for me to say more. I think back to yesterday, and my dad saying something about tuna fish. "You're the one who brings my dad food?"

He nods and smiles. He probably gets a lot of crap from my dad, and now here I am, running off as soon as he invites me to church.

"Thanks," I say, trying to sound nicer than my dad probably does.

He nods again.

"Thanks," I repeat out of sheer awkwardness, and then I duck out the front door and head to our place.

THE NEXT AFTERNOON, I'm in the shower when my phone rings. I hurry out and it's a strange 406 number I've never seen before. I dry my hands as quickly as I can and pick up.

"Hello?"

A female voice says, "So you're on a bus, and if you slow down to under twenty miles per hour, you'll *die*."

My face flushes. Aisha. She's calling. Me.

"Oh no," I say. "This is an unfortunate turn of events."

"What do you *do*?" Aisha asks, her voice dead serious.

"Am I in Billings, or New York?"

"Let's say Billings."

"Do I ever have a shot at going back to New York?"

"Let's say no."

"I slow down."

She laughs. "True 'nuf. Hey. You up for buying me a cup of coffee?"

"I could do that. In a few hours?"

"How about now?" she says, and silently I pump my fist five times.

---

Sweat drips from my eyelids as I walk into Off the Leaf, the nearest coffee shop to my house and the place where Aisha and I agreed to meet. I never thought I'd miss the noisy subway, but that was before a hot, last-day-of-June, late-afternoon, two-mile walk through Billings in which I saw not a soul. I'm going to need at least a bike to make this summer work.

Everything inside the coffeehouse is crisp, bright, hospital clean, and huge. You could place a regulation basketball court in here. It's the antithesis of a hip New York café.

Also quiet. Unlike most coffee shops I've been in, there's no music playing. Consequently, I can hear very clearly the four beer-bellied guys by the door bellowing about the Broncos, and the two middle-aged ladies in orange sweat suits reclining on a dangerously low pink vinyl couch. I glance around and there's Aisha, positioned next to a metal-framed fireplace, waving wildly at me as if she's trying to land a plane. I salute her and mouth, "Want a latte?" She nods her head enthusiastically.

One of the perks of being dragged to Billings against my will is that my mother gave me a bribe: my own credit card to use, for all expenses "that seem reasonable." I've never had unlimited fundage before, but I guess Mom thinks I'm a responsible kid who won't, you know, go buy a Jet Ski or something. She is not exactly made of money, but I'm pretty sure that so long as I don't go crazy, I can do what I want this summer and it'll be courtesy of the Bank of Mom.

"Whut can I git for ya?" asks the guy behind the counter. He looks like no barista I've seen in New York, ever. His belt buckle is bigger than my head, his hair is buzzed to within a centimeter of his scalp, and he has the confident swagger of a deeply unpleasant person.

"I'll take me two of them there lattes," I say, and he nods his thick-necked head in a way that makes it unclear whether he thinks I'm making fun of him or not. He takes my card and gives me a cowboy smile, which I return, and then I wait while the other barista, an alt-looking girl with black lipstick, makes the drinks.

*I'm hanging out with Aisha,* I think while I wait, allowing the words to swim around my brain. *No big deal. I'm cool like that. I am a dude who hangs with girls who look like models.*

My mom the therapist calls these affirmations. I call them lies, but whatever. There's no turning back now. I'm going to make this work.

The Hollywood studio that created this ultramodern café and put it next to a place that appears to be named Casino Grand Liquor has filled it with random pieces that don't make sense. Aisha is sitting in one of four comfy-looking leather chairs next to the fireplace, and they've put a shiny piano right up against one of the chairs, so that a pianist would have to fight anyone sitting in that chair for elbow space while playing. There are flat-screened TVs all set to Fox News, and a bunch of beanbag chairs strewn around as if this was hipster heaven.

It is not hipster heaven.

The lattes are taking awhile, so I walk over to Aisha, who pats the chair next to her facing the fireplace. A fire is burning, despite the fact that it is a Wednesday afternoon, the first day of July, and I am sweating like a pig. Aisha is wearing the same tank top she was wearing on Monday at the zoo. Not that I'm complaining; she looks unreal in it.

"You have any good misinformation for me?" I ask, attempting to air out my shirt a little.

"This place is really happening, for one."

"I expect Kanye West to come in here any second," I say back, and then the girl calls my name and I go get our drinks.

The drinks are sitting on the counter, and I'm about to take them when a meaty hand whisks one and then the other away.

"I think those are mine," I say, but the same guy who took my order seems not to be listening. He pours the contents of the coffee cups into the sink.

"Um, excuse me?"

He does not look up. He walks back to the front counter as if he needs to take another order. There is no one there.

"Are you kidding me?" I say, thinking about the eight dollars, tip included, I just spent for nothing. The alt-looking girl offers me a quiet look of sympathy.

I look back at Aisha. "He just poured our drinks out and is now ignoring me," I say, loud enough so that everyone will know. The orange sweat-suited women either pretend not to hear, or they don't. The football-talking guys are oblivious, as football-talking guys tend to be.

Aisha motions for me to come to her.

"What's his problem?" I say.

"Long story," she answers. "Just ignore him. Or better yet, when he goes in the back, get the girl to make us some new drinks. She'll do it, I'm pretty sure."

"Hmm," I say, still talking loudly. "That's really weird and possibly illegal."

36

"Pick your battles," Aisha replies, and I sit down next to her, latteless.

Conversation comes less easily today. Possibly it's because I just charged drinks to Mommy's credit card and I didn't get them and that makes me feel like a wimp. But it's also because Aisha called me, and I don't know why. I mean, can't she do better? I think she can.

"The Alamo," I say, after a lengthy silence.

"What?"

I shrug. "You said, 'Pick your battles.' "

She rolls her eyes, and I imagine permanently sewing my lips shut, because clearly she was at her dorky humor limit the other day at the zoo.

"The Bulge," she says back, and I look down at my crotch without thinking about it.

She raises one eyebrow. "Mm-hmm," she says. "I don't know what you're thinking. Me, I was picking a battle. I should have said, 'Of the Bulge.' Sorry."

I crack up, relieved yet embarrassed to have so quickly brought the focus to my dick.

"So, Billings. Why?" she asks, and I'm happy to have the topic changed.

"Well, you know. It was South Beach or the French Riviera or here, so" — I cock my head and motion around us — "obviously we made the right choice. For me, anyway."

"Obviously," she says. "That's what brought us here too, my family. Well, that and the huge black population."

We look around the café. Fifteen or so people, all white except

Aisha. Not a brownish hue to be seen. Not even a tanned person, really.

"So it's massive," I say.

She nods. "There are a hundred thousand people in this city and almost five hundred of us are black, so that's . . . something."

I laugh. She does not laugh. "Oh. You're serious."

She goes back to nodding, but this time really slowly.

"Oh my God. There are like five hundred black people at my *school*."

"Take me with you," she says.

I get a semi hard-on. "Um. Okay."

"My dad was the offensive line coach for the Indoor Football League team here. Got the job and moved us here from Lincoln, Nebraska, when I was in ninth grade. Two years later, the team folded, and guess what? Still here! He coaches at Rocky Mountain College now."

"Billings has a pro football team?"

"Had. The Billings Outlaws. Raised the black population of the city about ten percent."

I do the math and realize that she is potentially not exaggerating. I don't know whether to laugh or what, so I open my eyes wide to show her I know that's crazy and sad and all of that. She accepts my reaction with a similar eye widening.

I hear a "psst" behind me. It's the alternative barista girl. She has two steaming lattes on the counter. The barista guy is not in sight. I jump up and grab the coffees. The nice barista has sketched a pretty heart in the foam on our lattes.

"Isn't that sweet?" I ask, handing Aisha one of the mugs.

Aisha looks down at her drink. "I love foam art," she says.

"You do?"

"My favorite thing in the entire world."

"Is this more misinformation? Should I assume that a lot of what you say isn't true?"

She nods twice.

"Well, it's my favorite thing too. It's modern cave art. Years from now, anthropologists will study foam art formations and make sweeping generalizations about our lost coffee culture."

"Most probably," Aisha says, sipping her latte, thereby smudging her coffee heart. Now it looks like a cursive L.

She tells me she just graduated from high school and she's looking for work, although obviously not too hard, since we're sitting in a coffee shop in the middle of a Wednesday afternoon. I explain the basic facts about coming to visit my dad, leaving out the parts about him dying and my not having seen him in fourteen years. There are some things you don't tell a girl on your first date.

And yeah. This is definitely a date. The eye contact. Way crazy eye contact.

"So tell me a long story," I say. "Why did that asshole pour our drinks out?"

She bites her lip. "I may have dumped the contents of a lunch tray on his head once."

I laugh. "Ooh! Sounds like a good long story. Why'd you do it?"

She seems nervous, maybe. Her eyes keep darting around instead of staying focused on me, as they have been for the better part of ten minutes.

"I wouldn't have come here if I knew he worked here."

"What did he do?"

"He was being nasty to someone I care about," she says.

"A friend?"

"Well . . ." She pauses, glancing back at me. "Me, actually."

"Well, good for you," I say, like someone would say to a child who has just painted a stick-figure portrait of his family. I cringe when I hear it. "I mean, that is — sticking up for yourself and all. Not to jump to conclusions, but, racial stuff?"

"Something like that," she says, looking away again. I follow her glance and notice that the skinhead barista guy is back and now mopping the floor in front of the football guys. He looks kind of funny in an apron, and I hope he feels embarrassed.

"Maybe we should go someplace else?" she says.

This time I get fully hard. I'm about to invite Aisha home, which may or may not be okay with my parents, but I don't care. I have a basement, and the stairs are right off the back door. If they have to know, I'll make it okay with them. This is really happening. Aisha. Me. Really. Happening.

"Uh, sure," I say, and Aisha is standing now and I'm really not in a good position to stand, so I stay seated and cross my legs.

The barista comes over to our area with his mop, and I feel my chest tighten. A part of me wants to hurt this guy, even though he's bigger than me. As he mops around the table between us, he mumbles, "How do you like living on the streets, dyke sauce?"

"Piss off, Colt," she mumbles back.

"Couldn't have happened to a nicer man-girl," he whispers.

"You say one more thing and I'll stab you in the fucking neck. Don't think I won't."

He blows her a kiss and moves on. I look at Aisha, who glances at me and then turns away.

I stare down at my feet as I try to figure out what just happened. I feel as if someone stole the air from my chest. Like a second ago I was pumped full of all these possibilities, and now they're gone, and the air around us is thick and troubled.

I look back at Aisha. She is still not looking at me. I want her to tell me that I misheard. That this didn't just happen. That this ass-hole barista guy didn't just imply that she lives on the street, and she is, what, a lesbian?

And then Aisha just leaves. Walks to the door and leaves. I jump up and follow her.

"I'm sorry," I say once we're outside, but I don't really know what I'm sorry for.

"You're sorry?" she says, not nasty exactly, but maybe a bit bewildered. "What for? Because some asshole called me a name? Because I'm a dyke? Because my dad found out and kicked me out and I'm sleeping in the fucking zoo? I'm at the end of my rope here, and you're sorry? What exactly are you sorry about?"

I really don't know what to do. So I do something I don't do. I put my arms around her and gently hug. She smells lightly of sweat and something I can't place, almost like olive oil. Her thick hair wraps around my ear and envelops it, and she hugs me back a little. I want to memorize the feeling of her body against mine. When she whimpers in my ear, I pull her closer.

"All of that. I didn't know," I say. "I'm sorry for whatever's going on."

We are standing in the parking lot of the coffee shop. It's about half-full. She walks over to a gray fence and sits down next to it on a patch of grass, so I sit down too. It feels a little homeless, actually, sitting there. Like now that I know she's homeless, sitting in a parking lot by a fence takes on a different meaning.

"Talk to me," I say. "What's going on? What happened?"

She sighs. "You want the long version?"

I nod.

"It happened last week. You sure you wanna hear this?"

I nod again.

"Well, let me back up. My dad and me, we've always been real close, especially around sports. I'm big into track and volleyball. He's also real religious. Took us to church every Sunday of my life that I can remember. Ate that shit up. I did too, when I was younger. All that junk about a personal relationship with Christ and offering up my sins and stuff.

"So anyway, I guess early last week, he got suspicious that I was dating some boy, because I was away from home a lot. So he tracked my cell phone. He rang the doorbell and scared the crap out of my girlfriend, Kayla, who answered the door in a robe. He barged in to Kayla's room, and I was in her bed and I'm like, 'Dad.' Shit. Well, this ain't great.

"And that wasn't cool, because it showed no trust, and I never gave him any reason not to trust me. I never showed the man anything but respect my whole entire life. We have one of those 'Get in my truck right now' moments, and he drives me home. We don't

42

talk, don't say a word the whole way. The next day he sits me down at the dining room table and explains that he's made some calls. I'm going to this place called Flowing Rivers in Mesa, Arizona. I have an aunt who lives there. And this place, he explains, is going to make me straight, through the Jesus."

"Jesus," I say. My mind is running wild. It's like, who does that to their daughter? Try to change her? And this other, tiny part of me is thinking, *Well, could that work? Could we be a couple if you went there? Because I'd totally wait for you.*

"Right?" Aisha says, rubbing her eyes. "Because let's just say I'm no longer a believer. So I ask him, 'What if I won't go?' My voice is shaking. And my voice never shakes.

"And he says, 'I don't know, baby girl. But whatever you do, you won't do it here under my roof.'

"My mom didn't feel that way, but in our house, Dad is in charge. So I went into my room and thought about it. And for a few seconds there, I was thinking, *Just go to Arizona. It won't work, you'll leave, and either you'll come home again and Dad will calm down, or you'll start a new life down there.* But then I thought, *What if it does work?*

"I saw my reflection in the mirror. I thought about how, if I changed, I'd be someone else. I like me, you know? I thought, *My dad has no right. He has no right to take me out of me.* So I went out and I said, 'Dad, we can work this out. We'll get a therapist over here, and they'll help. I'm not a bad person; I'm just a lesbian. Have been since forever. You know me. I'm your daughter. I was always exactly this way.' But my dad. He just wasn't having it. He said, 'You're going to Mesa.' And I said I wasn't, and he said 'Get out,' and I got out."

"Jesus," I say again. I try to imagine being kicked out of my home. Thousands of times in New York I sat on the radiator in my room, looking out the window at the mostly closed blinds of strangers across the air shaft, thinking about what it would be like to live in one of those other apartments. Thinking maybe I should just leave. And then I was like, *And do what?* And that's when that idea goes away, because a fantasy is a fantasy. And the reality? I can't imagine a reality of being on my own with no resources that doesn't suck.

"I packed a bag, and that night I slept in my car," Aisha says. "The next day, I went back to Kayla's place, but she disappears when the going gets tough, I guess, because she wasn't so much about me staying with her. I tried a couple friends, no dice. I couchsurfed a couple days with a family I found online before I wore out my welcome. There's a women's shelter downtown, but the idea of living in a shelter made me feel a little too much like I was really and truly homeless, so I nixed that. I guess it was Saturday night when I decided on the zoo, mostly because it seemed remote and safe, and I like zoos. Animals. Someday, I want to be a vet. Well, I did. I was gonna study veterinary medicine at Rocky Mountain this fall, but my dad withdrew me."

"Shit," I say.

"And then Dad turned off my phone. Had to get a new one on my own. And it ain't easy getting a job for the summer, and even if it was, it's not like you can just get a job and get an apartment. You need to bankroll some cash first. I have some cash saved up, but I've been petrified that if I start to use it, I'll run out and then I'd really be in a situation.

"So I slept there in the zoo, where I showed you. The last four nights now." She sighs. "What I really want to do, I guess, is get the hell out of Billings. I mean, this place sucks, and if I'm not part of my family anymore, why not go somewhere else? But part of me feels like I have to try and make it right with Dad. And anyway, I don't have that much money. I'm a realist. I don't want to end up on the streets of Portland or somewhere. I don't know what's gonna happen, but it better happen soon," she concludes.

"That's . . . wow," I say. I can't do any better.

"I know. Not what you signed up for, right?"

I take her hand. She looks at me and tilts her head slightly, and I remember that we're not actually boyfriend and girlfriend. I drop it. She half smiles.

"Sorry," I say.

She shrugs.

"My dad's dying," I say.

"Oh," she says. "I didn't know. Sorry."

"I mean, for what it's worth. I don't want to be all, 'Poor me, my dad is dying, *waah waah waah*.' But yeah, that's why I'm here. Before Monday, I hadn't seen him since I was three."

"Wow."

"He's a drunk. It's a lot of fun over at our house."

"I bet."

"Fathers," I say.

She snorts. "Right? What really pisses me off is the whole 'man of God' thing. What *is* that? You disown your daughter in the name of God? I grew up with that evangelical shit. I'll tell you, the second he kicked me out, that was *over*. Looking up at the stars in the zoo one night, I just realized. Religion is supposed to be all about loving thy neighbor, but religious people are hypocrites. Kicking your daughter out is an act of love? Please.

"I'm glad I'm out of there," she says, scooping some gravel up in her fingers and then throwing it back onto the ground. "I'm glad."

I think about religious zealots, like the ones who flew into the towers on 9/11, and the people who preach damnation for sinners on the subway. Once on the downtown 1 train, this cross-eyed guy started screaming about the wrath of God, and how it's all the gays' fault. This militant gay dude got in the guy's face and told him to shut up, that he didn't need some preacher to tell him right from wrong. When he was done, most of the car clapped for him. The preacher guy got off at the next stop. I clapped too. I mean, isn't God (who doesn't exist, by the way) supposed to be this all-loving Father to Us All?

"Religious people suck," I say, and Aisha nods and continues to trace a pattern in the loose gravel around her, like a sole figure skater practicing.

We sit for a while, and somehow I feel a little relaxed, which is weird because nothing is okay, not really.

"So wait," I say. "How come that felt kind of like a first date? Am I crazy?"

"I'm sorry," she says. "That wasn't cool."

"Were you, like, playing me?" I ask.

She takes a deep breath, looks up and to the right. Then she looks directly at me.

"No and yes. I mean, I knew you dug me, and I thought maybe . . . But I like you, Carson, really. You crack me up. I need a friend, and this isn't the best place to be a lesbian, you know?"

I stand up. "C'mon," I say, sure of myself while knowing that it's not my call to make.

"Where are we going?" she says, slowly standing.

"Home," I say. "You're staying with me."

# 6

"I WISH THERE was a way I could make sure my mother wasn't, like, in the kitchen," I say as we stand in front of the door to the house.

Aisha looks at me and raises an eyebrow. "You don't really *get* lesbianism, do you, Carson?" she says.

I turn away from her and pretend to have trouble with the lock. I mean, as far as *getting* lesbianism is concerned, I do and I don't, I guess. I mean, I get that she's a lesbian, and that she likes girls, aka *not me*. But that doesn't mean that I'm a lesbian too, if you know what I mean. Just because visiting a guy's house doesn't do much for her, that doesn't mean that having a hot girl come over doesn't do something for me.

"I would just rather tell them, I don't know, tomorrow, I guess," I say.

Aisha drove us back to the house in her red Dodge Neon, and on the way, I'd formulated about ten arguments for why we need to let Aisha stay. While my mom barely notices my existence and is very chill about almost everything always, I can't really picture her going along with a strange girl moving into the house. And not knowing my dad, whose place we're in, it's really hard to imagine everyone will be like, *Sure! Why not?*

"This isn't a hookup. You get that, right?"

"Yep. Not into me. Got it."

She exhales loudly. "Forget it. Let's just. I don't know. I'll see you tomorrow."

"Okay, see ya," I say, and this actually surprises her, because she turns quickly toward me, her eyes wide. "I'm kidding, God," I say. "Like I'm really going to let you sleep with the monkeys because you won't put out. Gimme a break. C'mon."

I open the door for Aisha, and as she passes through, she says, "No monkeys at the zoo."

And I reply, "Big shocker."

Mom is searching through the refrigerator when we walk into the kitchen. Her hair is wet and she's wearing a beige floral-print robe.

"We're out of Greek yogurt," she says to me when she hears my footsteps. When I don't answer right away, she turns around.

"Oh," she says, seeing Aisha and fiddling with her robe to make sure it's closed, which it is. "You've brought a friend. How lovely."

"Sorry, I should have called," I say. "This is my new friend Aisha."

They both say hi, and then we stand there, awkwardly.

"Would you like something to eat?" my mother asks.

"Do you have any Greek yogurt?" Aisha asks, and it's spot on, because my mother, who isn't always about the quirky humor, smiles.

"As a matter of fact, we don't," she says. She then pulls out a Tupperware container. "Strawberries?"

Aisha says she'd love some, and I realize she probably hasn't been eating well. I pour some out on a plate, and I ask my mother if she and I can talk in the other room for a second. As Aisha sits at our kitchen table and gobbles berries, I follow my mom into the living room. My brain spins through all of the arguments I've come up with.

"What do you need, honey?" my mother asks. There's an edge to her voice, and I hear it as, *I can't take one more thing, Carson. Not one more thing.* She's been here with Dad all day, which has probably not been great. The bags under her eyes look dark and heavy, like fruit scales at the supermarket.

"Aisha's a lesbian and she got kicked out by her dad," I say.

"Oh," my mother says, and I realize the counselor in her will totally get this.

"It's really bad. She's been sleeping outside, and she's an amazing person. You have to talk to her. She's just so cool."

"How long have you known her?"

It's obviously a rhetorical question, since I have to have met her either Monday, yesterday, or today.

"We met at the zoo."

"I see," my mother says.

I stare at the ground and tap my foot a few times. "I'm just trying to figure out the right thing to do," I say. "I mean, obviously, what would be best for her isn't possible, probably, because, even though she's a lesbian, she's still a girl and all. So obviously she can't stay here, right?" I lower my head and peer at her face.

My mother sighs. I don't know what it feels like to have her tell me no, because I don't ask for a lot, usually. I just sort of take what I need, and I'm pretty self-sufficient. But I think I'm about to find out what no sounds like. When she doesn't say anything, I add, "She's looking for work, so it's not like she'll be here except for at night."

My mother sighs again. "If it's okay with your dad, it's fine," she says. "Do what you feel is right, honey."

50

I admit I'm a little shocked. Because even though it's what I want, it just seems like, *Wow. That was really, really easy.*

I knock on my dad's door. He opens it up, and it's the first time I've seen him since our first meeting. His eyes are glassy, and I don't know if he's drunk or not.

I tell him the situation, and amazingly, he asks more questions than my mom did.

"You sure you're not just saying she's a lesbian so you can get some?" he asks, smirking.

I shake my head. I have no idea if he's kidding or not. "No. She's an actual lesbian."

"Are you gay?" he asks.

"No, Dad. I'm not gay. Thanks for asking, though."

He laughs. "So there is a part of you that digs this girl, right?"

I shrug and keep my calm. "It's not gonna happen. She's cool, though."

He continues to smirk at me. "Attaboy. And just so you know, I would've been fine with you being gay too. I'm not like that and all."

"Duly noted," I say, and he laughs again.

"A lesbian in the basement. I like it," he says. "I dig it."

"Nineteen seventy-something wants its word back," I reply, and my dad's smile gets a little wider before he retreats back into his cave and shuts the door.

"He's fine with it," I say to my mom as I pass her, and she nods her head. I can't quite tell, but it looks like her jaw is really tight.

I walk back into the kitchen. "Welcome home, I guess," I say, and Aisha gives me an animated look of shock.

Once settled in the basement with me, Aisha heads off to the shower, saying it's her first home shower in a few days, since she had been limited to showers at the Billings Athletic Club. I can hear the spray of the water from my room, and my heart starts beating fast. All I can do is think about what excuses I could come up with to go into the bathroom and somehow sneak a peek inside the shower curtain.

"Oh hey, I was just making sure there was enough soap. . . . Do you need me to hand you — oops! Sorry."

"Oh hey, do you like music while you shower? I'm just going to put my iPhone dock in here — oops! Sorry."

But I do none of these things. Instead, I count to 84 by sevens, and then 232 by eights. She comes out of the bathroom in one of my shirts and a pair of clean-ish shorts and puts her dirty clothes in the washer. I take her out for dinner at Wendy's because frankly I'd rather shave my head than subject Aisha to dinner with my parents. After, we hang out in my room for hours and watch clips from YouTube on my laptop. I let her sit on the slowly sinking air mattress I had the pleasure of sleeping on the first two nights here, since she's going to sleep there, and I sit on the carpet, aka my new bed, and lean up against the mattress.

After a while, she asks, "So aside from watching fascinating YouTube videos, what do you like to do?"

My perverted mind comes up with a few ideas of what I wish she means by that, and then I swallow those thoughts down. I think about it and come up blank. What do I like to do? Nothing. I like to do nothing. What's wrong with me, and is it fixable?

"I don't know," I say. I click on a news video about this trend where kids sucker-punch strangers on the street. It's a game called Knockout. We watch it, and I say, "Oh my God, people are stupid." Aisha nods.

I click on another clip, a news story about two drunk guys stealing a penguin in Australia. Aisha laughs as they show the losers being dragged away in handcuffs. She says, "I wonder how they did it. Is it like, if you want to steal a penguin, you have to think like a penguin? Or maybe they dressed up like penguins and were all, 'Come with us, buddy.' And the little guy just went along?"

"So they dressed as fancy waiters?"

She laughs again, and I sigh a bit as I see how her tongue flicks up against the back of her front teeth. I think, *I made that happen. I did that.* Making Aisha laugh is like the big win I've never had. It's what I like to do. It makes my insides flutter and my shoulders relax and I am home.

And then I think, *Excellent, you are falling deeper in love with a lesbian.*

"That's not even the hard part," I say. "The really hard part is stealing a penguin's *identity.*"

Aisha leans back on her elbows. "What would you do with a penguin's identity?"

I allow my eyes a little glimpse of her flat stomach and then I look away. "Maybe you'd give felons a second chance? I mean, it's hard to start again, find a job and such when you've robbed a bank."

"True."

"So you go up to this felon, and you hand them a document, and you say, 'You are now officially known as Mitchell T. Penguin. You have not committed any felonies, and all you've done thus far is mate for life with Lucille J. Penguin."

"I think penguins are gay. I think I heard that somewhere," she says.

"You know, not everyone is gay," I say, and she gives me the finger. "Well, probably not *all* penguins are gay. I mean, that would be not the smartest strategy from a Darwinian standpoint."

"You don't know," she says. "They could have surrogates."

"Oh yes, penguin surrogates," I say. "I've often heard of them."

"You're really weird," she says. "I like you."

"I like you too," I answer, and I close the laptop. As the light in the room evaporates, I hear her exhale, and it sounds like the kind of breath you let out for the first time in a long time.

"Thanks, Carson. Really. Thank you. You are a good person."

"No biggie," I say, grinning widely because I know she cannot see me. "I simply saved your life."

She snorts. I wrap myself in the blanket and settle in for a night on the carpet. And for the first time in a long time, I don't feel alone.

# 7

I WAKE UP in the morning when I hear breathing in my ear. I open my eyes to find two eyes staring into mine from literally six inches away.

I start to scream, and a hand covers my mouth. Aisha's hand.

"What the . . . ?" I say into her palm.

"I always wanted to do that to someone," she says, a silly look on her face. "Looked like you were about to wake up, so I just . . . hurried that process up a bit."

I look around the still-dark room. "What time is it?"

"It's six thirty," she says.

"So yeah," I mumble, turning over onto my stomach, a pale orange blanket the only thing between me and the carpet. "I probably wasn't about to wake up."

She pounces on me and wrestles me onto my back, and my ribs press hard into the floor, knocking the wind out of me. I can tell she's kidding around, but I tense my whole body and fight against her.

It's futile. She pins me on my back by holding my shoulders down with her hands, and she sits on my thighs. She looks down on me with this grin on her face, and I have to avoid her eyes. I'm in a pair of shorts, no shirt, with only a blanket over me, and she's wearing just a T-shirt and panties. Girls don't get it. They don't get what they can do to us. It's terrible and embarrassing.

"What?" she says.

"Leave me alone," I mumble.

"Oh, come on," she says, and when I don't look at her, she gets off me. "Sorry. I was just foolin'."

I sit up and curl my arms around my legs. I can feel the brooding coming on, but I don't want to be that guy, so I shake it off. I yawn and stretch my arms out. "I'm not a morning guy. I am not a guy of the morning."

"We need to talk," Aisha says. She is sitting up on her bed, which is to say she is sitting on a fully deflated air mattress.

"Talk, woman," I say.

"At what age did you become a hoarder? Have you considered going on the TV show?"

I raise an eyebrow, or at least I attempt to do Aisha's one-eyebrow raise. I fail. "Huh?"

She points across the room at the boxes piled atop each other against the far wall. I saw those the first time I came downstairs, but the truth is I haven't thought of them since. I look back over at Aisha, whose tank top is loose in all the right places. It's early and my brain is barely functioning, and I have to remind myself not to gawk.

"Bring it up to the actual hoarder," I say. "My dad."

She stands and stretches her legs. "We're living down here, not him. Can we clean this crap up? I mean, the smell." She pinches her nose.

I sniff and I don't really smell anything anymore. I must have gotten used to it. Is that a bad sign? Does that mean I smell too, and I don't even notice anymore? I resist the urge to check my underarms.

"Ugh," I say. "Cleaning? Really? Worst summer ever."

She gives me that inimitable Aisha smile that engulfs her whole face and says, "Well, you've obviously never cleaned with Aisha before. . . ." She does a spin and a little jump, and I watch her, wondering where the hell this is going. She stops with her arms out wide, facing me. "Sorry, I got nothing," she says. "Can you take care of the boxes? I'd rather scrub floors than deal with boxes that have been gathering spiderwebs for decades. That freaks me out."

After we do our morning stuff, we get to work. The boxes are, in fact, covered in cobwebs. Some have been numbered with orange Magic Marker — a "1," a "3," and a "4." Some are damp on the bottom, like maybe there was a flood, and I imagine a box with an orange "2" on it floating down a river. When I lift "3" off the pile, it feels soggy on the bottom and begins to collapse into itself. I wrestle that one safely down to the ground and open it.

The box is filled with old photo albums. It's pretty clear to me that this is my grandmother's stuff, and that my father must have decided, upon moving in seven years ago, that everything should be put away and tended to at a future date that never quite arrived.

The top one is a wedding album. I flip through and the photos are all black and white — more like black and yellow, really — and the setting is some sort of banquet hall, in some town where smiling was illegal or at least really frowned upon. Of the posed shots, not a single one is even a little bit joyful. A few show strangers on the dance floor having maybe a moderate amount of fun. In one shot, my grandfather appears to be smiling as he dances with my grandmother, but she's glowering up at him. When I get married, I probably won't keep any of the glowering shots.

My grandfather looks even more like me than my dad does, which is weird because he's, like, a missing person. His face is long and thin like mine. My dad, with his rounder face, looks a lot more like my grandmother.

"I wonder how long these have been here," I say, closing the box and then placing another on top of it. Aisha doesn't respond. She's busy scrubbing a dirt stain off the carpet near the stairs.

I open another soggy box — the one marked with the "4." Unlabeled folders are stacked on one side, and on the other, random trinkets have been tossed in together. I pick out a wooden cross with peeling green paint, a lone turquoise earring that appears to be rusted, and a jewelry box. Inside the jewelry box are four baby teeth. Someone has written, on a small piece of paper thrown into the box, "Matthew's first teeth, 1971."

"If you were wondering where my father's baby teeth are, I found 'em," I say.

Aisha laughs. "Mystery solved."

"You think there's a good baby teeth market on eBay?"

"Probably Craigslist," she says.

I grab one of the files, sit down, and open it up. The front page is stuck to the file, and as I pull it back, I can see that blue and black ink has tattooed the inside of the folder itself, creating blurred backward words, unreadable. The top page of paper is illegible, and a few more pages are stuck to it. Some of the inside pages are readable, though, and I flip to a form called "Petition for Dissolution of Marriage with Children."

"More workin', less sittin'," Aisha calls over.

I ignore her and turn through to the final page, and there, under the title "Petitioner," is my grandmother's name, Phyllis Helen Smith, and her gritty, harsh signature.

Across from it, under the title "Respondent," is my grandfather's name, Russell Alan Smith. In his more animated autograph, the letters seem to be battling for attention.

There is also a witness's signature: John Francis Logan. Everyone's favorite pastor slash neighbor. The date is listed as May 23, 1983.

I'd never heard anything about my grandparents getting a divorce. I mean, according to my mom, my grandfather just up and left one day, never to be heard from again. I guess not. I wonder if my dad knew that they were having trouble, and that they had gotten divorced?

I riffle through the trinkets. Other than the baby teeth, most of the stuff is religious — crosses, a little round thumbnail picture of blond Jesus on a silver necklace, a cracked picture frame with an embroidered angel inside bearing the phrase, "With God all things are possible."

I roll my eyes. *Yes. All things. Like happy marriages and well-raised children. All possible.*

I GET BACK to cleaning, and soon I have the boxes stacked neatly against the wall and Aisha has the room smelling a little less musty.

We go up for a snack, and my father is sitting in the kitchen in a pair of tattered blue shorts and a ratty white T-shirt, eating frozen waffles with Aunt Jemima syrup. His legs are pasty white and skinny, and I'm a little embarrassed to have Aisha see him like this. Dad smiles when he sees her. "So you're the lesbian in the basement," he says.

I blurt out, "Dad!"

But Aisha laughs. She walks over and sticks out her hand. "Thanks for letting me stay here," she says. "Really."

"No sweat," he says, smirking as he shakes her hand, and I realize my dad is a bit of a charmer.

"And yes, that's how I like to be known. As the lesbian in the basement."

Dad laughs and takes a chomp of his waffle. "Good, 'cause I'm bad with names."

She says, "And what should I call you?"

My dad thinks for a bit, and then he coughs a couple of times into his hands and wipes them on his T-shirt, leaving an amber smudge. "The drunk upstairs," he says.

She nods like this is normal fatherly behavior. "Nice to meetya, the drunk upstairs."

"Nice to meetya, basement lesbian."

I want to play with them, so I find myself trying to come up with the funniest thing I can, but nothing comes to me. "So Grandma had quite the collection of religious things down there," I say. Dad looks at me blankly, and I add, "We did a little box organizing."

He nods. "Oh yeah, all sorts of shit." He turns to Aisha and says, "That religion crap gives me serious butt cramps."

Aisha laughs. "Butt cramps. Thanks for that . . . image, Mr. Smith."

He shrugs. "What can I say? I'm a poet."

"I'm not a fan of religion either," Aisha says. "I mean, I only became the lesbian in your basement after my Bible-thumping dad threw me out."

My dad shakes his head. "That's rough," he says. "A guy shouldn't do that to his kid."

I feel my jaw tighten. *Have another drink, Dad. Maybe you should choose that over your son?*

Aisha sits down next to him. "He was all about the Jesus," she says. "I guess the Jesus told him to do it."

"Oh yeah. Jesus tells people to do a lot of shit, seems like," my dad says, chewing with his mouth open. "You have no fuckin' idea how much I hate those Jesus people. Act all holier than you and then do all sorts of crap. Your religious dad kicked you out. You know what mine did? Left us. No note or nothing, just left. Man of God."

"Wow," Aisha says, looking at me. I shrug. "I didn't know that."

"And then my mom, she goes and gets even more religious on me. After he leaves, suddenly she's the fuckin' church lady. I don't have time for that crap. None of it."

"Amen to that," Aisha says. "If I never see the inside of a church again, it'll be too soon."

I sit there thinking about the construction of that sentence. *If I never, it will be* . . . *When I don't do something, it will be* . . . It's a sentence that means nothing. I've never noticed that before. My dad gets up and ambles over to the refrigerator. I sit down across from where he was sitting. He takes out a Coke bottle, swigs from it, puts it back in the fridge, and sits down again.

"So a priest and a rabbi are walking down the street," my dad says. "They pass by a schoolhouse. Priest says, 'Hey, let's screw some kids.' Rabbi says, 'Out of what?'" He leaves his mouth open after, like waiting for the laugh.

Aisha snorts, which is more than I can do, because as much as I like a good joke, I'm not sure this is one. This one just seems like it's in bad taste.

"Ahh!" he says, pointing wildly at Aisha. "You get me. You're not so butt-scared all the time like someone I know." He looks directly at me. "You're like the son I never had."

I cross and uncross my arms, stung. I count by thirteens to 273. He puts up his hand for Aisha to high-five. She just gawks at him.

"Too much?"

"A bit," she says. "I think you just told your son that you don't have a son."

My dad closes his eyes and concentrates, and then he shakes his head. "Ahh, fuck. I'm always too much. Born that way, I guess. Sorry, kiddo. I know I'm a moron."

"Yeah, I definitely get that," I say.

Dad ignores the insult and motions at me. "What about you? You don't believe in that crap, do you?"

At first I think he's asking if I believe he feels like he doesn't really have a son — which is debatable — and then I realize he means religion.

"Nah," I say. "I don't subscribe to the Jesus stuff. Not a Jesus subscription holder."

"I believe in waffles," my dad says. "Lots of waffles."

"I believe in strawberries," Aisha says. "You think there are any left?"

I shake my head, because I know we're out. "I believe in the Porcupine of Truth," I say without thinking about it.

"The porcupine of what?" Aisha asks, leaning back in her chair.

The rules of improv with the group at my school are simple: One, just come up with stuff on the fly. Two, anything anyone else comes up with you have to treat as true, meaning you can't deny anyone else's reality. I nod at her like everyone knows about this stuff and let my brain play. "You never heard of the Porcupine of Truth?"

Aisha gives me that arched-eyebrow look from when I first met her at the zoo. My dad shakes his head, and I feel like we should be sitting out around a campfire. I place my hand over my heart.

"In my, uh, belief system," I start, "when you get to heaven — which isn't called heaven, by the way, but is instead called, um, Des Moines — you aren't greeted by Peter or any saint or Jesus or anything like that."

"So who greets you?" Aisha asks.

"The Porcupine of Truth. He meets you at the gates of Des Moines, which are less like gates and more like, you know, a velvet rope in front of a club. And when you get there, he asks you, 'Truth or dare?'"

She says, "Wow. This is good to know."

"Well, yeah. This is important stuff. And if you say, 'Dare,' and the Porcupine, say, dares you to run naked through the fields leading up to Des Moines and you won't, he pushes a lever and you are sent to hell, which is actually Paramus Park Mall, the day before Christmas."

"The what mall?" Aisha asks.

"New Jersey," I say. "What were you, born in Billings?"

"Nebraska," she says.

"And if you do what he says, you get to go into Des Moines, which as you know is a beautiful place with lots of trees and stuff."

I sneak a look at my dad. His mouth is wide open, and it takes me a second to realize he's a little awed. He hasn't seen my improv shows like Mom has. He has no idea about any of this.

I continue. "And if you say, 'Truth,' the Porcupine, who is omniscient . . ."

"Where'd this all come from?" Dad says, but there's a smile on his face, and it's hard for me not to break character and smile too.

I repeat, "The Porcupine, who is omniscient . . ."

"Like all porcupines . . ." Aisha says.

"Exactly. Like all porcupines, *she* is all knowing."

Aisha cracks up. "I like the 'she.' "

"Know your audience," I say. "So she scans through your life files and finds the four moments that are most embarrassing, and she asks you questions about those moments. For example, it could be the time you were on the school bus and you peed yourself laughing and left a puddle and pretended it was Jamey Foster who did it."

Dad laughs. His face is lit up like I haven't seen it before. I want to bottle this moment. This feeling. For all the times I don't have it. Which is every other moment of my life ever.

Aisha says, "For example, not like that's something that happened to you, right?"

"Right," I say. "And the Porcupine of Truth asks you about this in front of a studio audience of all the people who have ever known you who died before you."

Dad, still smirking, puts his hand under his chin and rubs. "Okay, so what if you're a baby and you didn't know anyone who has already died?"

"Good question. Then they fill the audience with dead child sitcom stars," I say, trying to ignore the nauseous feeling in my chest. All this talk about death with my dying dad. Too much.

He starts to laugh again, hard, and that turns into a cough. "Of course," he says as he tries to stop coughing.

"And you have to tell the truth in front of everyone, and if you do, you get to go to Des Moines. And if you don't, you wind up in the pits of Paramus Park Mall. Or, if you're lucky, suburban Chicago, which is what they call the place in between heaven and hell. I forget what it's usually called."

"Suburban Chicago, I believe," Aisha says.

"Exactly. So that's the Porcupine of Truth, and I swear on a stack of Bibles, or, where this particular story comes from, *Entertainment Weekly*s."

My dad applauds, clapping his hands above his head. "Bravo, bravo. Now that there's some good shit," he says.

I can't help but smile.

We bullshit some more, and it's awesome. I kind of want my mom to see this, because of all the times she bad-mouthed Dad as I was growing up. And really, he isn't that bad. Or maybe he is, or was, but he has good qualities too. He's actually fun.

The conversation begins to stall, and Aisha stands up.

"Found some interesting stuff in the files downstairs," I say, staying seated. "Divorce papers, stuff like that."

He screws up his face like he's annoyed. "My parents never got divorced," he says.

"But I just saw —"

He shakes his head. "Nah. I mean, maybe after he left, she filed. I don't know. But we never heard from him again."

"But he signed —"

My dad interrupts me. "Stop. Enough. I don't give a crap about any of that."

"Okay," I say. "But it was in the —"

"Seriously, kiddo. Stop."

I tense my shoulders.

Dad exhales. "Relax, Carson. I really don't worry about that anymore. When you're dying, you don't have time for that junk. The shit people did to you? It's over."

I nod and look away. The conversation stops, and my dad and I are just sitting there. Aisha looks over at me and says, "Awkward turtle." She puts her left hand on top of her right with her thumbs out and then rotates her thumbs forward.

"What the hell's an awkward turtle?" my dad asks.

Aisha shows him again, and I think about what funny thing I can say. Nothing comes to mind. And then, I once again do something that doesn't feel normal to me. In a quiet voice I ask, "When did he leave?"

Dad makes a frustrated noise, but then he takes a deep breath and actually answers.

"It was the year my Brewers finally made the World Series. I remember because my father and I used to watch baseball together. Sometimes they'd be the game of the week on Saturday afternoons, because that year they were finally good. Harvey's Wallbangers. Yep. The Wallbangers."

He smiles at the memory.

"That summer. I was, what? Seventeen? One day I woke up and he was gone. I asked my mom. She had no clue. I figured he'd write or something. Never did. And of course that's the year the Brewers got to the Series. Finally. We'd waited my whole childhood for that, and there they were, and he wasn't there to watch it with me. Lost to the Cardinals. Stupid, fucking Cardinals."

He shakes his head, and I can hear the despair. All these years later, and he can say whatever he wants to, but it does still matter to him. Like, a ton.

It's hard to know what to say. So I just say, "Sorry," and Aisha says, "That sucks," and he nods and shrugs, and soon Aisha and I go downstairs and hang out.

"Well, that was, um, educational," Aisha says.

I bow my head. "Yeah," I say. "Sorry about that."

"Not at all," she says. "Apple didn't fall far from the tree."

*What does that even mean?* I think. *He's a deserter, dying of alcoholism. What a horrible thing to say to a guy.* But I don't say that, of course. I just say, "Yeah, well."

She says she's gonna chill on the porch for a while, and for kicks, I get on my computer and look up the Brewers' World Series history. I've never been big on baseball, which is the world's dullest sport. But imagining my dad and his dad watching it in this very house makes me feel a little nostalgic.

There it is. The Brewers and the Cardinals in the World Series.

I look closer, and the hair stands up on the back of my neck.

It took place in 1982.

The year *before* my grandfather signed the divorce papers.

WHEN I WAKE up from an afternoon nap, I find that Aisha has created the Porcupine of Truth.

She is outside, under the big pine tree, lying on her back with her hands clasped behind her head. The Porcupine of Truth — and I know what it is immediately — is sitting up, staring down at her.

The porcupine's core is poster board that Aisha has traced and cut out with God knows what, since I can barely find a pen around here, let alone scissors. She has festooned this core with what appear to be bristles, probably from the broom she used this morning when we were cleaning up the basement. For eyes she found black buttons, and the snout appears to be wadded-up waxed paper. The buttons are not inset on the poster board, but instead have been attached to the bristles, like an afterthought. It is not so anatomically correct, but I have to give it to Aisha — it's a pretty impressive art project. The porcupine stands about eight inches tall, and when I lean down to straighten one of her quills, she teeters back and forth.

Aisha, still lying down, picks her up and holds her high above her in both hands. "Behold! The Porcupine of Truth!"

I sit on the grass and applaud. Aisha does a horizontal curtsy.

"On an unrelated note, do we need a new broom?" I ask.

"We might."

"Well, clearly we must worship her."

"Well, clearly."

"What does one do to worship the Porcupine of Truth?"

"Good question." She sits up, and a brown pine needle is stuck to her tank top. I want to be that pine needle. "Buy a new broom, possibly."

"Of course, it is the Porcupine of Truth, so there is truth telling."

"Of course," she says.

"And if I recall correctly, there's the Guacamole Festival."

Aisha shakes her head. "I think you're just hankering for guac, which is way different than an act of worship."

"You're breaking the rules. You aren't supposed to deny my reality."

She screws up her face at me, and I realize she doesn't do improv comedy or know the rules, so I let it go.

"So there's a thing," I say.

"What thing?" she asks.

"A thing. I looked up that World Series my dad was talking about. It happened in 1982."

"So?"

"So, that's the thing. The form I saw, the divorce form, the one my dad said didn't exist because his dad left one day and they never got divorced and no one ever heard from him again?"

"Yeah?"

"It was signed in 1983."

Aisha is quiet for a bit. I glance over and she is biting her lip, lost in thought.

"Okay," she finally says, slowly. "So what do you think that means?"

"It means my dad's dad disappeared back in 1982. But my grandparents actually divorced in 1983."

She nods a few times. "I mean, it could just be that they divorced by mail."

"Right, but my dad has no idea about it."

She chews on her lip a little more. "You heard your dad. He doesn't care about this stuff."

"Yeah, I don't buy that."

She seems to consider this. "So who could we ask about the divorce thing?" she asks.

"The pastor next door signed the form too," I say. "He knows more than my dad does. That's weird, right?"

"Oh good. A pastor."

"You just want to meet a real, live pastor. Because of your deep love of religion," I say, and Aisha says, "That's exactly it."

# 10

THE PASTOR IS watching the local news when we arrive, and he seems overjoyed to have company.

"Who's your friend?" he asks me as he ushers us into his living room, which still smells like pinecones and old folks.

I introduce him to Aisha and we three sit down on his couch.

"You're very striking," he says.

Aisha bows. "Thank you, sir. It's always been my life goal to bring a little taste of sub-Saharan Africa to central Montana."

He clearly has no idea how to respond, so he says, "So are you from here, dear?"

She nods, not looking at him, and then we suffer through the world's most awkward three-minute conversation about nothing. No topic is safe, and I can tell Aisha is thinking about turning "striking" into an action verb. Finally, thankfully, she asks if she can use his bathroom, and the pastor points the way down the hall.

"So I was actually wondering if I could ask you some questions," I say once Aisha is gone.

"Of course," he says, visibly relieved that it's just the two of us.

"It's about my grandfather. He was your friend, right?"

"Oh yes," the pastor says.

"You have any idea where he would have gone?"

The pastor takes a deep breath and gives me a deeply sympathetic look.

"I really don't," he says.

"You never heard from him again after he left?"

He shakes his head. "I'm sorry."

"Did my grandparents ever, like, get divorced?"

He looks up and to the right, like he's trying to remember.

"I don't think so."

"Huh," I say.

He crosses his legs. "Your grandmother and I went through this same process, thirty years ago," he says. "We tried everything. We wanted to understand what happened. Nothing panned out."

"Nothing?"

He puts his head down and lets it hang there. "You have no idea how hard it was. For all of us. His . . . disappearance. Your grandmother . . . just about fell apart after. Your father, well. He took to drinking, even though he was just a kid, and he never got back on track. I know this all too well. Believe me. I wish I knew how to help. I've been trying to help all these years, but your father, he doesn't want me around. I know that. I just . . . keep looking after him because I think Russ — your grandfather — would want me to. We're family, Carson. I wish I could say the one thing to make it all better, but I simply can't. Do you understand that?"

Aisha returns from the bathroom and comes to stand by my shoulder.

"I get it," I say, wondering how to bring up the fact that I know about the divorce. And his signature. "And thanks. It's just. There's this one thing I —"

Aisha jams me in the back, and I stop talking. The pastor is waiting for me to finish.

"This one thing I . . . wanted to say. To you. Thanks," I say.

"Yes," Aisha says. "Thanks."

He smiles, and our good-byes are even more awkward than the last time I saw him.

We walk back across his yard to our house. When we get down to the basement, I say, "What just happened?"

"I needed to get you to stop talking," she says.

"Why?"

"Because," she says, jutting her hands out wide. "He has one of your boxes. In his office. I opened the wrong door on the way to the bathroom, and I saw it."

"What?"

"I saw a box that's definitely one of your grandmother's. This one had the same flood mark. That line across the bottom, about four inches up. I've seen that line. I swear to you. It's one of the same boxes."

I shake my head at her. "If there was a flood in this house, there was probably a flood next door."

"Nope," she says. "This one had an orange '2' on it."

My stomach drops. "While you were in the bathroom, I asked about the divorce. He said it never happened."

"He lied," Aisha says. "And this isn't like one of those things he forgot."

"How do you know?"

"The box. It was open. It was next to his desk chair, and it was open."

We stay up late formulating a plan to get a chance to look at the box. It's tough, because there's no conceivable way to get Aisha and him talking while I sneak back to his office.

"Maybe you could do an exotic African dance for him?"

She shoots me a sideways look, and I realize that she can joke about race. I can't.

We simply can't come up with a way to get me in there.

"We need to see the box when he's not around," I say, and Aisha nods.

"How bad do you want to see it?" she asks.

"Pretty bad," I say. "I mean, the fact that he's actively lying is creepy."

"Well. What if I told you we could get in without breaking and entering?" she asks. "Did he have an alarm system?"

"The dude doesn't have a computer. I'm sure he wouldn't know what do with an alarm system."

"Up to you," she says. "I have a feeling there's an easy way to get in."

I have trouble sleeping, and I wake up around three in the morning and curse myself for not having a glass of water nearby. I go upstairs and pour myself one, and I drink it by the light of the moon, next to the open window over the sink. I stare up at the gray-black Billings sky, barely lucid, and I let my eyes wander over to the pastor's place, where, tomorrow — today, really — we will be entering-but-not-breaking. How? And what will happen if we get caught?

My eyes scan over a small, round, second-story window, right under an arch. I see what I swear are eyes, staring back at me.

And then, just like that, they are gone.

# 11

FIVE MINUTES AFTER the pastor leaves for work in the morning, Aisha leads me to his front door and illustrates her devious plan. She turns the doorknob and pushes open the door.

"This is Billings. Lots of people don't lock their doors here," she says as we walk into the living room. It feels weird to be in there without him knowing, but on the other hand, at least we haven't broken and entered; we have simply entered.

The door to his office is closed. She pushes the door open.

She exhales. "Shoot." There is no box there.

"Damn," I say back.

We wander the house, peeking into other rooms. The box is nowhere to be found. I begin to wonder if she was seeing things yesterday. We scour his bedroom. No box anywhere. Then I think about last night, and seeing him in an upstairs room. I know it's a two-story house, but we open all the doors and don't come upon a staircase.

"There has to be a way upstairs," I say, leaving out the part about me seeing him last night. I don't need to make this any creepier than it already is. Aisha takes the lead, wandering until she comes to a stop next to the bathroom. We look up. A string dangles from a square in the ceiling.

"Yes," she says. "Yes, there is."

She pulls the string and slowly a hatch opens. A ladder comes down, and we climb up. She goes first, and I follow, staring at her apple-shaped ass.

The room upstairs has such a low ceiling that we both have to hunch our shoulders. At the far end sits a window alcove with a brown, high-backed, weathered leather chair facing the attic. I maneuver behind it to the window and see that it looks down into our house, through the window above our kitchen sink. As I do, the chair swivels a bit.

Next to the chair is a small table with a half-full coffee cup on it. Probably from last night, when I saw him up here. There is an album cover next to the cup. At the mouth of the alcove is a record player with a record on it. I've never seen one in real life before.

"Uh," Aisha says, pointing across the room. I turn around. The "2" box. A shiver runs through me.

She opens the box, and I walk over to the pastor's chair. On the table next to the coffee cup, the album cover reads "Steve Forbert" in big red letters. Mr. Forbert has a mullet and a pug nose. He looks like no one who is alive in the world currently. The eighties. Wow. I pick up the album, turn it over, and a name is scrawled across the top in black Magic Marker:

*Smith.*

"My grandfather's," I say, almost like I'm croaking out the words, and Aisha comes over and takes the album cover from me.

"It was just out on the table?" she asks. I nod. The album itself is on the record player.

She hands the album cover back to me, and as she does, an

envelope falls out. Its corners are frayed and yellow. I pick it up, and the first thing I see is that it is addressed to "Pastor John Logan, 923 Rimrock Road, Billings, MT 59041." There is no return address, but there is a postmark in the upper right corner, on top of a twenty-cent stamp with Eleanor Roosevelt on it. The postmark reads, "Thermopolis, WY, 7/19/82." The envelope has been opened carefully with a letter opener, with the letter neatly folded inside.

I remove the letter from the envelope. Even the paper feels old.

I turn the letter over and back again, scanning for a name. I find it on the bottom of the second page: *R. S.*

"Those are my grandfather's initials! Holy crap!"

We look at each other, amazed.

"Well . . . Read it," Aisha says.

I read the letter out loud.

*July 17, 1982*

*Dear John,*

*A leper walks into a bar, sits down. Bartender looks over, vomits all over the place. Leper says, "Hey, I know I'm not an attractive man, but I have feelings too." Bartender shakes his head, says, "It wasn't you. The guy sitting next to you keeps dipping crackers in your neck."*

I look at Aisha and crack up. She looks horrified, so I keep reading.

*Sorry. I figured you'd want to know it was still me. A leper can't change its spots, you know. Although that is what I'm trying to do, I guess.*

I'm writing from Thermopolis. I've decided to stay an extra day with Thomas and Laurelei. An extra day can't hurt, can it? I have to get my head together. It's not close to together.

Last night I dreamed of Phyllis and Matthew.

"My dad and my grandma," I say.

Aisha nods. I look back at the letter and speed up my reading.

Her face as I told her. His face, his profile, as I left the house the last time, and he had no idea. I know you didn't want me to tell her. I promise, she's the only one who knows, and she's not going to say anything, believe me. She has no idea where the money came from anyway, so don't worry too much. You did good. A good thing.

John, if I'm not back soon enough, please look after them. It tears me up that it's even a possibility that I'll never see my wife and my son again, and I know it's all my fault. And at the same time, I know you'll be there and you are family too. I know you would always treat them as you'd treat me.

Thomas and Laurelei are good people. You never cease to amaze me with the people you know. The number of possible Leff puns is astronomical, and after the first two didn't hit, I gave up.

Sigh. I have never doubted you before, John. That's the hardest part of this. This mustard seed of doubt. What if this is bigger than you? What if it's bigger than God? Man oh man. Why'd I have to go and choose the world's most dangerous and expensive grid? But I have faith in the KSREF. I have to.

Last thing. And I'm only saying this because everything is so up in the air and I want to say everything:

If you are looking out for my best interests and those of my family, why does it feel as though you're protecting the church and not them? If I had followed your advice, Phyllis would not know where I am now, and it's hard enough having Matthew in the dark.

This is but a mustard seed, John. Mostly I am beyond grateful for what you are doing for me, for what the church is doing for me. Your friendship literally sustains me, and I love you for that always.

I truly hope that someday we'll see each other again, and this will be behind us, a nightmare and a secret we take to our graves.

Your leper friend,

R. S.


I look up at Aisha and hiss, "What the . . . ?"

"Wow," she says. "Just, wow."

Suddenly, I'm very aware that we're in the pastor's house without his permission, and I am in possession of something he surely does not want me to have. A piece of information, maybe, but there are more questions than answers in it.

"It was in the album the pastor was listening to?" Aisha asks.

"Yup."

"He must have been rereading it," she says.

I think about him watching our house last night, and I get this chill, like he's been thinking about me. It's super creepy. "Well, we're definitely taking this," I say.

She nods slowly. "Just know, if we take this stuff, he's gonna know it's missing. You were just asking about your grandfather and the divorce. He's gonna know you took it."

I think about that, and then I stuff the letter into my pocket. My grandfather had a secret. *A nightmare and a secret we take to our graves?* I have to find out what this is.

She goes back over to the "2" box and opens it. Inside are neatly stacked envelopes, a notebook, several folders, and a couple cassette tapes and albums. It's my grandfather's stuff. I just know it.

Aisha rushes to the window as if she hears something. She peers as far right as she can.

"Shit shit shit," she says.

"What?"

"That would be the pastor's car," she says, panic obvious in her voice.

We rush into action. I repack the box as neatly as I can, and Aisha dashes over to the stairs. She pulls them up with all her might. They barely budge.

"They're stuck. Maybe they don't close from up here," she says, sounding desperate.

"Fuck," I say.

"Okay," she says. "Hang tight."

Before I can even react, Aisha leaps down the stairs, and in one quick movement she pushes the stairs up and slams them shut. I stare at the closed attic hatch like an idiot, thinking, *What the hell just happened?* Then I run over to the window, and, to my right, I watch the pastor slowly ambling toward the house from his car. I quickly shut the box, turn off the attic light, and hide behind the chair. The back door creaks open downstairs, and I glance out the window to my left just in time to watch Aisha scamper from the back door to the front yard of our house. She's safely out.

That's a lot more than I can say for me.

# 12

I SIT MOTIONLESS behind a leather chair in a window alcove of my neighbor's attic, thinking about betrayal.

If I ever get out of here, Aisha is gone. She couldn't have taken one extra second to explain to me that we were going to leap down the stairs? She had to lock me in? I am so pissed with her that I don't care where the hell she sleeps. Just not in my basement. I'll go back to being the guy with not too much going on, stuck for the summer with his crazy, dying father and his weird, psychobabbling mother.

I take out my cell phone. I make sure it's on vibrate, and then I text Aisha.

wtf???

She doesn't respond. My blood boils.

seriously. wtf.

Nothing.

If I'm stuck here for a full day, or worse, overnight, I'm in trouble. There's no bathroom up here, and I already have to pee, damn it. I could crawl across the floor to the box and go through it. But when I press down on the flooring below me, it creaks. I'm not going anywhere. I'm stuck behind this chair.

Finally, after seventeen minutes, my phone buzzes.

**Didn't want to text you when I got out cause I figured your sound was on. Forgot to keep my eye on my phone. Trying to get you out.**

I type back furiously.

Well try harder. You abandoned me!

**Wtf choice did I have?**

I need to pee

**Well, pee. Mice probably do it.**

Mice?!?

**Sorry. Not good in a crisis.**

Wait. Is this a crisis?

**See what I mean?**

I put my phone away. Clearly I'm gonna need to figure this one out myself. How do you get out of an attic without taking the stairs? The window doesn't open, and even if did, it's a small, round thing, and it's pretty high up.

I hear a noise and I tense my muscles. It's a sliding sound. And then the slide gets louder.

Shit.

He's lowering the stairs.

He's coming up to the attic.

*Shit shit shit. How am I going to explain this? Oh hi, Pastor. I just enjoy crouching behind chairs in strangers' attics. It's my thing.*

Slow footsteps enter the attic, and then the light comes on. I crouch down low, and from my angle I can see the pastor's shoes and the bottom of his pants as he walks directly toward me.

I used to play this video game set in Nazi Germany where you hide from the SS guards. They march right at you, and you only see their boots and the bottom of their legs. Sometimes they stop before they get to you, and other times you hear them yell something in German and then gunfire, and you're dead. This feels exactly like that.

Pastor Logan strides slowly to the chair, and then to the left, like he's going around it. I close my eyes, as if that will make me invisible when he steps on me.

I brace for contact. But there is none. Then I hear some sounds coming from a speaker at ear level. He's put on a record.

I take a silent, slow, deep breath. The song starts with a harmonica, then a steel guitar comes up, and the beat starts. Then there's a huge rustling noise. The pastor has sat down in the chair, inches from me. There's no way this ends well.

The pastor starts tapping his foot to the beat. It must be that album that my grandfather had put our last name on — Steve something. It's old music. The lyrics are all about going down to Laurel to see a girl. I try to imagine the pastor being young enough to think about going somewhere to see a girl. Surely my granddad felt that way about my grandmother when they were young. It's all so impossible to imagine, the past — when old people were young and had the pervy thoughts I have today.

A cell phone rings, and I automatically tense up. But it isn't mine.

The pastor stands up and strolls over to the record player to stop the music. He answers the phone. I stay as still as I can and try not to breathe.

"Hello? . . . This is he. . . . How can I help you? . . . Well, I should be heading back that way in an hour or two. . . . Oh my word. . . . When you say emergency, what do you — . . . Okay. . . . Of course. . . . I'll be happy to — okay. Good-bye."

The pastor mutters, "Dadgummit," and I watch as his lower legs carry him back toward the stairs. He takes a long, long time to climb down, and I find myself holding my breath longer than I need to. The stairs slowly rise up into the attic, and the trapdoor gently closes.

I exhale. Out the window, the pastor ambles to his car, the car lights flash, and he backs up and pulls onto Rimrock Road.

I text madly, **Get here! Now! He's gone!**

No response. Damn it. C'mon, Aisha. C'mon.

I hurry over to the stairs and try to push the trapdoor open. It won't budge. I check my phone again. Nothing. I call, figuring maybe she'll hear the ring.

And then I hear a ringtone — something sort of jazzy — playing within the house, and the stairs are pulled down, and there's Aisha at the bottom, smiling at me.

"Thank God," I say. "He got a call and left."

"Who do you think made the call? Give me a little credit," she says. I'm about to climb down when she adds, "We oughtta take the stuff — the box. Clearly can't stay here. He comes and goes too much."

I figure, *What the hell?* I pass the box to her. I climb down, we close the hatch, and we run out the back door as quickly as we can.

# 13

BACK IN MY dad's basement, Aisha explains what she had to do to get me out of there. She wanted to call Pastor Logan right away, but she didn't have his number. My mom was on the phone with someone back in New York, so Aisha bugged my dad, who was not too happy that she actually wanted to speak to the pastor. He almost didn't give her the number, but finally relented, telling her she was crazy for wanting to talk to some religious dude.

"I'm sorry," she explains. "I know you must have been freaked when I left you up there."

"I was fine," I say, lying.

The first thing we take out of the box are a stack of letters, some opened and most not. Every single envelope looks like it's been through a flood. In some cases, the ink has washed off entirely. In others, it's just been smudged beyond recognition.

On one, I can just about make out a postmark with the date October 19, 1988. The place it comes from, however, I can't decipher — only what appears to be an *S* or an *E* as the first letter. On another, the month and day are unreadable, but the year appears to be 1985. The stamp is Duke Ellington, and it's twenty-two cents.

There seem to be about twenty of these letters. A few have opened from the moisture, but I can tell that the letters inside have never been removed or read. I take one out of an open envelope, and the ink has bled over the entire piece of stationery and dried.

"Do you think these are from your grandfather to your dad?" Aisha asks.

I don't even have to answer, because I lift away an old, empty photo frame, and underneath, in a plastic baggie, is another opened letter. I grab it and just about tear the baggie open. Aisha takes the box and keeps digging.

The letter is short, and it's in the same handwriting as the letter my grandfather sent to the pastor. Unlike most of the other letters, this one has no water damage. I read it out loud.

*December 21, 1982*

*Dear Matthew,*

*Happy birthday, son. I am so, so sorry I am not there with you to celebrate. I wish I could explain, but I can't. Just know that I hope to be back soon, and then I will apologize for the rest of my life.*

*I miss you so much, son. I was a bad father and I know that now, and when I come home, I will try to be better.*

*The Brewers in the World Series! It would have been great to watch it with you, but I sure as heck am glad you weren't with me for Game 7! Talk about a disappointment!*

*Love always,*

*Da*

I look up at Aisha in amazement. She returns the look.

"You think my dad ever saw this?" I ask.

"He said he never heard from him again. And yet this is open," Aisha says. Her eyes are wide. Wider than I'd expect, like she's even more shocked by all this than I am. "You ready to get your mind blown?"

"Um," I say. "Try me?"

Tentatively, she hands me another opened letter. It isn't water-logged, and it is very readable.

"It was stuck on the side, like it was hidden away on purpose," she tells me.

It is postmarked December 21 of last year, no return address. I look at Aisha. "Holy —"

"I know," she says, blinking. "I know."

She watches as I open the letter.

The handwriting is a little different now — maybe older, more shaky, the letters less controlled, perhaps. Like my grandfather grew up over the course of thirty-two years.

Dear Matthew,

I cannot blame you for not responding all these years. I do think this will be my last letter, though, seeing as you're fifty now. Where did the time go?

Happy birthday, Matthew. I so wish I could see you, but I know it is your choice, and I respect it. Take care.

Love you.

I feel my head go numb, and I struggle for air. "My grandfather is alive! And the pastor knows it. Holy . . ."

"I know," Aisha says. "This is crazy."

"You want to be there when I show it to my dad?"

She shakes her head hard. "Not my drama. I'll stay down here."

My heart pounds as I climb the stairs. My dad. He doesn't seem like the kind of guy who takes things well, at least not without alcohol. But this is good news. Shocking news, maybe, but also good. His dad is alive.

He answers his door bleary-eyed, and I quickly sniff. I don't smell any alcohol on him, but I'm not sure which is better — him drunk or him not drunk — for something like this. "Hey, kiddo," he says.

"Hey." Suddenly I'm at a loss for words.

"Your lesbian friend wanted to talk to the pastor. I don't know about that girl," he says.

I laugh. "She's something, all right."

"Pretty, and nice," my dad says, and I wonder if he knows just how pretty I think she is.

"She's cool. So I have to ask you something. Did you ever see this?"

I hand him the letter from 1982 first. I don't want to freak him out all at once.

He brings the letter close to his face and squints, and then he holds it as far away from his face as he can and strains his eyes.

Something registers. He looks up at me, shocked. "Where the fuck did you get this?" He thrusts the letter back at me, and I take it.

"I . . . We found it in a box."

"How the . . . ? What the . . . ?" He stumbles backward a couple of steps.

"Dad," I say, walking toward him.

He puts his arms out to stop me from following him. His face is a mask of pain. Agony.

"Don't you ever," he yells, his voice thin. "Don't you . . . Did I ask you to — fucking . . ."

He grabs his chest and he starts to cough, and then he keeps coughing and coughing. I stand there, paralyzed. My mother comes running. By the time she gets to him, his face is turning slightly blue and I'm still standing there like a helpless moron.

"What happened?" she asks, sitting him down on the bed.

"I was telling him about something I found. It's from his dad," I say. "There's more —"

She doesn't look up at me. "This isn't a good time to upset him," she says. "Go downstairs."

"But —"

"DOWNSTAIRS," she barks. It's as angry as she's ever been with me.

My blood freezes. I walk, numb, through the kitchen to the basement stairs. I descend. I count to 255 by fifteens. It does nothing for me.

When I see Aisha, I try to breathe normally. I feel underwater. I sit back down next to her.

"What'd he say?" she asks.

My phone buzzes in my pocket, and I go to pull it out, but the case gets stuck against the fabric. I pull harder, and it won't come out, and then I'm tugging with all my might, and it just won't budge. When I give up and remove my hand, the phone slips out of my pocket and onto the floor. I stomp on it. I slam my foot down, again and again, and I keep slamming my foot down until my phone is in pieces, strewn across the basement carpet.

Aisha is expressionless. Just sort of there. This is a dealbreaker. She thinks I'm totally messed up, and she's going to walk away, out of my life, and I'll never see her again. Which is perfect, because finally I have a friend. Someone who kind of gets me. It's been a long time, as in forever, and now she's here, and soon she'll be gone, because that's what happens when people get close to you. And I'm so frustrated that I walk into the bathroom and slam the door behind me.

The tub is still a little wet from this morning's showers, but I don't care. I sit down in the cold puddle, lean back, and close my eyes.

I just kind of disappear into my brain for a while and allow the world to go away. It's what I do sometimes back home in New York. Sometimes it's better to be nowhere than somewhere. So that's where I go. Not mad, not sad. Just nowhere, nothing. I go there for a while.

# 14

WHEN I OPEN my eyes, Aisha is sitting cross-legged on the bathroom floor, looking at me. I have no idea how long I've been out.
More importantly, a hot girl has been watching me sleep. I check my
breath to make sure it's not terrible, then I rub my eyes and sit up.

"Sorry," I say, about nothing in particular. Or maybe everything.

She shrugs it off, digs into her pocket, and pulls out my phone.
She has Scotch-taped the pieces together. It's clearly never going to
work again, but it feels like the kindest possible thing for her to have
done while I slept.

"Thank you," I say, taking it from her. "It's perfect." I pretend to
make a call on it. "Hey, Dad? Great to hear from you! I miss you too.
I always love our conversations. You aren't the shittiest father on the
planet at all!"

"Hey, at least he didn't kick you out," she says.

I nod a few times. "Yep, he's a gem." I pick up the phone again.
"Hi Mom! Thanks for making me feel like it was my fault that my dad
turned blue!"

Aisha reaches out and touches my forearm. "I saw your mom
upstairs and filled her in a little. She felt bad. She said he was having
a tough day before all that. You just talked to him at a bad time."

I nod and nod. I don't know what to say.

"So are we gonna look at more of your grandpa's stuff?"

I don't have to be asked twice. I start to climb out of the tub.

"But first," she says. She reaches into her pocket and hands me a smartphone. It looks new. "I thought you might need another one without all the tape on it," she says.

I look at her and then look back at the phone. "You got this for me?"

She nods. "Consider it the least I could do. You're putting me up and all."

I shake my head. I have never had a friend who would do something like this for me. Surprise me with a gift. "You don't have the money to waste on this," I say.

"It was fifty bucks at Best Buy, and your mom went halvsies with me. She told me you're on Verizon. She gave me your password. I already activated it with your number."

I feel this tightness in my throat and I have to avoid her eyes and look at the floor. "I'll pay you back," I finally say, still studying the carpet beneath my feet.

"Forget about it."

"Thanks," I say, and I remind myself to thank my mom too. That was pretty surprising, and pretty darn nice.

We walk out of the bathroom and go through the rest of my grandfather's box. I find a spiral notebook with a mustard-yellow cover. Some of the pages are yellowed and water-stained. I open it to the first page.

*February 7, 1978*

<u>*Russ's Book of Puns*</u>
*Those who jump off a bridge in Paris are ~~in Siene~~ in Seine.*
*Dijon Vu — the same mustard as before.*

*Why does a man* A man needs a mistress just to break the monogamy.

*When two egotists meet, it's an I for an I.*

*What's the definition of a will? It's a dead giveaway.*

*A chicken crossing the road is poultry in motion.*

*Funny?*

*An eyeless fish is a fsh.*

*What do you call an invisible child? An invisible couple had a child. The kid was nothing to look at.*

I crack a smile. These are puns I could have come up with, definitely. And something about seeing his edits makes me feel like I'm watching his brain work, that he is alive and with me. I say, "Listen to this," and I read the page to Aisha.

She snorts a few times. The dead giveaway one makes her laugh.

"There's like pages and pages of this stuff," I say, thumbing through the notebook.

"Save it," she says.

"For when?"

"When I'm not around? I dunno."

I read another page or two to myself. One page is titled "Little-Known Bible Verses," and the first one listed is "The Parboil of the Evil Farmer." The second starts, "In the beginning, God created light bulbs. Wait. That was General Electric."

While I don't know much about the Bible, it seems wacky funny. I like wacky funny. And as much as I know my grandfather left his family and was a drunk and is mostly responsible for my dad being the way he is, I feel like the person who wrote these might actually understand me.

"I think I want to find him," I say.

"You think we could?" Aisha asks, and I like that she uses the word *we*.

I pull out my laptop and Google the name Russ Smith, and I find out that there's a college basketball star with that name. I try Russell, and I get a Wikipedia page devoted to all the famous people with that name. There are eleven. I am about to click on one who is a writer when I realize what I'm doing. *Yeah. He's probably not famous. Not a lot of people disappear and escape detection for thirty years by becoming famous.*

I do a census search, and there are 6,713 Russell Smiths. I narrow it to Montana and suddenly there are only thirty-five, and my heart jumps. Then I look closer, and I see that the census search results stop at 1940.

"Dang," I say.

Surely someone must have done this. My dad must have searched for his own dad online, right? But how the hell can I be sure of that? He's a drunk. It's hard to predict what he's done in his life or on Google. I have no idea.

I soldier on to ancestry.com. I put in Russ's name, choose a birth date of 1940, and set the parameters to plus or minus ten years. I figure if my dad was born in the 1960s, that's about right for my grandfather. I specify Billings, Montana.

A bunch of newspaper articles come up with what appear to be baseball box scores with the name Russell in it. Not helpful. This search is futile.

"What about those references in the letter to the pastor?" Aisha asks. She's busy going through the box.

"Oh yeah." I pull the letter out of my pocket and scan it. I type KSREF into Google and study the results. "Kenya Sugar Research Foundation. Yeah. Unless he moved to Africa or was looking to become a soccer referee in Kansas, that's not so helpful."

I type in "world's most dangerous and expensive grid." All sorts of stuff about clean energy and airports come up. I sigh deeply. "Meh. I think we're back to step one."

"Who were those people in the letter? From Wyoming?" she asks.

"Thermopolis. Thomas and Laurelei. He also says something about 'Leff.' Maybe that's the last name?"

She grabs my laptop from me and goes to whitepages.com, where she types "thomas and laurelei leff thermopolis wyoming." As the cursor spins, I think about whether we should ask the pastor again. He must know something. But he didn't tell us before, and now we've stolen stuff from him. It won't take him long to figure that out.

Up pops an entry for Laurelei V. Leff, age sixty-five to seventy. There's an address in Thermopolis, but no phone number. Aisha elbows me and she pulls up Google Maps and types in the address. The location appears on-screen, and Aisha asks for directions, putting Billings in as the origin. It's 190 miles away, and it would take a little over three hours to drive there.

I realize what's happening, and it fills me with shivers. "We don't have to," I say, but I don't really mean it.

"Of course we do," she says. "You want to find your grandfather.

We have one lead. I got wheels, you got a credit card. We can leave in the morning and be back by dinner."

I think about the credit card part. I mean, it all comes down to what's a "reasonable" expense. Coffee is reasonable. A movie. But a trip to Wyoming? Is this reasonable? It's tough to say. The whole thing is so unreasonable it's hard to find a lot of reason.

We are interrupted by the sound of footsteps on the stairs, then the back door opening. A strange voice says, "So you'll give him the morphine rectally when needed?"

My mother says, "Yes."

I give Aisha an embarrassed look, but she doesn't react to it.

"He's in a lot of pain," the man's voice says. "That's typical and to be expected. When these things progress . . ."

"And it's progressing?" Mom says.

"Sadly, it appears that way."

"How much time do we have?"

The man clears his throat. "Maybe a few months."

"Well, thank you," my mother says.

"Call if you need anything," the man says, and we hear the door shut.

Aisha and I look at each other. There are footsteps on the stairs. My mother is paying her first visit to our lair. She rounds the corner, a brave smile on her face. She doesn't look like my mom, the practiced, controlled woman I know. She looks like she's trying to be someone else.

"I assume you heard that." Her voice is softer than usual. This is her in crisis mode.

I nod and keep my head down.

She addresses Aisha. "I'm sure it's odd to be here for all this family drama."

Aisha shrugs her shoulders. "I wish I could help."

My mother says, "Did you give him the phone?"

Aisha nods.

"Thanks, by the way," I say to my mom. "Really."

She nods, and then addresses Aisha again. "I feel very glad to know you're here with Carson. He needs the distraction." Mom faces me. "I understand that you must feel terribly sad about your father. And I want you to know I feel that too. And it's okay to feel that."

I nod, and the chilly, empty feeling in my gut returns.

"I don't know exactly what it is you've found down here, kids, but I have to ask you to not bother your father with that right now. What he needs is to rest."

I nod again.

"It must be very hard for you to understand what this is all about. Aisha told me you found some information that might mean your grandfather is still alive. What you need to understand is that even if that's true, he walked out on your father. Even if you found him, your father does not have the strength for some kind of reconciliation. He doesn't want that. Do you understand what I'm saying to you?"

I nod a third time.

"Can you say something, Carson?"

"I get it," I say.

She smiles. "Good. And I do understand that what you were doing was done from the goodness of your heart. What I want to say to you is that you're a beautiful young man, and the impulse to help is exactly what I'd expect from you. Just not in this way, perhaps."

"Gotcha."

My mother heads upstairs, and Aisha and I sit on the bed in silence for a bit. I'm trying to put it all together. My grandfather is still alive. My father is dying, and he doesn't know his dad is still alive. My father doesn't want to know. And he's got maybe months left in his life.

"I just want to know where he is for *me*, you know?" I say finally. "He's my grandfather."

"Yup. Me too, now that I'm like your honorary sister."

"Yeah, congratulations on that," I say ruefully.

"Hey, I like your family," she says.

I'll have to think about that one for a bit. Like a long bit, probably.

I spend a few more hours poring over the contents of the box. I open every letter. They are all illegible, soggy, faded, blurred. I stare at the unreadable words and try to will them to be as they were before the flood. It's mostly useless, this box we've found. It's a pulsing beacon in the dark recesses of our basement, pulling us toward a mystery that may never be solved.

# 15

SLEEPING IS IMPOSSIBLE, what with the box, and the fact that my neighbor might know by now that he's been robbed, and that the robbers are next door, and if he knows this, he must know that we have in our possession all sorts of clues he doesn't want us to have. And then there's my dry mouth, and I want a glass of water, and I curse myself again for not getting one before I went to bed, because, of course, the sink window is visible from his attic. And I don't think I can take that. Seeing the pastor again, ever.

I turn on the flashlight app on my phone and grab my grandfather's journal. The weathered pages crinkle as I turn them, and I try not to wake up Aisha. The notebook is a weird combination of jokes, ideas, and diary entries.

*July 7, 1980*

*Too many thoughts in my mind. I can't sleep. Phyllis is the noisiest damn sleeper in the world. She snores like her uvula is sawing lumber.*

*Skit idea: A dainty lady gets hired by a bunch of lumberjacks to saw difficult wood with the powerful instrument in the back of her throat. Funny?*

*Sometimes I get so sick of my brain and I want to escape it all. How do you escape your brain? Do you run away? Do you cut your head off and let your torso run? How about a lobotomy? Worth a try.*

I lie down again, and I open the journal wide and place it face down on my chest. This was two years before he left. Why was my grandfather so tired of his brain? What was so wrong? And did he run away? It's all so hard to understand. Who is this person who jokes like me and wants to escape just like I do sometimes? I pick the journal back up, flip ahead a few more pages, and he's written a scene.

November 11, 1980

SCENE: Standard pharmacy

A man walks in and gets in line to speak to the pharmacist about a prescription. There are three guys ahead of him. The first guy says to the female pharmacist, "Haven't we met before?" She smiles, and he pays her. The second guy says, "That white coat looks beautiful on you." The pharmacist curtsies and takes his money. At this point, the man who just walked in notices no one has dropped off a prescription or anything. The third guy says, "If I said you had a beautiful body, would you hold it against me?" To this, the pharmacist frowns. He walks away, dejected. Finally it's the man's turn. He says hello to the pharmacist and puts the prescription down in front of her. She stares blankly at him. "Can you help me?" he asks. Nothing. Finally, he says, "May I drop off this prescription here, and have you fill it?" She shakes her head. "Sorry," she says. "This is the pickup line."

Is this, like, the funniest thing ever? No. But I can completely imagine coming up with something like this, and writing it down, and feeling that sense of pride that you get when you make yourself laugh. I don't know if that's universal, but I totally get it. And so does Russ.

How is it that two people who have never even met could be so much alike? Does sharing the same DNA make people do the same sorts of things, and where does that end, and, like, upbringing take over? How does heredity actually work?

These thoughts swirl through my head for a while, and then, when I get so restless on the carpet that I could scream, I creep up the stairs.

The pastor's attic light is off, thankfully. I grab a glass and turn on the faucet and gulp down a couple glasses of water.

A slight noise comes from my dad's room. My heart quickens. What if he's struggling? Does my mother have some sort of baby monitor in there so she can hear him in case he needs her?

I softly step toward the hallway. The noise is muffled and strange, high-pitched almost. I approach the door. It sounds like he's hyperventilating in his sleep.

I stand there for what feels like hours, alternately trying to psych myself up to go into his room or go back downstairs. Neither works. I just stay planted until my feet feel stuck. And when I'm as close as I can get to ready, I take a deep breath, knock on the door, and walk in.

I can see his outline faintly in the moonlight. He is on his side in his tattered blue sweatpants and white undershirt, cradling a pillow in one arm and an empty Jack Daniel's bottle in the other.

Goddamn alcohol. He's dying. He's on morphine. And somehow he still has a bottle of whiskey.

He is rocking back and forth, forth and back, and he's sobbing. The staccato sobs sound like they're coming from his nose. Every time he makes a noise, it feels like somebody is choking the air out of *me*.

I approach the side of his bed. "Dad," I say softly. "Wake up, Dad." Looking down at his body, I can see clearly that he's dying. He's dying. He's sick and frail and human. All the things your dad is not supposed to be.

"Dad," I whisper again. He doesn't have many nights left, according to the doctor. And the fact that he is sobbing one of those away is too much to take. "Wake up, Dad."

He doesn't wake at first, so I softly knee the mattress near his head. His eyes creep open. He looks at me, dazed, for quite a few seconds, and then his eyes get bigger.

"Da!" he says, his face seeming to illuminate. "Daddy!"

"No," I say, meaning it. "No."

"Daddy!" he repeats. He's smiling broadly now. It's a bit delirious, this wide smile, and I know he's drunk.

"No," I say, taking the bottle from his grasp and setting it on the floor. "I'm your son. Carson."

"You came for me," he says, his unfocused eyes boring into my upper forehead. The area feels like it's burning. "I've missed you so goddamn much, Da."

I'm frozen. There are certain scenes you're not supposed to have to play when you're a kid. Something inside of me is shaking, like, *No, no, can't do this, no, no,* but the other part of me, the physical part that can do stuff, is tentatively sitting down on the bed, next to his head.

He nuzzles his head against my leg until I gently lift his skull up onto my lap. I stroke his hair. It feels weird, wrong. And it also feels something else, something that's not wrong, and that part I have to choke down because this is my dad, the joke guy. Even if he's crying right now, I'm afraid he'll switch it up and laugh at me if I take this too seriously.

I stare at his profile. His chin is a stranger's chin. I don't know this chin. His nose is not one I know, not well. And yet also I do know it. Which is fucked up. He smells sour, like alcohol, and also like he hasn't showered in a day, maybe two. The base smell is like me when I don't shower. Families have scents, I guess. I was not aware of this. Is it in the DNA?

"I've been good," my dad says as I stroke his hair. His eyes are closed and he looks peaceful. "I'm glad you came back for me. I knew you'd come back."

"Yes," I finally say, through gritted teeth. "I came back."

"I missed you so much."

My jaw relaxes a bit, and I breathe into it. "I missed you too."

He opens his eyes and looks up at me. The look is still spacy and unfocused, and the thought comes to me that when he dies, this is the image I'll have of him. And I don't want it.

"I'm glad we're a family again, Dad," he says.

I close my eyes. "Me too," I say.

"Do I have long?" he asks. I open my eyes, and his unfocused glance seems to be searching for connection, and it's like neither of us can find it.

And his question. I don't know what he means. Does he have long? With me holding him, or to live?

"No," I say, as kindly as I can.

He doesn't cry. He just breathes and coos like a content little baby. And then, after a few minutes of that, there is shaking, and he does cry some more.

I pet his thinning brown hair gently. I don't say anything, because I can't. All I can do is breathe and breathe and breathe. This is all I'm capable of doing.

# 16

WHEN I AM safely able to extricate myself from my father's dream, I walk, numb, back down to the basement. Aisha is lightly snoring, but I figure if she can wake me at six thirty to clean, I can wake her up for this.

I sit down on the edge of the air mattress and tap her shoulder gently. "My dad," I say, when she finally leans up, resting on her elbows.

"What about him?"

"Crying. For his dad. To me."

I can't say more, because if I do, *I'm* gonna cry, and I don't cry, ever.

"What?"

I suck in as much air as I can, and I set my jaw tight, and I do my best to explain to her what just happened.

"Man," she says. "Heavy shit."

"Yeah."

"So . . ."

"So," I say. "So we have to find him. We have to find my grand-father, I mean. Before my dad . . . you know. We need to get my grandfather back here for him."

"You think?" she asks.

"I know," I say, and maybe the way I sound so sure makes her sure too, because she nods in agreement. "We have to go to Thermopolis and talk to those people. See what they know."

She stretches her arms over her head. "Let's do it. What're you gonna tell your mom?"

"I have no idea," I say.

I decide to take the journal, and Aisha says we have to take the Porcupine of Truth. We put these things on the ground next to the stairs. Neither of us can sleep much more, so we get up around five. I decide I'll text my mom once we're on the road, just in case she says no for once. Once we're both showered, we creep upstairs so we can sneak out to the car without her or my dad seeing.

We're all set to go around five thirty, and just as I close the passenger-side car door, my mom comes out the back door in her peach robe and slippers, her face so tense I can see the creases from ten feet away in the side-view mirror. She looks nothing like the calm woman who came down to the basement in crisis mode last night.

I get out of the car and salute her. Aisha gets out of the car too, and Mom waves to her tentatively.

"What's going on, Carson?" my mother says, her tone clipped, controlled.

"Got stuff to do today," I mumble.

She tenses her jaw and takes a deep breath. Then she puts her hand on my shoulder, which is apparently the official mother greeting. "Seeing your dad like that must have been very difficult for you," she says.

At first I think she means my nighttime visit to his room, but then I'm pretty sure she doesn't know anything about that. Pretty sure. "It was delightful," I say.

She lowers her chin to her chest and speaks to my kneecaps. "I'm hearing a great deal of anger at your father. I want you to know that I know it isn't easy for you to be here. I appreciate you coming to Montana, and I know that there will be a great deal of growth for you if you continue to be the bigger man."

"Thank you," I say, and my mother taps me on the shoulder twice like she's my teacher and I just got a hundred on my sixth-grade geography test, like maybe I was the only one who knew where the fuck Botswana was. She goes back inside without asking, for instance, why we're getting in the car at five thirty in the morning.

I look at Aisha and hold up a finger, telling her to pay attention. I cross to the house and open the back door. "Hey, Mom," I yell. "We're gonna head out to Wyoming for the day. Okay?"

A couple beats of silence, then she yells back, "Whatever you think, honey."

"I'll just use the card for any expenses, 'kay?"

Slight pause. Sigh audible from twenty feet away. "Sure, honey."

Aisha gives me a quizzical look as I walk back to the car, like, *Really?*

I shrug. "Yep, that just happened," I say.

And with that, the journey to find my grandfather begins.

# PART II
## West of
## Not New York

# 17

THE PORCUPINE OF Truth perches precariously on the dashboard as Aisha pulls the Neon onto I-90 and starts us on our journey west and south from Billings.

The Porcupine is our new, prickly mascot. When Aisha makes a sudden stop at a yellow light, the porcupine lurches forward into the windshield and then off the dash into my lap.

"Ow," I say, pushing her onto the floor. "Our God is a painful God."

I recline in the passenger seat. When I take my shoes off, kick up my legs, and place my bare feet against the windshield, Aisha swats me in the biceps and says, "You crazy?"

I pull my feet away from the glass and see that I've left toe marks. I rub them and that just makes a smudge. She turns up Tegan and Sara, which is not what I would choose, but it's not terrible. I find myself bouncing my head exaggeratedly to show her I approve, and then I stop because it's like, *Overcompensate much?*

Conversation is tougher this morning. Maybe it's that we're stuck in a car for three hours, and that's different from being in the same house, because in a house, you can always get away. Also, I'm not in a real jokey mood, what with the whole *My dad is dying and last night he thought I was his dad* thing, not to mention the *My grandfather is still alive* thing. But joking is what I do. So as we career through the outskirts of Billings, the billboards on either side screaming for our attention, I look out the window and riff on whatever I see.

"Candy Town. The largest candy store in Montana. Do they get a medal for that?"

"It's a cool store," she says, almost defensive.

"I'm sure. Far be it for me to diss candy." I keep scanning for more material. "Pelican Storage? Did someone really name their store Pelican Storage?"

"Apparently," Aisha says.

"Is it for the storage of actual pelicans only? Or can you store other fowl there?"

"You want me to stop and ask?"

"I think they probably prefer only pelicans, but if someone has an osprey, or maybe a flamingo, even, they're like, 'Fine. So long as we don't get to a point where we have fifty percent flamingos, we're set. We don't want to have to change our name.' "

"Right," Aisha says, monotone. "All the new signs."

I look over at her, grateful that she's playing along. "What about the self-esteem of birds?" I say. "I worry about things like that. Like if you're an osprey, you're set. Everyone fawns all over you and you can hold your beak high. But if you're a pigeon? Do you think pigeons have inferiority complexes?"

"Probably they do," she says.

"Some of them walk around with their chests puffed out, but I think it's a false pride."

We exit onto a rural highway, and now we are entirely alone on the road. There is nothing remotely like this on the east coast. Not that I've seen, anyway. It makes me feel important, like, instead of being one of a million people to travel through the Lincoln Tunnel one day, I'm the only one on a lonely stretch of highway. Maybe that's what I've been missing in New York? The thought that I matter?

Fifteen miles past Bridger, the first town we pass through with an actual stoplight, I spot a yellow deer sign surrounded by flashing lights.

"So that's where flashing deer cross, I guess? Are they doe? A deer, a female deer? Do they flash for money?" I ask.

Aisha is lost in another world, because she doesn't answer. Tegan and Sara melts into jazz explodes into the hip-hop sass of Janelle Monae, and ours may be the only car in all of Wyoming at this very minute in which Janelle Monae is playing. We let "Q.U.E.E.N." envelop Aisha's Neon. How cool would it be to be able to rhyme like that? So flawless and smooth and quick. And then I think about how she gets to go into a studio, and she gets do-overs. The recording we hear is her final cut. Maybe in life, most of us feel inferior because we compare our dress rehearsals to Janelle Monae's final performance. If I could just broadcast the *Best of Carson Smith*, and erase all the thoughts that go flat, all the jokes that don't go anywhere, maybe I'd be amazing too.

"So if you could create an app, any app, what would it be?" I ask.

"Is this where we've gone now? What happened to prideful pigeons and flashing deer?"

I laugh. "You gotta keep up," I say. "My brain does this."

"I think there are medicines for that."

I look down at my fingernails. Is she trying to pick a fight? "If I had to create an app, it would be one where you give haircuts to feral cats, or maybe one where you chase witches around a plant nursery. If I had to create a reality TV show, it would be called *America's Next Top Podiatrist*. Contestants would face increasingly bizarre and disgusting foot diseases."

Aisha sighs. "I would not watch that show."

"Aw, come on. Scabies of the foot? Pinky toe rot?"

"Oh my God, Carson," she says, raising her voice a bit. "Am I actually going to have to murder you in the first hour of our road trip?"

"You want to kill me over pinky toe rot?" I ask, blowing air against the window and then wiping up the mist that forms.

We drive on in silence, and I find several spots on the window to breathe against and then wipe up. When we are ten miles outside of Belfry, the sun comes up on the left, and the buttes begin to illuminate on the right.

"Nice butte," I say, and Aisha says nothing.

"I like big buttes and I cannot lie," I mock-rap.

Aisha groans. "Everything is a joke with you."

"Whoa," I say. "Where did that come from?"

"I'm serious. Why can't you just not make a joke once in a while? Silence. It's golden."

"So silence is a color now? When did this happen?"

"Just — shut up, Carson. Shut up."

I stare out the side window at the blur of pine trees. I imagine each of those tree branches slapping me in the nose, my stupid, annoying nose.

"You just . . . Why can't you talk about what's up?" she asks. "With your dad, I mean. Like say something real for once, and not hide behind some stupid joke."

"So you're a psychologist now?"

"It doesn't take a psychologist," she says.

I close my eyes. Am I this bad now? Am I being psychoanalyzed by homeless chicks? I feel like the anger could just bubble out of my mouth, like the acid could ooze out and smoke could billow from my ears and I wouldn't be able to stop until there was nothing left inside me anymore.

"Yeah, you're nothing like that," I say finally. My voice doesn't really sound like mine. "It's not like the first time I met you, you said the tiger was at the zoo because his father kicked him out for being gay. It doesn't take a psychologist to figure that one out either, looking back. Thank God *you* don't use humor as a shield."

I hear her inhale. But she just keeps driving, and we say nothing.

"So now you're not talking to me? Great. Real mature," I say.

She turns up the rap song that's playing. Then she turns it up louder, and the thumping bass starts to rattle my brain. It's one thing to be angry, but giving me hearing loss seems a little aggressive.

Aisha turns down the music when it starts to bug her too, I guess. She mutters, "Fuck. You know what the worst thing about car fights is?"

When I don't reply, she says, "You can't leave."

I feel something that is way too big for a Dodge Neon boiling in my bloodstream. I don't need this shit. I don't need my fucking crazy family, and my mom and her psycho-fucking-babble and my lame-ass dad and his dying and my one friend of the moment and her bullshit.

Maybe my dad had it right all along. A glass of whiskey. Beats people.

The miles slip by, and my anger washes over me in waves. I play the conversation over and over in my mind, and I think of other things to say, meaner things, smarter things. Aisha slaps a button and the music goes from soft to off. I steal a quick glance at her face and her eyebrows are arched high in much the same way as when she's excited. The only way I can tell she's angry from her face is the tightness of her lips.

Then something inside me shifts, and I remember that when she's not being a total B-word, she's my best friend. In under a week, Aisha has become the best friend I've ever had, and maybe I wouldn't say that to her, because it's undeniably pathetic, but it's also true.

So I take out my phone and text her.

im sorry

I put my phone away so she won't see me holding it when hers buzzes. She gets the buzz, pulls her phone out of her pocket, and glances down to read it.

She starts to text back.

"Texting while driving?" I ask. "Really? Why don't you just steer us directly into a tree?"

She gives me an annoyed look, but then she does something that surprises me. She slows and pulls over to the side of the two-lane highway.

**I'm sorry too**, she writes.

> i didn't mean to bug you
>
> and i didn't mean to piss u off

**I was being a bitch.**

> no comment. me too. a male version of a bitch

**Bastard.**

> hey watch the name-calling

**Let's be nice to each other. I'm sorry.**

**Upset about Kayla today.**

> you're too good for her

**I guess.**

> do u think it says something bad about us
>
> that we are texting our apologies?

**It's not a great sign.**

> i kinda love u, u know

**I know. Love you too kinda.**

We hit the road again. We're quiet, but at least the tension is gone.

"You text in full sentences, and you use punctuation and capitalization," I say.

"Does it take that much longer to hit shift?"

"I think I'll start doing that," I say. "I mean, with all the many friends I text."

That makes her laugh. That. Not all the awesome ideas I came up with earlier, but the sad fact that I haven't had a textual transmission in a week except what she's sent me. And she must know it, because we're together all the time.

And then I realize: *Her too.* I've never seen her text either. I laugh back.

"We are quite the popular duo," I say, and she shrugs.

"Maybe not, but hey. Today I'm on a road trip with a friend. That's better than I was doing a week ago."

I don't want to admit it, but yeah. So am I. "Ditto," I say.

# 18

I CHEER AS we pass the WELCOME TO THERMOPOLIS billboard, which alerts us to the fact that the world's largest mineral hot spring is here. There's a picture of two kids on a waterslide, and it says SWIM, SOAK, SLIDE, STAY.

We follow Google's directions to a deserted, treeless dirt road, and for a moment I think we're lost. But then we come across a rickety green-and-white wooden sign swaying in the wind: FOUR PEAKS MOBILE HOME PARK.

Aisha and I look at each other. "Here goes nothing," she says.

I've never been to a mobile home park before. The homes are marked with numbers, and we keep our eyes peeled for the Leffs' place.

What we find is a small, narrow trailer with a covered parking spot out front, a dilapidated, olive-colored Chevy under it. In the front yard, a squat old man in work boots is standing over a foldout table, painting a piece of pottery.

We stop the car but keep the engine running. The man looks up from his painting and gives a half wave, clearly trying to figure out if he knows us. Aisha cuts the engine, and we both get out of the Neon.

"Hi," I say, taking the lead.

He nods. "Can I help you?"

He's old, chubby, and has a silver mustache, with round, rosy cheeks. He looks like what the captain of the football team at my school would look like if he were melted down for a bunch of decades and then artificially inflated with air.

"Are you Thomas Leff?"

"That's what my driver's license says."

"We're sorry to bug you. I just have some questions about my grandfather. Apparently he stayed with you a million years ago. Russ Smith?"

The man's face animates for the first time, and he approaches us on stubby fire-hydrant legs. "Get outta town," he says. "Russ Smith. You're his grandson? You don't say."

"That's me. I'm Carson Smith. This is my friend Aisha Stinson. Do you know him?"

"Knew him, yeah. How's he doin'?"

"Okay. Well, not okay. Actually, I don't know. Do you have a few minutes to talk to us? We're kind of trying to figure out what happened to him."

He slaps me on the shoulder. "Any family of Russ Smith is certainly welcome at our place. You up for some lunch?" He motions toward his trailer.

This does not seem like a great idea to me, but Aisha starts to nod. I excuse us and pull her away for a moment.

"Might as well. We're here," she says to me.

"I'm from New York City," I say. "I don't generally go into strangers' trailers for lunch. Everyone in New York is a potential serial killer. I'm pretty sure that's true out here too. I mean, he seems harmless, but really?"

She shrugs. "I'm not afraid of him. Seems like a nice old dude."

"That's how they get you!" I'm not sure I even mean this, but now that I've started it, I feel the need to follow through. "Isn't there some 'Don't go in the attic' thing?"

Aisha turns and looks out at the horizon. "I don't know," she says. "I think at some point, if you're going to have a life, you have to start going into the attic."

"Wow," I say, remembering how going up into an attic nearly got us in trouble yesterday. "Just, wow." But I don't have any other arguments, so I walk back over to Thomas, who has been watching us from a distance.

"We'd love to, thanks," I say.

"Well, good," he says. "Nice of you to come up to my attic."

I jump a bit. Thomas's laugh is unexpected and melodic. His face lights up and his mustache twitches like a caterpillar.

"You need to talk more softly if you don't want people to hear you," he says. "Life isn't a movie."

I blush, and Thomas keeps smiling. "You're kind of funny," I say, genuinely surprised.

"Me?" he says, looking all shocked. "I'm just a nice old dude." He leads us over to the trailer and opens the screen door. We follow him in. "Oh, dearest!" he bellows.

The door to a room at the far end of the trailer opens, and an old woman with a radiant smile peeks her head out. "There you are!" she says, and then she sees us and says, "And guests!"

"This, dearest, is the grandson of one Russ Smith!"

She puts her hand to her chest. "Russ Smith? Oh! Oh my goodness!" The woman scurries over to us, arms out wide. "It is so lovely to meet you! I'm Laurelei."

"His name is Carson," Thomas says. "His friend, who is clearly the second most beautiful person ever to step foot in this home, is Aisha."

She clasps Aisha's hands in hers, and says something like, "My, aren't you gorgeous." Then she looks at me. She raises her left hand to my head and instinctively I open my arms to hug her. As I do, she says, "Oh!" and I pull back. In her left hand is a leafy thing that she must have pulled from my hair. I say, "Well, that's awkward," but she shakes her head like this happens all the time.

Then she does hug me, and I am amazed at how much I feel like lingering in the hug of an old lady I don't know. I feel starstruck, like I'm meeting the trailer park version of Oprah Winfrey, maybe. She's got to be at least sixty, but something about her is also eighteen, like on the inside. Her face seems to glow.

What appeared from the outside to be a small trailer is surprisingly wide and long, with low ceilings, maybe eight feet high. Thomas heads into the small kitchenette area and gets busy washing, chopping, and plating fruits and vegetables. Laurelei sits us down on twin couches near the front door and brings us a bowl of trail mix to snack on. She asks us about our trip and tells us what an amazing day she's had. It consisted of walking through the trailer park and seeing a handful of neighbors. She also interacted with a neighbor's dog.

That's it. And she seems happy. Not like pretending, but actual joy. I kind of want to move in with her. I look at Aisha, and I can tell she feels the same way.

"What would you like to drink?" Thomas yells from the kitchen.

"How about some wine?" I ask, half joking, and Aisha frowns at me.

He laughs. "Nice try." He brings out a salad bowl for each of us, a medley of raspberries, strawberries, melon chunks, and broccoli on a bed of sprouts, no dressing. We sit on the twin couches and eat with the bowls on our laps.

"So my grandfather," I say. "You knew him well?"

"As well as you can know someone who was in your life for, what, two days? Three?"

"That's all? You acted like he was your best friend when I said his name."

Thomas laughs again. "Out here, we don't get tons of visitors. He was memorable. Looked like an older version of you, you know. I coulda guessed if you'd let me. It's in the cheekbones."

I feel my face and then, self-conscious, move my hands away. "I just hope you can help us figure out what happened to him."

"Well, I'm not sure what we can say that will help you," Laurelei says. "We enjoyed his company, but I'm sure we never heard from him after he left us."

"Wasn't it Wyatt Thurber who introduced us?" Thomas asks Laurelei. "The pastor. From Billings, wasn't it?"

"John Logan, maybe?" I ask.

His face lights up again. "I think that's right! John. It's been so many years."

"He's my dad's neighbor."

"How is John?"

"He's fine," I say. "But my granddad hasn't been back to Billings since he visited you. And it's kind of a big deal, because my dad hasn't seen or heard from him since either, and now he's dying, and —"

"Oh! Poor dear," Laurelei says, and even though it's lunch and we're eating, she actually stands up, comes over behind me, and puts her hands on my shoulders while I sit. She rubs them softly. It's the weirdest thing ever.

"It's fine," I say, my body rigid. "I hardly know him. He's a drunk. I mean. My mom and I left when I was three. We're like . . . just taking care of him now while he's —"

I can't finish the sentence, and I find myself counting by elevens to 209.

Laurelei continues to massage my shoulders, and I see that Thomas has stopped eating and is looking at me with very kind eyes.

"There's a lot of feelings in there," he says, pointing at my chest, and I'm like, *Whoa, fella. Buy me a drink first. I'm just fine, thanks.*

Then I realize I haven't been breathing.

Laurelei goes back to her seat, and I must be two people now, because part of me thinks, *Awkward turtle*, and the other part thinks, *Come back, please. I'm not done being touched.*

"So, um," I say, trying to get my head back. "Do you have any idea what was going on? Why he left without telling my dad?"

Thomas and Laurelei look at each other. "Not a whole lot," he says after a beat. "He was a nice man and we enjoyed him. If I recall, it was a tough time in his journey."

Laurelei nods. "Such a sweet man. Like you, Carson."

I look down at my food.

"So, nothing else?" Aisha asks.

"Sorry," Thomas says, looking at Laurelei. "I wish we could be more helpful."

Our only clue, a dead end. Then I remember the letter my grandfather sent.

"Wait," I say. "Yeah. He wrote this letter to Pastor John from here. We have it." I pull the letter out of my pocket and read it aloud to them.

Thomas looks up at the ceiling like he's pondering the whole thing. "What's the world's most dangerous grid?"

"That's what we're trying to figure out."

"Maybe an electrical grid?" he says.

"It's expensive too," I say.

"Right. Of course. An expensive and dangerous electrical grid, run by a church choir director." He chuckles. "Doesn't ring a bell when it comes to Russ. I know it's been a lot of years ago, but I don't remember much going on about expensive grids."

Laurelei shakes her head. "No. That one doesn't mean anything to me either. Sorry."

"Anything come to mind when I tell you to 'have faith in the KSREF'?" I quote the letter again.

Laurelei squints. "I'm afraid not."

"Oh well. And you're sure you never heard from him again?" I ask.

Thomas wipes some salad dressing off his chin. "I'm pretty sure."

"Sorry. Me too," Laurelei says.

"Oh well," I say again.

Aware that our visit has just become a lunch with nice people we'll never see again, we move on to other subjects. Thomas talks about how he fell in love with Laurelei in college in Colorado. She wanted to be an artist, and he was into religion. After college, they traveled to third-world countries like Borneo and Uganda, where they built homes for people and taught them how to sanitize their drinking water. In their thirties, they settled in Wyoming, and he became pastor of a church in Thermopolis.

"I liked it at first," Thomas says, "but then the pressure came." He looks at Laurelei, and she offers a sad smile.

"Misguided people," she says. "Ugliness."

The head of the church asked him to speak out against the Equal Rights Amendment in his sermons. Laurelei explains that the ERA was a proposed amendment to the Constitution in the 1970s that would guarantee equal rights for women. It passed in many states, but not enough to make it into the Constitution.

"I told him to follow his heart," Laurelei says, and Thomas laughs.

"You told me that if I said a word against equal rights for women, you'd divorce my ass and move to California."

She laughs back. "Tomato, tomahtoe." He reaches out, and her hand clasps his. They squeeze each other's hands like they're doing Morse code. I feel like I'm glimpsing something intimate and sweet, and I wonder what it takes to find a Laurelei.

Thomas explains that they gave up organized religion years ago in response to the rise of the religious right in the early 1980s. They didn't care for the politics. He'd met Pastor John at religious conferences, though, and when he received a phone call from him asking for a place for his friend to stay, he was happy to help.

"So you remember this from, like, over thirty years ago?" Aisha asks.

Thomas spreads his fingers wide. "I can count on this hand the number of friends we've had come stay with us since we've settled here. Our life is very simple. We like it that way."

"No Facebook?" Aisha says, and Laurelei smiles as a response.

"We don't have television and we don't own a computer," Thomas says. "One of our friends urged us to start an email account using his computer. We did, but I'm sure we haven't looked at it in ages, have we, darling?"

Laurelei shakes her head. I try to imagine not having a TV or a computer. It's such an unbelievable idea that I involuntarily gasp.

"My life is so different from yours," I say, and they all look at me. "I'm from New York. I pass by thousands of people every day on the streets, and on the subway I'm shoved up against strangers all the time, yet nobody ever says hi to anyone else. I text and I email, and I almost never feel like I'm really connected. And you had a full morning," I say to Laurelei, "because you got to play with a neighbor's dog. That's crazy. Crazy good."

She gives me the warmest, sweetest smile, and I feel myself falling for these people and their world. I really don't want to leave.

"Stay for a few days if ya like," Thomas says, as if he's reading my mind, and Aisha and I, without even looking at each other, say yes in unison.

Laurelei asks if we're a couple.

"Gay girl, straight guy. Buds," Aisha says before I can respond, and Laurelei smiles again, and Thomas says, "Well, it's settled then. We're so glad you'll stay!"

I quickly call my mom and tell her that we are in Wyoming staying with friends of Aisha's, and we'll be back tomorrow. She does her usual thing, which includes passive-aggressive breathing followed by a "Whatever you think, honey." Instead of it bothering me, I just feel relieved, because right now I don't want to be part of my broken family. I want to be part of this family, and I wonder if there's some way I can get the Leffs to adopt me. Us.

Thomas looks at his watch and says they have meditation class at two. It centers them, he says, and I can't help but imagine them literally centered in every room, every photo they're in. It's now 1:10.

"We can cancel," Laurelei says. "Unless — would you like to come?"

I've tried something like meditation only the one time, with the gentle yoga, and it was not the most successful thing. Could I do better now? I want to think that I could do better, but I'm scared that I won't, and I don't want to let Thomas and especially Laurelei down.

Aisha says, "Sure."

This is exactly the kind of invitation I'd normally decline, because it's new and different and maybe a little scary. What if I suck at it? And then I look at Laurelei, smiling expectantly at me, and I drop all that stuff. "Yep," I say. "Sure. I'm in."

# 19

BY THE TIME we get to the meditation place, I am calm and even a little excited to try it. *I will keep an open mind*, I keep repeating as we drive over. *I will not make jokes out of every little thing.*

This is immediately challenging, because Thomas and Laurelei did not tell me that we would be meditating in a kids' classroom in a church. All around us on the walls are colorful posters with Bible sayings on them. One features an electrical socket and a cord plugging into it. It is unclear why, or what the hell that has to do with the accompanying saying: "Since I live, you also will live." Another has a lightning bolt and reads, "Go into all the world and preach the Good News to everyone."

I get the feeling you get when some girl you really like and want to talk to has food stuck in her teeth and you think, *Oh no, not her too.* I thought Thomas and Laurelei said they gave up religion. Aisha has an alarmed look on her face as well. I tug on her sleeve. "We don't have to do this."

She doesn't give in to my tug. "I kinda want to try."

"We can meditate outside. Or you can, and I'll just pretend, since it isn't actually a thing."

Aisha walks over to Laurelei, who is helping a woman clear desks out from the middle of the room. "All the religious stuff pretty much makes my head explode," she says.

Laurelei finishes moving the desk and puts her hands on Aisha's shoulders. "This isn't a Christian meditation. Don't worry about any of that. It's simply the room we use because it's empty at this hour."

Aisha nods and says, "I guess I can always leave if y'all start with the Jesus."

Laurelei laughs. "Tell you what. We'll leave too. Okay?"

Aisha looks back at me, and I shrug. Fine. Whatever.

Thomas and Laurelei put down their mats and greet the other six or seven meditators warmly. The leader, an old woman with gray hair and a body that looks almost elastic from the way she sits tall while folding her legs in front of her so effortlessly, explains that we will use the next thirty minutes to simply *be* together, in silence. We are grateful for this time, and we thank our higher power for it.

At the mention of a higher power, my throat tightens. That sounds like God to me.

"Praying," she says, "is talking to God. Meditating is listening."

I look over at Aisha. I'm not so sure God is tuned to our church in north-central Wyoming. He may be a little busy with the people in Africa and the Middle East to talk to a bunch of happy old folks and two wayward teens in Thermopolis.

The leader ends her introduction by saying that we will accept exactly where we are. Sometimes thoughts are hard to put away. If they come, we will welcome them. We will acknowledge them, and then we will let them float away. We don't need to focus on them. We will allow our minds to be as they are, and we will not judge ourselves harshly.

The last part almost makes me laugh. *Right, starting this very minute, I will stop judging myself harshly.* This seems likely.

I take a deep breath, trying to move past the idea of God and into our harmless little meditation session. *Okay,* I think. *I guess this is fine. I guess it's cool. I can try this.*

Then the silence begins, and my brain is on fire.

*Okay, thoughts and visions,* I say to myself. *I welcome you. Howdy.*

*Howdy howdy howdy howdy howdy.*

*Hello hello hello hello.*

*C'mon. Nothing. Think of nothing.*

*God! God! God! HELLO THERE, YOUNG CARSON! YOU SHALL KILL YOUR FIRSTBORN SON, OR I SHALL SMITE YOU.*

I shake my head, trying to spin the thoughts out. I toss them onto the floor beside me. I open my eyes and look around. The room is very still. Aisha is very still.

A rare Billings memory floats by. Watching cartoons with Dad on Sunday mornings. He'd bundle me up in blankets on the floor in front of the television, and he'd lie on the couch, and we'd watch *The Mouse and the Monster* and *Space Strikers,* plus old-school cartoons like *Road Runner.* I was warm and whole and happy. Dad made me feel that way.

My throat catches. Something unwelcome trembles my body, a wave of cold and static and tingle. I close my eyes tighter, shake my head.

*You're free to go,* the voice says.

*No. No. No.*

*No.*

*Let the thought be?*

*Okay. Fine. I'll let the thought be.*

*You're free to go*, says the voice. A male voice.

We are in the kitchen. They are, anyway. Mom's head is buried in her hands, and she is making cat noises, it sounds like. Dad is saying words. I am holding a red ball. I stand in the hallway alone. It's play-time. Dad said he'd come home and we'd play in the backyard, but he's late. It's too dark to go out, but I've been waiting up. I've built a fort in my bedroom out of pillows. I fell asleep under the fort, but then the door slammed and voices shouted and I came out to see, to listen, and Mom is on the kitchen floor and and I am confused.

"You're free to go," Dad says, and to my three-year-old brain, she seems to be meowing.

I hold the ball between my hands. I try to crush it. I can't. The harder I push, the harder it pushes back. Mom's wailing hurts my ears. It makes my chest feel like it's going to cave in. I want to make it stop. I need to make it stop. Moms are big people. They are not cats. They are not supposed to wail.

*Daddy? Mommy?* Did I say those words? I think I did. But no one heard. No one came.

Then the world ripped in half.

Her: "I'm taking Carson. We'll leave in the morning. Is that what you want?"

Him: "What I want is for you to leave me the fuck alone."

Her: "You're a disgrace. You're a failure of a man."

Him: "Tell me about it."

Her: "You're losing your son."

Him: "Bound to happen."

My throat feels so tight. *I don't want to think about this. I never goddammit want to think about this why did you make me think of this stop it stop it stop it!*

I jump up and run out of the room. I swing open the church door and sprint to Aisha's car. This was a big mistake. Aisha will come out soon, and we'll say we're sorry but we can't stay. I tried and I failed.

Minutes go by. A lot of them. I check my cell phone. No messages. Why would I have messages? I never do. I turn and look out into the distance, this mountain range with just a hint of snow on the top, framed by a juicy blue sky that makes me thirsty. Across the street there's a bar, and I get this crazy idea again. Maybe just one drink? Maybe they'd serve me?

I stare at the bar until my eyes blur and there are two of them, two bars, side-by-side, drifting in and out of each other as I focus and unfocus my eyes. This is how it starts, probably. This is how I become my destiny. My dad. My granddad. A drunk. I make myself turn away.

And then I turn back toward it. I can do this and no one will know. I'll sit in a bar in Bumfuck, Wyoming, and drink a beer like an adult who is free to do whatever the hell he wants, because my dad is dying, and my mother doesn't care, and my best friend is better than I am. Why not?

I walk to the bar, and again I'm two people. One is saying, *What are you doing, Carson? You know better than this.* The other is saying, *One, shut the fuck up. I'm living my life.*

Inside, the bar is dark and somber. There's a guy at the far end, nursing a beer. His grizzled, pruned-up face makes him look maybe a hundred and fifty, give or take ten years. A bartender in overalls sits on a stool behind the bar, reading a newspaper.

He looks up as I approach. He doesn't smile; he doesn't frown. He is not the kind of person who rubs your shoulders when they find out your dad is dying.

"Can I have a beer?" I mumble.

"Got ID?" he barks.

"C'mon, man," I say.

He gives me the finger. "Out," he says.

There's something really depressing about being given the finger and turned away at the world's bleakest bar. Like, I'm not even good enough to be a miserable patron there. That's how it feels as I walk back toward the church.

The meditation is still not over. I sit on the hood of the car. The minutes pass slowly, murderously slowly, and I need Aisha now. I need to make fun of this bullshit. More minutes pass. Then more. An unbearable number of minutes. I count to 336 by fourteens — up and then back down again. It doesn't help.

By the time Aisha comes traipsing out of the meditation area, I want to tear her apart.

"Was that a lot of fun for you?" I ask, seething in my gut.

She shrugs. "It was interesting, actually."

I laugh. Right. Sitting in silence in a church classroom, listening to God. Real interesting.

She stretches her arms up. "I liked it. Sorry if you didn't. It's okay. It's not for everyone."

I laugh harder. "Oh my God. I know you're not going to get all holier than thou on me, because I will seriously . . ."

She raises her left eyebrow. "Seriously what?"

I don't know why Aisha makes me so pissed sometimes. "Come on, Aisha. You're always making fun of the Jesus."

"What does meditating have to do with the Jesus?"

"Are you going crazy? Is everyone going crazy? Religion is bullshit. God doesn't exist. We believe in the Porcupine of Truth."

"I agree," she says. "Religion's the worst. This isn't religion, Carson."

"Um. Meditating means 'listening to God.' God is religion. You're out of your mind."

"You don't have to be religious to meditate, Carson. I'm not even sure you need to believe in God. I don't think I do."

I put my hands over my head. I don't meditate for the same reason I don't pray to God. Similarly, I don't have long, one-sided phone conversations with a dial tone. It's a waste of time and energy and anyone being honest with themselves knows that.

"That is the dumbest thing I ever heard," I say. "So you're communicating with something that you know doesn't exist?"

"I can't explain it, but it's not like that at all," she says.

I'm disappointed in Aisha. I thought she was this freethinker who came up with her own answers, and now I see that I misjudged her.

"Okay then. If you say so," I say.

As we drive the Neon back to the Leffs' place, Thomas and Laurelei ask Aisha about her experience, and I feel more alone than ever.

I flash on an image of young me, at three, sitting on the front stoop of our Billings home. Minutes before Mom and I left.

Some things you remember, and some you forget. Of the things you remember, you have to wonder what's real and what's translated into a memory from a story you heard. Like in this memory, my dad is wearing Bermuda shorts. I don't think I knew what Bermuda shorts were back then, so how would I know that? Except I remember it.

It's early that last morning, and I'm sitting on the stoop outside the front door in my yellow pajamas. Mom is cradling a green duffel bag to her torso. Icy tears stream down her face like rain on a windshield, except there are no wipers to sweep them away. Mom is melting, and moms are not supposed to melt. Dad is I don't know where, but wearing Bermuda shorts. I know something irreversibly terrible is happening. The earth is shifting below my feet, and there's a rumbling earthquake like when the subway comes into the Seventy-Ninth Street station, shaking the entire platform. It rattles my entire body, rearranging my insides, changing my chemistry. But that part of the memory can't belong in Billings at all, because I'd never been on a subway then, so that means it's not quite true.

I am holding a red die. Not sure why I'm holding it, or where it came from, but I remember the feeling of its dull corners pressing against my tiny fingers. I remember thinking that if I hold on to the die a bit longer, a bit harder, an all-loving God will make this earthquake stop, will stop the flood of icy eye water that is turning my powerful mom into a puddle. God like the one Grandma Phyllis believes in. The one she says prayers to.

Dad walks out in his red Bermuda shorts, no shirt, smoking a cigarette. It's like watching a movie now, because I am not there. Mom and Dad, on a screen, yelling at each other, way too loud for how close they are standing. Mom with tears streaming down, turning my stomach inside out. I remember watching and thinking, *No. Let's stop.* Like I'm asking God. Like I'm asking my parents. I don't know if I say this or I think this. I have no idea.

And the answer to my words or prayers is that my mom grabs my left arm and pulls. Her hand wets my arm, makes it feel slippery. She says, "C'mon, honey," and I am dragged away. I scream. I scream to my dad. I scream to the universe. *Stop this from happening. The world is ending! The world is ending! Stop this!*

I drop the die. I never get to see how it lands, if it stays on the stoop or falls to the ground. And no one stops the world from ending.

So no, I'm not gonna just sit here and be like, *God is listening.*

Not so much, in my experience.

# 20

YOU HAVE NOT lived until you've sat in a rickety old chair outside a trailer at night in north-central Wyoming. This is just crazy beautiful, with so many stars glimmering above me that I feel like if I believed in anything more than the Porcupine of Truth, I'd be praying to it right about now, saying, *Thank you Jebus, you amazing son of a bitch*. It's just un-fucking-believably gorgeous.

I'm half depressed as shit, half in awe of the world. I'm sitting like a fool in a trailer park and I don't know why. I guess I'm chasing a mystery about my dad, who doesn't give a crap about me, and his dad, who doesn't know I'm alive. But my dad is dying. Dying. It scares me for my life. How random is it all gonna be? How do you meet a Laurelei, or a straight Aisha? And even if you do, how do you not let them annoy the crap out of you, or disappoint you to death? What's the point of it all?

The door creaks open and Laurelei ambles out, wrapped in a puffy pink blanket. Even though I'm wearing baggy gray sweatpants Thomas lent me and it's July, it is chilly, and my teeth are chattering. She sees me sitting there uncovered, and she goes back inside and comes back out with the blue-and-white quilt that I left on my couch. I wrap it around myself, and she grabs a second lawn chair and drags it over to me. The sound cuts into the otherwise silent Wyoming night.

"Do you know that your grandfather did the same thing you're doing?"

"Huh," I say.

I hear her smile in her voice. "He couldn't sleep. Grabbed himself a blanket and sat in a chair in just about the same spot you're sitting in. Came and looked at the stars, and he cried like a baby."

I smile, though it's hard for me to imagine my grandfather crying like a baby. "That's cool. Sad, but cool."

"He was a good man."

I don't know if I believe her, but it's nice for her to say. We sit quietly and look at the sky.

"Goddamn," I say, and Laurelei laughs.

"Isn't it perfect?"

"Yeah. Sorry about the 'goddamn' thing. I know you probably aren't big on using God's name in vain or whatever."

She flicks me lightly across the back of the head. When I look at her, she says, "God fuck damn shit."

I laugh, and she laughs.

"Don't idealize me," she says. "I'm a human fool. We all are, and it took me a long time to become the happy person I am today. A long time. Okay?"

I look back at the stars, and so does she.

"So do you believe in God?" I ask.

"I do."

"But you're not Christian."

She sits up abruptly. "Surely you're aware that not everyone who believes in God is a Christian, right?"

"Well, yeah," I say, though in fact I have temporarily forgotten that, like, a majority of the world isn't Christian. How did I forget? Thomas and Laurelei meditate. They're probably Buddhists. How stupid am I?

"So you stopped believing in Christ and started believing in what?"

"It's hard to explain," she says. "I would say that I'm more spiritual than religious at this point."

"What does that even mean?" I stare upward at the gleaming stars.

"To me, religion is the Walmart of spirituality."

I laugh. "It's all cheap stuff made in China?"

"Exactly." She flicks me in the back of the head again. "Exactly what I meant. I mean it's prepackaged. Lowest common denominator. People just have to follow the preset motions and rituals and rules. They don't have to think about how the words reconcile with their own hearts. Their own experience."

"Huh," I say, considering that. "And what do you believe in now?"

She raises her hands to the sky, then puts them behind her head. "Everything."

I snort. "Weak sauce."

She laughs. "You don't believe."

I shake my head. "I'm sorry. I just have trouble believing in things that don't exist."

"What doesn't exist? The stars? The sky?"

"God," I say. "God is a concept used by people who want to feel better about the pointlessness of being alive. You live, you die. The end. Sorry, but that's what's real."

"For you," she says, as if to add it to the end of my sentence.

"Hey, call it what you want. That's what I know to be true."

"So can I teach you something I've learned?"

I look over at Laurelei, who is beautiful in a mom way, who I would be okay spending the rest of my life listening to, even if she's batshit crazy. "Go for it. Knock yourself out."

"I've learned that the answer to every question about God is 'Yes.'"

"What if it isn't a yes or no question?"

"So judgmental for such an otherwise delightful young man. I'm saying that whatever it is that a person believes about God is totally, completely, irrevocably true — but only if you add two words."

"Check, please?"

That one earns me another playful smack, and then she stands up and says, "I think I'll head back to sleep. You?"

I nod and stand up too. "So you didn't tell me what the two words are," I say.

She opens the screen door and holds it open for me to walk through, and then she follows me. I see Aisha's sleeping cheek illuminated by the starlight.

"*For me*," she whispers, and she disappears into the darkness of the trailer.

# 21

I WAKE UP to loud clanking above me, like a pinball game played by someone who is seriously bad at it. The pings come in quick succession, and then nothing for a minute. Then more pings. I look over to the other couch. Aisha is gone and her blanket is nicely folded. Light pours into the trailer from the semiopen blinds above me. I must have overslept.

I find my shoes, check my breath, decide it's not terrible, run my hand through my hair, and step outside in the sweatpants I slept in. Then I scream.

A man is crouched on the ground. With a rifle. Pointed at me. I cover my face with my hands and duck.

"Oh hey!"

It's Thomas's voice. I peek through my fingers as he slowly hoists himself to his feet and puts the rifle down. "Didn't mean to scare you."

"No worries," I say, as if it's a typical Carson morning to wake up in a trailer, go outside, and almost get shot.

"Sorry for the noise. Damn pigeons. Drive me crazy."

I walk out to where he is and look up. There on the pitched roof of the trailer are three pigeons, milling around.

"Isn't there like a 'Thou shalt not kill' rule or something?" I ask.

He glances at me sideways and laughs. "For pigeons? Don't

think so. Wait 'til one day you have these dirty things pooping all over your front yard. You'll want to shoot them too."

"Hey, I already kind of want to shoot them," I say, and he grins. "Is it legal?"

"BB gun," he says.

"Oh." That doesn't really answer my question, but I don't care.

He cocks the rifle, lays it on his right shoulder, and squints one eye closed. I've never seen a BB gun before. I've actually never seen any gun up close before. We're not big recreational shooters, we who take the 2 train to school.

He shoots. The gun emits a little pop, followed by a clank when the BB hits the metal roof . . . about fifteen feet away from the trio of birds, who don't look remotely alarmed.

"Where is everyone?" I ask.

"The girls went to meditate," he says, and I feel glad that Aisha found something she likes, even if it's something stupid. Then I think about the "for me" thing that Laurelei said, and I let it go.

Thomas aims again and shoots. Oh for two.

"Aisha is so pretty," he says.

"Don't I know it."

We share a look, and it's like he knows that I dig her. He reloads. "I heard you and Laurelei talked about God last night."

"We spoke about God, and we concluded that God is dead."

The ends of his thick mustache dance when he laughs. "You're a tough nut to crack."

"When you're trying to sell me on God, yeah." I put my hand out. "Can I try?"

He hesitates for maybe just a nanosecond, and then he hands me the rifle.

"Nobody's trying to sell you anything. You believe what you believe. That's all."

"If you say so," I say.

"So what exactly does this God I'm trying to sell you look like? What does he do?"

I fiddle with the rifle, unsure of what to do. "Oh, I don't know."

Thomas takes the rifle from me and shows me how to hold it. He places the butt of the rifle against his right shoulder and puts his right hand on the trigger. His left hand holds the rifle steady. Then he tilts his head down to look down the barrel.

"You see how there are two sights? This little slot near your face and the bead at the end of the barrel? Line 'em up."

He hands the rifle to me, and because I'm a lefty, I reverse what he's shown me.

"You're a natural," he says. "Wanna shoot?"

"I guess." I concentrate on aiming at the birds, unsure if I'll be able to pull the trigger. I've never killed anything before.

"So what does this God look like?" he asks again.

I put the rifle down and look at Thomas, and I think, *You*. Which is weird. God doesn't exist, so he doesn't look like anyone. But if he did, I realize, to me he would look and act like Thomas. He'd be authoritative and manly, not silly and prone to emotional outbursts like my dad. He'd be kind and serene, or whatever you get from meditating (aside from bored).

But that's the kind of thing you really can't say to a person without having them question your sanity — that he looks like God. So I say something else instead.

"He's a big white dude, and he has a white beard and he wears flowing white gowns, but not in a gay way. He has thousands of switches and levers in front of him and they're labeled, like, 'Middle East Violence' and 'Bali Earthquake.' Some of them he just flicks on and then laughs, a real deep laugh. Others he can adjust, such as the weather — someone's gotta control the weather. What with global warming and whatnot, that's almost a full-time job."

Thomas laughs really hard. "That's quite a busy schedule for God. You'd think he'd have some helpers, like Santa's elves."

"He does," I say. "They are called God's leprechauns."

He laughs some more. "God's leprechauns. I like it."

"I try," I say. I pick up the rifle and force a frown, so that I look the way a guy holding a rifle should look. I aim at the roof, and then, before I can think about it too much, I squeeze.

The pop jolts my head. Dust flies about five feet from where the pigeons are. Better than Thomas, but still a miss.

"No pigeons were killed as a result of this shooting demonstration," I say. He grins. I put the gun down and add, "Anyway, I'm cool that y'all are spiritual or whatever, but just for the record, I'm pretty sure God doesn't exist."

He shrugs and takes the BB gun back from me. He raises the gun, aims, and says, "Reminds me of a joke I saw written on a bathroom stall. Someone wrote 'God is dead,' and signed it 'Nietzsche.' Then someone crossed that out. Underneath it, they wrote, 'Nietzsche is dead. Signed, God.'"

I laugh. "So here's what I don't get," I say. "You believe in God, but you've been to Africa and seen all the hardship and crap."

He nods, his gun still aimed at the roof.

"So God lets that crap happen? Why? Why is God so mean?"

Thomas fires, and this time, the pop is accompanied by a pigeon tumbling off the roof.

My hand involuntarily grasps my own throat.

It's funny, because it's just a pigeon. And it's not like I wasn't just shooting at it myself. Maybe I didn't put it all together. That the activity we were doing while having a nice talk could actually end a life. Even if it's the life of just a pigeon.

I look to the other pigeons to see their reaction. Are they aware of what just happened? Do they know they've just lost their family member? Was that a mother? A father? A child?

That pigeon is over. Life done.

Thomas is too focused on his kill to notice me. He strides over to view the bird. I look down and see that its wing is still flickering some. Thomas lifts the BB rifle, aims, and fires down into it.

I sit down on the gravel, numb. Thomas goes inside, and moments later he returns with a dustpan and a black garbage bag. He uses the end of the rifle barrel to push the lifeless pigeon onto the dustpan, and then he throws that life away.

I sit there with my chin on my knees, watching and wondering what just happened to me. Because it's just a pigeon. And Thomas is just a man, not like a god. Or maybe he is just like a god, because God smites things every day, every second. This all-loving thing you're supposed to pray to, who loves you and provides for you.

He's a killer. He's all-powerful, and terrible stuff just happens, over and over and over again, and God doesn't stop it. Like with my dad. I think about this and I hate the world.

Thomas takes the garbage bag down the road to a green Dumpster and deposits the expendable just-a-pigeon life, and then he comes back and he sits next to me on the ground. We both sit there, arms wrapped around our knees, staring at a roof with one less bird.

"I don't think God is mean. God just is," he finally says. "A long time ago I gave up the idea that God was some great puppet master, that one day he decides there needs to be a tornado in Kansas. Things happen, and then there's God."

I don't respond, because what would I say? Real men don't have feelings over pigeons. I 100 percent don't know what a "real man" is, but he doesn't cry over spilled pigeon.

He looks over at me and swats me on the shoulder. "You okay, kiddo?"

"Tired," I say, rubbing my eyes.

Thomas scoops up a handful of pebbles and shuffles them around in his hand. He sifts a couple of pebbles back onto the ground through the hole between his thumb and his forefinger. "Okay," he says. "Just checking." He says it in the way that people talk to damaged goods, and I don't want to be damaged goods. But obviously I am.

Thomas heads inside, and I'm left sitting on the gravel, pondering bird families. Somewhere out there, a pigeon dad is in mourning for his son. He is wondering what he could have done differently, like tell his kid to stop playing on trailer park roofs. And he wonders: Where do all the bird memories go after death?

And what happens when you die? Do you just stop breathing? Try to imagine: You are breathing. Then you stop. Breathing. Forever.

# 22

I'M STILL SITTING outside, trying to get a grip, when Laurelei's old olive Chevy spirals a cloud of dust toward me as it pulls in to the covered spot next to the trailer.

Aisha springs from the passenger seat like a totally different person than she was yesterday. Laurelei waves at me and heads inside, and Aisha jogs over.

"I know, I know. You hate meditation," she says. "But that was . . . That was seriously serious. I'm all, like, Zen'd out and shit."

I recline on the gravel, my elbows scratching against the rocks, which is not at all comfortable. Aisha kneels down the way basketball coaches kneel to check out a hurt player. Elbows on knees. Calves flexed.

"You okay?"

I nod.

"You don't really look that okay."

I look up at her and I don't know what gets communicated, but in about a half a second she's yanking me to my feet and we're walking away from the trailer.

We silently stroll the dirt ring of the trailer park, past a trailer that has multicolored toilets in front of it, like some sort of art project gone terribly wrong.

"You wanna talk about it?" she asks.

"It's stupid. I don't know what it is," I say. "It's just . . ."

"Yeah," she says, and I have a feeling she doesn't have a clue what "it" is. Since I definitely don't.

I concentrate on kicking up dust as we continue to walk. All the trailers are covered with crazy, tacky stuff that's hard to categorize. Street signs taken from the side of roads; macramé masks that would make a two-year-old cry; lonely, forlorn lawn ornaments; and other castoffs from the isle of misfit trash. I feel like I belong here.

I keep walking, and finally I begin to think that if I don't say something, Aisha's gonna just decide I'm fine, and I'm not fine. Part of me wants that, for her to not know what's going on in my brain. Another part of me is so fucking tired of people not knowing.

So I just talk. "Do you think, like, pigeons mourn when a family member is shot?"

"You and your birds." She laughs. I don't, though, and she stops laughing when she realizes that I'm not.

We stop walking. She looks into my eyes, and I avert them from hers.

"I'm such a loser," I blurt. "All Thomas did was, like, shoot a pigeon off his roof with a BB gun, and my head got all wacked, and —"

I look down at the dusty road beneath us. I say, "I'm a loser and a freak and an idiot."

Aisha does the weirdest thing. She puts her hand on my forearm and squeezes. She speaks really softly, which I don't expect from her. "I feel messed up sometimes too," she says, looking directly in my eyes.

I can't quite return the look. "You?" I ask the ground.

"Ugly," she says. "I feel ugly."

"You are the least ugly person in the world, and you can trust me on that one." I am studying a patch of gravel-less dirt. It's so much easier to talk without eye contact.

"You are the least loser person in the world," she says, but I just can't believe those are the same thing. I am definitely more loser than she is ugly.

I know that if I say that, she'll just tell me again I'm not a loser. And that won't make even a little bit of difference in my mind, because I know I'm at least something of a loser, or else we wouldn't be having this conversation. But I don't say anything. I just continue to feel her hand on my forearm, which now feels good, actually. Not in like a sexual way. Just in the way of something that feels nice.

She lets go, and we stand in the dust, close to each other, like we need to stay close now. I am finally able to look up into her eyes.

"We're wounded," she says softly.

A funny idea crosses my mind. Maybe a joke will always cross my mind. I imagine two soldiers in a bunker during a war. There's a huge explosion and one of them loses his head. It explodes off and lands in his friend's lap. And the friend looks down at the head, and the head says to him, "We're wounded."

But I don't say that, because it's the wrong thing and the wrong time.

"I know," I say.

"I'll help you, you help me," she says, and I have to admit I like the way that sounds.

We find a place to sit in the shade, and we just hang for a bit until I feel better. Then we finish our lap of the park and go back to the trailer. Thomas and Laurelei are sitting on the couch where Aisha slept. I pretend I didn't just have this meltdown about pigeon shooting, and Thomas is cool and acts like I didn't too. We sit down and shoot the shit for a bit, and then Thomas and Laurelei share this look and she nods to him.

"So we have a little news for you," Thomas says.

"We were just talking it over and it came back to me," Laurelei says. "Peter and Lois Clancy in Salt Lake City. Russ went to them after he left us. We knew them way back when from those religious conferences."

Aisha pulls out her phone like it's a revolver from a holster. Thomas stops her. "We have all the information you need," he says. "We just called them. You ready for this? Lois absolutely remembers your grandfather, and she says she'd love to see you."

"What did she say?" I blurt. "Does she know where he is?"

"She said they lost touch, but she has something of his she wants you to have."

I look at Aisha, wondering whether she'd even consider a drive to Salt Lake City. "What is it? Can she tell us over the phone?"

"She said it would really mean a lot to her to meet you."

"But Salt Lake City is like . . ." And then I stop talking, because it's embarrassing that I have no real idea of how far away it is. Out West, everything seems super far apart.

Aisha is on her phone. "About eight hours," she says. "Give or take."

Thomas nods. "That's about right."

I think about our options. We can go back to Billings and be there in a few hours. We won't solve the mystery of my grandfather, but . . . Well, that's it, I guess. Or we can drive to Salt Lake City and meet someone who knew him. Who has something for me. They may have lost touch, but at least it will take us a step closer.

Aisha must be thinking the same thing, because she says, "I'm game."

"Really?" I ask.

"Yes, really," she says.

Thomas says, "If you leave now, you'll be there by eight, even if you stop a few times. Lois said they'd be happy to put you up."

My mind spins with the possibilities. What could she possibly have to give me? This is irresponsible. We haven't needed to get gas yet, but if we go farther, we will. What about food? We're definitely going to need to start using the credit card a whole lot. But then I figure, *What the hell? What's the worst thing that could happen?*

I look at Aisha. "You sure you're up for sixteen more hours of driving round-trip?"

She smiles and shrugs. "You got the funds, I got the wheels. Let's go."

I pull out my phone and text my mom.

Hey mom, on the road,
doing great. How's dad?

**He's doing Bette.**

**Better. Sorry. He has more energy today.**

Good! Okay if we take another day?

She's going to say no. There's just no way she's going to be okay with me being off with a girl I hardly know, who she hardly knows, wandering the Wild West while my dad is —

**I suppose one more day would be finish**
**Fine I mean. I hate this silver**
**Silly sorry**
**iPhone. Always charges what I type.**

I don't answer right away. I'm getting what I want, so why be upset? And I'm not upset. It's just. I don't know. It's too easy and it pisses me off, I guess.

Thanks. Luv u.

**xo. Please consider calling your fate**
**father**

Everyone's looking at me, so I put on a smile. And then I realize I'm going to freaking Utah with Aisha, and the smile becomes a smile for real.

"So, off to Salt Lake City," Laurelei says. "You're taking your grandfather's journey."

I hadn't thought of it that way. We're following in his footsteps all these years later.

Thomas gives Aisha the address and phone number. Then he quickly pens a note to the Clancys, thanking them for their hospitality.

"Now these are real religious folks," Thomas says, his tone a bit wary. "Can I count on you two to tone it down a bit?"

I look at Aisha, because I figure she's the problem more than me, what with the whole lesbian angle. But then I realize they're all looking at me.

"What?" I say. My jaw gets tight, but they won't stop looking at me, so I finally just say, "Fine, fine."

It doesn't take much for us to pack up our things, and Thomas notices. He says, "Take the sweatpants. Both of you."

"Really?" I say.

"Absolutely. You thought you were on a day trip. In fact —" He holds up a finger and disappears into the bedroom, and then he calls Laurelei in. After a few minutes, they return with a pile of shirts, some toiletries, and a ratty old canvas bag.

"There's no way you'd fit in any of our shorts or pants," he says. "But the shirts should do in a pinch."

"Thanks," I say, and Aisha says it too.

They walk us out to the Neon. Laurelei fawns all over Aisha, asking her did she get everything, is she sure we don't want to stay for lunch, does she want to shower. They exchange phone numbers, just in case.

"Man, I'm gonna miss you guys," Aisha says, burying her head in Thomas's shoulder in a hug. I feel both glad for her that she felt so at home here, and a little sad that it didn't work out that way for me exactly.

Laurelei takes my hand and squeezes good-bye. When she unclasps and lets my hand go, I look up and she is smiling at me, Thomas right behind her. There's this pang in my chest that I don't expect. He creases his lips in a way that tells me he's sorry our visit is over. I am too.

"Thanks again for the stuff," Aisha says.

Laurelei beams. "Don't mention it."

We get in the car, and the Neon kicks up trailer park dust as we take off.

"Bless you!" Laurelei yells to us.

"Bless you too!" Aisha yells back as we take a left out of the place.

I look at her. "Oh my God," I say. " 'Bless you'? Next thing you're going to tell me you no longer believe in the Porcupine of Truth. Which would be unfortunate, as it is, you know, the Porcupine. Of Truth."

She grins. "I would never deny the existence of the Porcupine."

We get back on the rural highway, heading south toward I-80. Wyoming is the windiest place I've ever been; even with the windows up, we can barely hear Fitz and the Tantrums over the gusts that whip across our windshield. We zoom past miles and miles of nothing but sagebrush, which I start calling the "broccoli of the West" as we pass cowless pastures filled with it. This makes Aisha smile.

"What's the worst thing that could happen on this trip?" I say, deadpan. "The Clancys are psycho killers and they kill us. Or they don't kill us, but they sell us into the sex trade."

Aisha shoots me a look. "Don't be such a pessimist."

I point at myself as if taken aback. "Me? Hardly. I'm an optimist. The biggest optimist. Eternal, even. If I were an eye doctor, I'd open a practice called The Eternal Optometrist."

I can actually feel Aisha roll her eyes. "Don't make me sorry I agreed to this before we leave Wyoming."

# 23

WHEN WE FINALLY arrive in Salt Lake City, it's just before eight on Sunday night. We've driven straight through without stopping for food so we can get to the Clancys' before it gets too late. The city's skyline at night is awesome — clean and crisp, like a Disney city — and I have to admit it's nice to be back somewhere with actual tall buildings. Even a city named after a lake of salt.

The address is in a crowded neighborhood on the north side of town, a tree-lined street packed with modern-looking houses. The Clancys' home is older, with paint chipping off the door. I ring the bell, clutching the letter Thomas wrote, my head buzzing with anxiety. Aisha looks much more calm than I feel.

We hear scampering feet, and then an elderly woman opens the door a crack.

"Hello?" she says. I can only see a sliver of her eye and nose.

"Hi, are you Mrs. Clancy?" I say, my voice trembling.

She opens the door a few inches wider, so we can see her lined face and wispy gray hair.

"I'm so, so sorry," she whispers.

I start to ask her why when a booming voice yells, "Lois, who is it?"

She shakes her head at me and speaks louder this time. "No. We can't help you."

She shuts the door.

Aisha and I are left standing there on her front steps, bewildered.

"What just happened?" I ask.

Aisha says, "I have absolutely no idea."

From inside the house, we hear a crotchety man's voice.

"They sent us a black lesbian. Goodness gracious."

Aisha and I look at each other, mouths wide open.

"He wasn't even at the door," I say. "How the hell would he know —"

She bites her lip. They must have learned this from the Leffs, and I feel a twinge of anger that the Leffs would have told them that information. Not to mention sending us to stay with a bunch of racist homophobes.

"That sucks," I say.

Aisha shrugs. "After a while you just stop listening," she says.

Part of me wants to pound on the door and tell the Clancys that they're hypocrites, hiding their hate behind a God who is supposed to be loving. But Aisha says, "C'mon," and we walk back to the car and sit there in silence.

I wish I could be half as strong as Aisha. Things that would destroy me just seem to bounce off her.

"So what do we do now?" I ask.

She thinks for a moment. "Do we go back to Billings?"

My stomach twists. I'm hungry and I'm tired and the idea of driving another ten or so hours right now is too much to take.

"Maybe we stay at a hotel?"

As Aisha considers this, her phone rings.

"It's Laurelei and Thomas," she says, and I perk up.

"Hey," Aisha answers, and she puts the phone on speaker. "We can both hear you," she tells them.

"Oh hi," Laurelei says. "I'm so sorry, guys. I'm furious right now about how the Clancys behaved. She just called me and told me. I'm mortified."

"It's not your fault," Aisha says.

"Well, it feels a bit like it is. I had no idea. When I spoke to Lois a few hours ago, everything was fine. Then, I suppose, she spoke to her husband. She just called me, and she sounded very upset. I'm so sorry, Aisha. I mentioned that you are homosexual just in passing. I did not expect it would matter, especially because Lois seemed so kind. I wish I hadn't said anything now."

"I'm glad you did," Aisha says. "I don't want to stay with someone who hates people like me."

"Well, me neither," Laurelei says. "But I also don't want you to spend the night on the street! I simply don't know what to do. We don't have any other contacts, and we don't use credit cards. I could try to call a hotel and talk to someone. . . ."

"Don't worry about it," I say. "I have a card. We'll be okay."

"Yeah," says Aisha. "Don't sweat it. We're fine."

"Well, there is something else. Carson, Lois still wants to see you and give you this thing of your grandfather's. She can't do it tomorrow, though. The first time she could get away from her husband is Tuesday morning, so she wants you to meet her at eight a.m. Tuesday in front of the Tabernacle in Temple Square."

I laugh. "Um. So she turns us away, then wants us to wait two days to meet her? Could she figure out how to see us tomorrow, at least?"

"I know, I know," Laurelei says. "I just don't know how to advise you."

I think about our options. We could figure out how to stay a couple of days in Salt Lake City. It'll mean spending money, and it'll mean taking some extra days away from Billings. I don't know. Even though my mom will probably never, ever say no to me, my dad is sick and I should be with him.

But how could I forgive myself for giving up my search for my grandfather? I picture him in the photo where he's holding my dad as a young kid. His face like mine. I remember one of his puns: "When two egoists meet, it's an I for an I." His jokes like mine. He's my blood.

I turn to Aisha. "I want to keep going. I really want to know what this lady has for me."

I don't know if I expect her to argue, but she doesn't. "Well then, I guess we're staying in Salt Lake," she says.

"I don't know how to help, but if you can think of a way, we'll do it," Laurelei says. "I feel partially responsible. We both do."

"Don't worry about it," Aisha says. "We'll be okay."

We ask Laurelei to tell Lois Clancy we'll see her on Tuesday. Laurelei wishes us well, and we say good-bye.

Aisha drives us to a nearby diner for a bite to eat. We're both famished. While we're waiting for our burgers and onion rings, she pulls up a site I've never seen before.

"After I was kicked out of the house, I couchsurfed a couple nights," she says.

I crane my neck so I can see her screen. "I think you mentioned that."

She explains that there's this site called surfingsofas.com. People open their homes to complete strangers for God-knows-what reason — insanity, possibly. She found a family in Billings and she stayed with them for two days before she decided she was in their way and left.

"It's worth a try. People review the folks they stay with, and vice versa."

And then the craziest thing happens. I think, *Sure. Why not? I'm doing all new stuff I've never done before. What's one more new thing?* "Let's do it," I say.

"Just no fucking Mormons. I'm over the fucking Mormons," she says as she scrolls through people. "My soul is not getting saved in Salt Lake City. I have limits, you know."

As I scarf down my burger, she finds two possible hosts who seem cool. She reads their profiles to me. One is a couple in their thirties who do organic farming, and the other is a lesbian couple in their twenties. I might as well just turn into a lesbian at this point, because that seems to be the direction things are going around here. She sends the requests, and then she dives into her cheeseburger while I tear into my onion rings and begin to steal hers. In between bites, we stare at her phone, hoping to hear the beep that would alert us to a message from surfingsofas.com.

"Did you know that the reason God burned down Sodom wasn't because everyone was gay, but because of a lack of hospitality?" Aisha asks as she sips her soda.

"Um. I did not know that."

"And of course the Clancys are religious. The husband's a pastor. That's very 'love your neighbor,' right?"

I realize getting turned away by the Clancys is bothering her more than I thought. More than that, she's right. Whatever their reasons for not letting us stay with them, the Clancys knew we were two teenagers alone in Salt Lake City. They had to know that if they didn't take us in, we'd have no place to be overnight. "Some people suck," I say.

She stares down at the last remnants of her bun. "The last person to turn me away was Kayla," she says, and I can tell from her tone that what she's saying is painful. "It's hard to find out someone you thought you might . . . love . . . doesn't love you back. At least not enough to give you a roof over your head when you don't have one."

Instinctively I reach across the table and intertwine my pinky with hers. She curls hers around mine, and I have to close my eyes because all I can think is, *I gave you a roof. Why can't you feel that way about me? I'd do anything for you. I would never, ever let you sleep in the goddamn zoo.*

After dinner, we drive the streets of Salt Lake City, which are completely impossible. N 200 W intersects with W 500 N, and you have to be just about a genius to know where you are in this town.

When the clock says nine thirty and there's been no beep, Aisha pulls into a Big Lots parking lot and checks her email anyway.

"Nada on surfingsofas.com. Oh well."

"Oh well."

"I think it's hotel time," Aisha says, and I know she's right, but I still wince. Right now my mom thinks we're staying with friends. How the hell am I going to explain a hotel charge to her? She says yes to just about everything, but I'm beginning to wonder if we're reaching the limit of "reasonable" expenses.

The cheapest hotel she can find online is a Days Inn for fifty-four dollars. That seems reasonable-ish, so we drive there. I'm feeling fried, so I know Aisha must be feeling even more so, since she's driven the whole way. She invited me to drive part of it, but the truth is, I don't even have a license yet. We who grew up with a crosstown bus don't have a lot of incentive to pass a driving test.

At the Days Inn, the guy behind the counter doesn't trust us from the start. He raises one eyebrow as we walk in, and his eyes dart back and forth like he thinks this is some sort of hookup. If only. He starts filling out a form anyway, and then he asks for our license and credit card.

I give my card to him, hoping we can do this without a license, or with Aisha's. He runs it through the machine and waits, looking at the screen. Then he shakes his head and flips the card back to me. "Declined," he says.

"What?" I say. "No. It can't be."

He frowns. "Declined."

I look in my wallet. Thirty-six dollars. We don't have any other way to pay. Should I ask Aisha what she has? I can't. So we leave, out of ideas.

We sit in the car and try to figure out what's next. Aisha's eyes look like they're beginning to close.

"Looks like we're sleeping here," she says, and I look around. There's the backseat, where the Porcupine is currently lying on her side next to a shiny, satiny lavender pillowcase, and there are the two front seats. The backseat could possibly be comfortable for one.

She offers me the backseat but I insist she take it, and we compromise on each getting it half the night. Before we close our eyes, Aisha checks surfingsofas.com and finds that both of our requests were viewed and not responded to. Yes, people do suck. In a last-gasp effort, even though it's almost eleven p.m., Aisha posts a message on the surfingsofas.com Salt Lake City bulletin board.

*My friend and I are sleeping in my car because our credit card wasn't accepted at a hotel. We're good people and we're just here overnight. Anyone willing to put us up? We would clean your house if you'd take us in. Seriously. Call or text me at 406-555-2355.*

Aisha curls up in the backseat, her head resting on the lavender pillow, and I recline the passenger seat back as far as it will go, so my head is inches away from her knees. I turn my head left and she's lying on her side, looking at me. She smiles, and I smile back.

"There's something kind of peaceful about this, isn't there?" she says.

"Yeah."

"The first night after my dad kicked me out, I slept like this and it felt like I was the only person in the world."

I imagine being alone in a car, and then alone in the world, parentless, on my own. It's an exhilarating and horrifying idea, and I have to close my eyes.

"Sometimes at home," I say, "I sit on the radiator in my room and stare out the window into other windows across the way. All the blinds are closed, so I'm not, like, a perv. I just sit and think what it would be like to be in another life completely. Like, not in mine."

Aisha nods. "What hurts you so bad, Carson Smith?" she asks.

I look away, out the front windshield at the mostly empty parking lot. Someone's parked a U-Haul truck that takes up two spaces. Whose truck is that? What does their life feel like? Where are they running off to? I think of sitting on my radiator at home, and all the times in my life I've fantasized about taking off. I want to believe these people are going someplace better, someplace warmer, maybe. Happier. I have to believe that. Because if I don't believe that, maybe life isn't worth living.

I hear Aisha sit up. I keep looking out the window at the empty parked cars, and then she hugs me from the side, around the seat. I hold my breath and start to count, and then I stop counting and try to just let the hug happen.

What is it that those people have that I never have?

Oh. This.

I've never had this. I've had lots of things, but never this sort of connection. Aisha's left arm falls across my chest, and a warm feeling radiates down my spine. I breathe a little bit into the hug.

When she releases the hug, I want to cut the tension with a joke, and I have three pulling at my tongue. Instead, I say, "Kayla had no idea what she was missing. And you're not the only person in the world."

She lets the words float there for a bit.

"Neither are you," she says.

I reach back with my hand, and at the same moment, she reaches her hand forward, and we hold each other's hands that way until we fall asleep.

---

In the middle of the night, I find I don't sleep so well sitting up. Aisha is softly snoring in the back, and I am suddenly wide-awake. I feel around down near my feet and find my grandpa's journal. It's like we're having an ongoing conversation, and even if it's one-way, I want it to continue. I read by the light of the moon.

*September 19, 1979*

*Russ's Book of Puns*

*She was only a seamstress's daughter. But she couldn't mend straight.*
*She was only a horseman's daughter. But all the horsemen knew her.*
*"A man's home is his castle, in a manor of speaking."*
*"Does the name Pavlov ring a bell?"*
*"She was engaged to a boyfriend with a wooden leg but broke it off."*
*"If you don't pay your exorcist, you get repossessed."*
*"The man who fell into an upholstery machine is fully recovered."*

And then, underneath, in shaky handwriting:

*Puns not funny, Phyllis says.*
*Why I drink:*
*I drink because I ruin everything. So why not drink?*
*Everything's already ruined.*
*Bottom's up!*

I feel numb. It's like my grandfather lives inside my chest. I'm not a drunk, but I know that exact feeling, like, *Screw the world, nobody loves me.* It's immature, but I've had that thought tons of times. Is that a Smith thing?

Do you grow out of it?

I think of my dad. He hasn't grown out of it. He acts like the world has screwed him. I get that, but I don't want to live my life feeling that way.

My grandfather has lived more than thirty years since writing this. I wonder if he still feels that way, or if he got over it. I try to imagine what he's like now. I have to believe he got past it. In that letter from last year, he sounded different. Wiser. How did that happen? Could he teach me?

# 24

MY NECK HURTS when we wake up. Aisha had the backseat the whole night, and I'm fine with it. More important is to figure out what the hell to do for a whole day in Salt Lake City.

Aisha drives us to a highway rest stop, and while she goes to the bathroom, I call my mother.

"Hey Mom."

"Hi honey. How are you doing?"

"I'm good. We're good. Really good, actually. Um, one thing though. The card was declined?"

"The credit card? It was? What were you trying to do?"

"Get a hotel room," I say, quickly scanning my brain. Did I tell her we had a place to stay?

"I thought you were staying with friends of Aisha's?"

Crap. "Yeah. Um. That fell through."

"Where are you, honey?" I can hear the icy concern in her voice.

"Um." I take a couple of seconds to think out my options. I land on the truth. "Utah."

"Honey. I thought you were in Wyoming. I'm not sure I care for you running around the country without my knowing where you are."

I don't say, *But you said, "Whatever you think."*

"Where did you sleep?"

I gulp. "The car."

"Honey."

"It's fine. It's just gonna be one more day. We have someone we need to see tomorrow morning, and then we'll come back," I say, knowing it's possible that's not true. If Lois knows something about where my grandfather is, we may need to keep going. But I guess I can come up with another excuse then.

"No," Mom says.

"What?" I'm actually jarred. I cannot remember her ever telling me no before.

"You need to come back. Your father. You're here to help me take care of your father."

"But you don't need my help. I sat around all day in Billings doing nothing. Can't I just have today and tomorrow?"

"No," she says, her voice gaining confidence. "That's enough now. I'll call the credit card company. No. Forget that. I'll wire you money, a hundred dollars. Just enough to get home and for an emergency. Okay?"

I close my eyes. My head is buzzing out of control. "No," I say.

"Excuse me?"

"Sorry, Mom. I don't mean to upset you. There's something we have to do. When have I ever done the wrong thing, like, ever? You need to trust me on this one."

She takes a deep breath. "I hear that you feel the need to spread your wings and have some adventures. But this isn't the right time. You need to come back here. We'll talk about this later, when you get home. Find me a place where I can wire you money for gas. Then I want you to just drive straight through. Promise me."

My throat feels cold. Every muscle in my body feels tight. She's telling me no for the first time in my life, and as much as I've maybe wanted that in the past, right now no is not an answer I can take. I need to go farther. I need to find my grandfather. It's the most important thing I've ever needed to do.

But I also need more money. We're low on gas. Aisha and I have maybe fifty bucks between us. We're stuck.

"I'll text you a place," I say, and then, as soon as she starts speaking, I hang up.

A few minutes later, a long text arrives:

**I understand you are upset and I want you to know that o hear that. What I want you to thin about is how much of this is you being upset about your father. I know this must be terribly difficult for you. I locate myself in that feeling.**

I've heard her talk like this before, like the psychologist she is, a million times. So why is it this time I start shaking?

I don't respond to the text right away. When Aisha comes back from the bathroom, I'm searching for a place my mom can wire us money.

"You figure out what happened with the card?" she asks.

"Yeah, sort of. No. It's fine. My mom is wiring us some money," I say, while texting my mom the information. I don't tell Aisha it's only a hundred bucks, which is not that much given that we no longer have a credit card. I also don't tell her that the money comes with a directive to get back to Billings immediately.

"Wow. My mom would not be that generous."

"Yeah, well," I say, trying to figure out how we're going to make this work. There's got to be a way. Failure is not an option.

170

# 25

WE PICK UP the money at a supermarket, where I also buy protein bars, because I'm famished. I give one to Aisha. As we're sitting in the parking lot eating, the phone rings.

It's a woman named Stacy Bailey, who saw Aisha's post on surfingsofas.com and invites us to stay with her and her family for the night. We check out her reviews, and they're flawless. A deal is struck, and we get the Baileys' address.

Driving there, it feels good to have someone care about me — us — even a stranger named Stacy Bailey. She will make everything okay for a day. She's our savior.

Casa de Bailey turns out to be this huge McMansion with a garage big enough for three cars. Stacy Bailey is a skinny, middle-aged blond lady who greets us warmly at the door, and we walk into a large, high-ceilinged main room with two leather recliners facing what must be a seventy-inch television mounted on the wall next to the fireplace. Two floral-print couches sit across from each other, and on one of them rests a college-aged guy with a beard. He's playing with his phone, and he doesn't say anything to us as we walk in.

Stacy says she has to get going, and she rushes to show us our rooms (separate!) and teach us how to use the TV remotes. She introduces us to her son, Gareth — the guy on the couch — who says, "No reality shows. Seriously. House rule," without even looking at us. Mrs. Bailey groans and playfully smacks him on the top of the head.

"Do something today," she says. "It's a Monday. Really. Please."

He says back, "Epic plans. Don't you worry."

We follow her to the kitchen, where we stand and watch as she sets a world record for cleaning up cookie-baking detritus.

"Thanks for taking us in," I offer.

She nods. "It was just, I listen to podcasts? And this morning's devotional was about how Heavenly Father wants us to share what we have with others. My mind flashed on surfingsofas.com and I thought, *We haven't done that in quite some time.* There your message was, waiting for me. I took it as a sign. I'm so glad you're here. I hope you'll forgive my busyness. We'd love it if you'd join us for a family dinner tonight, but for today, I'm sorry to say, you're on your own. Is that okay?"

"Thanks so much," I say again. "Really. This is so nice of you."

Aisha says, "I was serious about the house cleaning. Even a house this big. Totally worth it."

Mrs. Bailey laughs. "No need, no need. Heavenly Father asks us to welcome others as we would be welcomed." She explains that her husband, Robert, is at work, but he knows we're around, and we should help ourselves to some cookies, as she's made more than she needs for her committee meeting.

After she leaves, I look at Aisha. As soon as Stacy Bailey said, 'Heavenly Father,' I got that we were in a Mormon household, and I remembered Aisha's *No fucking Mormons* rule.

"I feel like I'm being tested," she says.

"Come on," I say. "She's really, really nice."

"Yeah, you don't get it."

For some reason, maybe because I'm tired and I am so looking forward to sleeping in a comfortable bed for once, I decide to push Aisha a bit. "How is you grouping all Mormons together any better than other people grouping all gay people together?"

She scowls at me and shakes her head. "Yeah," she says. "You really, really don't get it, do you?"

I put my hands on my hips. "I guess I don't."

She looks away. "Well, never mind, then," she says. She shakes her head as she walks out of the kitchen, leaving me with a slight pang in my chest and a plate of cookies to eat on my own. I'm so hungry that I devour two in about ten seconds.

"Cookies? Awesome sauce," Gareth says, bouncing into the kitchen. He puts an entire cookie in his mouth. Then he pulls a carton of milk from the fridge, chugs from it, puts it back, and belches.

I wince. I guess I won't be drinking any milk while I'm here.

The guy salutes me and says, "Gareth. As in the disappointing son. Are you the new converts? Did they baptize you yet?"

For once, I'm speechless. He grabs another cookie and smiles. "I'm kidding," he says while chewing with his mouth open. "I'm used to this by now. People come through all the time. My shrink says it'll broaden my worldview. I personally think it'll be the reason I need a shrink, when one of you guests tries to suffocate me in my sleep."

"Um," I say.

He looks up. "Don't listen to me. I talk before I think. Gets me in trouble. So who are you? Do you know you're the first interracial couple my folks have allowed in here? We're talking serious fucking progress, dude, serious."

I laugh. "Awesome," I say, not sure of what to make of this guy.

"They're totally rad now. Like, my dad saw a beer in my room and he didn't have a coronary. It was awesome, dude. Insane."

"I'm Carson," I say.

"Gareth," he tells me again.

"So you're Mormon and you drink."

"Jack Mormon," he says.

"Um. Like Jack Daniel's?"

He rolls his eyes at me. "Where are you from, Mars?"

"New York."

"City?"

I nod.

"Fucking awesome! Jack Mormons, we're like, we haven't left the church and we like the community and stuff, but we don't follow all the rules. Me, I don't follow any of the rules. Rules are for dickwads."

"They should put that on a fortune cookie," I say, but he doesn't seem to care.

My phone buzzes. It's a text from Mom.

**I trust your on your way. Please keep me updated on your progress.**

I put my phone away.

"How long you guys been together?" he asks.

"Oh, you mean me and Aisha?"

"Eye-eee-shuh. Dope name."

I hope to God she's not overhearing this conversation from her guest room.

"We're not a couple," I say, and then, for some reason I don't quite get, I lean in and whisper, "She's a lesbian."

"Right on, right on," he says, totally unbothered by this.

"I'm trying to change that, but I'm failing."

Gareth grins. He starts telling me stories of the various girls in and around his life, and suddenly there's a "we should" that appears, and I'm part of some group I don't really know, and that's weird, but I like it. He has to get going because he has a rollicking game of Frisbee golf to play, and he asks if I want to come along.

"Um, sure," I say.

"Great, and bring the chick," he says.

"Maybe don't call her a chick if you want to live."

"Ooh." His eyebrows arch. "I like feisty women."

"Yeah, maybe don't say that either."

He grins. "Aye aye, captain."

# 26

AISHA STILL SEEMS annoyed with me when I find her in her room, but she reluctantly agrees to come along. We get in the car with Gareth, who plays Phish too loud on the stereo and opens all the windows without asking whether it's comfortable for us, which it isn't. Once in a while, he yells out a question, but it gets carried away by the wind and we don't answer. He's totally cool with that, and I start to relax into the day.

We go to the Walter Frederick Morrison Frisbee Golf Course at Creekside Park. We wait for his friends, Mitch and Hodge, to arrive. Both show up wearing green argyle berets, which is . . . interesting. They fist-bump me and Aisha by way of hello, and then they open up beers, even though it says alcohol is prohibited on the course.

"Can I have one?" I ask, and Aisha gives me a dirty look.

"Never mind," I say, which is fine because Gareth doesn't give a shit.

Gareth throws first. He takes a running start on this concrete block that's the tee, I guess, and he lofts a small red disc a long way, way farther than I could hurl it. It lands about twenty feet to the right of the metal basket that acts as the hole.

"Hella nice, beyotch!" the guy named Mitch says. Mitch's most obvious characteristic, besides using decades-old catchphrases, is that his entire right arm is covered in tattoos. He throws next, and his throw is straighter to the basket, but shorter. Then Hodge, who has a soul patch and a gut visible under his tightly stretched polo shirt, flings the disc. It lands within fifteen feet of the basket.

I go next. Trying to copy how they threw, I run up to the edge of the concrete and let it sail. It surprises me how easy it is to throw a Frisbee, because I am quite sure I have never thrown one before. It streaks toward the basket and finally dies in a patch of tall grass, more than halfway to its intended target.

"Nice toss, dude," Gareth says.

That leaves Aisha, who is clearly the most athletic of us. She also seems the least interested. She stands still and flings the disc, and it flies a decent way, falling a bit short of my throw.

I get another text from my mother.

**I feel concerned that I havent heard from you.**

> Something came up. Can't get back
> today. Sorry. Don't want to upset you.
> Don't worry about us. We're fine.

We all walk out to retrieve our discs and make our second shots. "Put your back into it more," Hodge says to Aisha. "You're pretty good for a girl."

Aisha's lips stay tight and she says nothing, and I almost go over and say something encouraging, but I can just about feel the anger emanating from her, so I steer clear. Gareth's next throw hits the chains above the basket, and everyone goes, "Right on!" so I say it too.

My phone rings. I decline the call.

Mitch and Hodge take three flips each to reach the chains, and I do it in five. Aisha throws two more times and then says, "I'm gonna sit this out."

She doesn't wait for us to say anything in return. She just walks back toward the car, and I feel torn. Do I go to her? Or can I, for once, have some athletic fun with some guy friends, something that has happened just about never in my life, because I never allow it to happen?

My phone rings again. I decline again, and then I turn my phone off.

I wait until Aisha is out of sight, and I say, "You have an extra beer?"

Gareth looks at Hodge, who is wearing these huge cargo shorts that look like they could fit a baby kangaroo inside. "Beer him," Gareth says, and Hodge reaches into a pocket and pulls out a can.

"Thanks," I say. I have never had a beer before. I pop the top and when foam comes out, I sip it up. It crackles on my tongue, and the warmth pours down my gullet.

We keep playing, and I keep sipping, and soon my beer is gone, and Hodge beers me another without me even asking, and it feels fucking great, especially as my head begins to cloud. It's like the bad thoughts puff out of my brain through my ears, and my brain becomes calm with those bad thoughts gone. I've been waiting a million years to feel like this. If this is how my dad feels when he drinks, well, I still don't get the whole *I'm giving up my life and my family for this* thing, but I can definitely understand why he likes it. And I don't ever have to get that bad, because that's just stupid and reckless.

As we move through the holes and I drink a third beer from Hodge's bottomless pockets, the conversation moves on to girls. I don't want them to know how completely inexperienced I am, so I stay quiet. They start talking about girls they will set me up with,

178

next week, the week after. Which is weird because I won't be here, but my brain is on hiatus and I keep saying, "Yeah, yeah." They even make up a personality for me. I'm only about four throws behind as we walk to the sixth hole, and Hodge puts his arm around me and says, "Dude. You're the king."

And it feels . . . good. It all does. The guys, the conversation, the beer warming my gut and radiating out to my head and my limbs. Aisha-hugging-the-seat good, in a way. I am not alone, and even without me saying anything, they know how I feel. Hodge starts bitching about living in his parents' basement and how he has to go out and look for work. Part of me is thinking, *You live in your parents' basement?* But then I remember that back in Billings, I do too. That makes me laugh, and they all look at me, but I can't even come close to explaining right now. I salute them with the beer and they salute me back, and I do feel a little bit like the king. I find myself thinking, *Yeah. I could live here.* I could just call my mom back and be like, *Sorry, I live in Salt Lake City now. I'm a Jack Mormon.*

I finish my third beer as we approach the ninth hole, which takes us very close to the parking lot. Aisha is sitting on a bench alone, playing with her phone. I toss the can to the ground, knowing these guys won't mind me littering, because I don't want her to see it. Then I wave a few times at Aisha, and part of me knows that Aisha isn't going to like beered-up Carson. But either she doesn't see my wave, or she's ignoring me.

Gareth yells, "Tumble break," and he climbs a tall, grassy hill. We all run after him. It's hard to balance, but I don't fall. Aisha looks up and sees us, and I wave to her to come join us. She shakes her head, and I'm a little pissed. She needs to lighten up.

"One! Two! Three!" the three guys scream at the top of their lungs, and then they fall to their sides and roll, toppling down the hill until they land in a clump at the bottom, laughing hysterically. I'm left there at the top, my knees locked. Should I do it too? Will it look stupid? What will Aisha think? And then I decide to stop thinking, and I fall to my side and start rolling.

The world tumbles. I pick up speed, rolling and rolling. I knock into Hodge's side at the bottom, and we writhe in a pile, and I just let go and laugh and laugh.

Hodge yells out, "Shit! The beers!"

I feel the wetness just as he says it. One of the beers in his pocket burst open when he rolled down the hill. Now my shorts are wet too, and I smell like beer, but we just keep laughing.

Eventually we get up and wipe the grass and beer off of us as well as we can, and the guys run ahead. I look over at Aisha. I should probably go talk to her. Walking toward her, I feel the alcohol sloshing through my veins. It's a dirty, wonderful secret that Aisha can't know, so I make an agreement with myself never to tell her how much I drank.

"You have an accident?" she asks, frowning. She points at the wet spot on the front of my green cargo shorts.

"It's stupid," I say, lingering a bit away from her.

She smells it anyway. "Carson, were you drinking? Are you kidding me with this?"

Her voice is higher than usual, and it scares me, the emotion in it. I shake my head. "Hodge had beers in his shorts and they exploded when we rolled." I laugh, but she doesn't. She walks over and sniffs my face.

"Bullshit," she says. "You drank."

I nod slightly. "Just one."

"Jesus," she says. "Are you crazy?"

"In what universe is drinking a single beer crazy?"

She puts her hands on her hips and looks at me. "In the universe where your grandfather and your father are alcoholics. C'mon."

I look away. She doesn't get that these are the first drinks I've ever had. That's not quite alcoholic territory. And just because I liked it? People like beer. Please.

"Carson." She sits back down on the bench and pulls me to sit next to her. She grabs my head and forces me to look at her. "Seriously. You have even one more sip of alcohol and I am done with you. Not a joke. Done. Like I drive off and leave you here and you never see me again. You feel me?"

My brain focuses, suddenly sober. The world still spins a bit, but within it I am totally here. "I feel you," I say.

We sit there in silence. Getting yelled at for drinking is like this weird new place I didn't know I'd be in, ever. Was my dad here? My grandfather? A place where they were like, *I love this drinking thing. I'll make sure it doesn't get the best of me.*

"Will those guys be done soon?" she asks.

"I think so," I say. "Sorry about the drinking, by the way."

She responds with a tiny, tight-lipped nod.

"I'm sure they'll be back any minute. I know you hated that, but hey, it's almost over."

"Yay," she says. "Can we never, ever see those people again, ever?"

"Yeah, you don't really get them, do you?"

She picks at her fingernails. "You're right," she says. "I don't get them. I wanna smack that guy Gareth's head against the concrete. I don't want to do that with you. How come you actually wanna spend time with this person when I want to kill him?"

I bite my lower lip. I know the answer, in a way, but I also know she won't get it. "He's a 'sup, dude."

She screws up her face in a mask of annoyance. "A what?"

"A 'sup, dude. I've never had a 'sup, dude friend. You know. Someone who you'd meet for breakfast at a diner. Someone you'd order huge breakfasts with, and guzzle down milk shakes, and order more bacon, and talk about cars or Frisbees or baseball, maybe."

I brace myself for her laughter. It doesn't come. Instead, she says, "You want that?"

"Well, no. Yeah. I don't know. I want to try it, maybe."

"Can't someone who is not a total asshole be your 'sup, dude?"

"He's not a total asshole."

"He's not not a total asshole. . . ."

I laugh. Then she touches my shoulder, bats her eyes, and says, " 'Sup, dude?"

I kiss her shoulder. "I can't believe it. You're jealous." My skin tingles. The ego boost I get from making Aisha feel jealous of me is way more than I got from the entire Frisbee golf game.

"Not really. Maybe," she says, pulling away slightly.

I pull the shoulder back and plant three kisses on it. "I love you, Aisha Stinson. I love that you can be jealous of me, when you're you. That's just . . . I love you, okay?"

"Okay," she says, giving my shoulder a quick peck. "Love you too, asshole."

182

# 27

THAT NIGHT'S DINNER starts out with a prayer. Aisha and I are across the table from Gareth, while Mr. and Mrs. Bailey sit at either end. We see them grabbing hands, so I tentatively take Aisha's hand with my right and Mr. Bailey's with my left. Aisha takes Mrs. Bailey's other hand.

Mr. Bailey says, "Dear Heavenly Father, we're thankful for this bounty and for the chance to spend time together as a family with our new friends. We're thankful for the people who helped grow the food that went into this meal. Please bless them. Amen."

I say "Amen" when Mrs. Bailey and Gareth say it. Not sure if Aisha does or not. But for me, saying the word in unison makes me feel like part of something, and I want that. Thanks to this trip, I'm beginning to really enjoy feeling like a part. Rather than always apart.

And that prayer? It was just . . . thankful. It was nice. I didn't hate it.

Over dinner, Gareth talks about Frisbee golf, and about a new set of "rockin' discs" he'd like to buy. Mr. Bailey jokingly asks Gareth if he's considered putting half that much enthusiasm into a job search, and you can kind of feel the tension at the table, that there's a story and an ongoing drama surrounding this.

I guess no family is perfect. Though clearly, some families are more perfect than others.

I have never sat at a dinner table with both my parents that I can remember. When my mom took us back to New York and we moved in with my grandparents, the four of us had dinner sometimes, but that's it. Ever since my grandparents moved down to Florida four years ago, I mostly dine in front of the TV. Mom and I rarely eat at the same time. And meals are important, aren't they? I have never really thought about that before.

I turned on my phone before dinner. There were three long voicemails from Mom. The first one went like this:

*"Carson. I feel like we need to have a conversation about boundaries. I feel really surprised that you would violate my boundaries like this. I hear that you have your heart set on this trip you're taking, and if you would simply engage me in a conversation, perhaps I could come to understand why you think it's necessary at this time, of all times, to drive off with a friend you barely know. I want you to know that I recognize that you're individuating right now, and certainly that process is made no easier by spending time with your father. I know that's been terribly difficult for you, and I honor that. But you simply need to be aware that my boundaries are not to be crossed. If you do cross them, there will be repercussions. I intend for us to sit down when you return and really tackle some of these issues. Please keep me updated about when you'll be back."*

I looked at my phone. I thought about sitcom mothers. They run hot, not cold. They care too much. They meddle in their kids' business. They yell and scream or they work hard not to yell and scream even though they want to. I thought, *My mom would not make a great sitcom mother.* I didn't respond. I turned my phone off again.

The conversation bounces between our journey, and Gareth's lack of a job, and Mr. Bailey's exciting yet fascinating career as an accountant. Then Aisha says to Mrs. Bailey, "So what was your committee thing this morning, if you don't mind me asking?"

"It's a church thing. I counsel abused women," Mrs. Bailey says, her voice taking on a more serious tone we haven't heard before.

Mr. Bailey, who looks a bit like a TV senator with his khaki-colored hair parted at the side, says, "I encourage Stacy to get out into the community."

Aisha asks, "Counsel them how?" I hear the edge, but I'm hoping Mrs. Bailey doesn't.

Mrs. Bailey swallows the bite of food she was chewing. "Do you know what righteous dominion is?"

We both shake our heads no.

"Well, in the Mormon church, men are charged with providing a righteous dominion over our families. Most Mormons are probably more like us, where Robert is the head of the household but we're all involved. But in other homes . . . We have a growing problem with unrighteous dominion. Men who use neglect, or physical, emotional, or even sexual abuse, to rule their families. I counsel women who have to deal with unrighteous dominion."

"How do you counsel them? What do you tell them to do?" Aisha asks, that edge still in her voice. I'm guessing she thinks that Mrs. Bailey tells them to endure it. I want to kick her under the table because, well, not that the question isn't a good one. But these are our hosts.

Mrs. Bailey's face is a mask of patience. "Well, it depends. Oftentimes, we're teaching them to protect themselves. Some of

185

these women are in danger, and we help them get themselves and their families out of harm's way."

Aisha doesn't have an answer for that one. "Cool," I say, covering for her.

Mrs. Bailey gives me a kind smile. "It's a dangerous world out there. Here in the Mormon world too. Women can be victims, and they shouldn't have to be."

We all go back to eating for a bit. And then Aisha starts another conversation.

"You supported Prop Eight."

"What's Prop Eight?" Mr. Bailey asks.

"It made gay marriage in California illegal for a while. It was overturned," Aisha says.

"Oh," he says, like someone just poked him in the ribs.

"I'm a lesbian," she says.

"Oh," Mr. Bailey says again. "Okay. I respect your lifestyle choice. To me it's a sin, but that's between you and God."

Aisha raises her voice. "I didn't *choose* a *lifestyle*," she says. "Did you choose to be Mormon?"

The table is quiet for a bit, but we can all feel the grenade under the floor.

"That's not the same," Mr. Bailey says.

"No?" Aisha says, scooping up a forkful of potato.

"My religion is my belief system. Yours is about who you . . ."

She looks directly at him. "Who I what?"

He shrugs. "Choose to love."

Aisha shakes her head. "Right. Because who wouldn't choose to be a second-class citizen?"

186

I want to disappear. I want to crawl under the table.

"We didn't support that," Mr. Bailey says, frowning. "That proposition."

"Sure you did. The Mormon church funded most of it."

"We're not the Mormon church," he says, his frown becoming more pronounced.

"Do you go to church? Do you give money?"

I realize that as rude as Aisha is being, she's right. If the Mormons gave money to an antigay cause, anyone who gave money to a Mormon church also supported it, indirectly at least.

"You seem to think you know where I stand on issues based on my religion," he says, his voice clipped and practiced. "Do I know where you stand on issues because you're a lesbian?"

"No," Aisha says. "I guess you don't."

"So maybe instead of telling me what my beliefs are, you should ask."

Aisha doesn't respond. She just grips her fork tight. Mr. Bailey doesn't know what she's been through, and I wish I could find a way to tell him to lay off, to let this all go. But I can't.

"I have nothing against gay people," he says. "And I don't have a strong opinion about gay marriage. All people should be equal."

"Don't tell me," Aisha says, her lips tense. "Tell your damn leaders."

I stand up. "Can you excuse us for a second?"

"Hey," she says to me. "You don't have righteous dominion over me. I can say what the hell I want."

"You're right," I say, my head buzzing. "But it's rude. These people are our hosts."

Aisha takes a deep breath and shakes her head. "I can't ever do anything right." She looks up at them. "I'm sorry. I apologize. Can I be excused?"

Mr. Bailey nods, and Aisha just about runs back to her room. I sit back down, but I don't pick up my fork. I can't. Earlier I chose hanging with Gareth over her. I can't do it to her twice in a row.

I give a weak smile. "I'm going to have to —"

"Sure," Mrs. Bailey says. "We understand."

I go to Aisha's room and close the door behind me. She's on the bed, propped up, a pillow on the headboard behind her. She's staring into space.

"I guess I should have seen this coming when they started with a prayer," I say. "Sorry."

She doesn't look at me, but she also doesn't seem about to explode, either. I sit down next to her, pick up a pillow, and put it behind me as I lean back.

"You know, I didn't even mind the prayer," she says, her voice soft.

"Me neither. I was surprised, but I didn't hate it."

"It's the rest of it. They're so nice, and they're so perfect, and yet."

I wait for her to finish. "Yet what?"

Her eyes are rimmed in pink. "This place is melting me."

I don't know what that means, but I nod and I put my hand on her arm.

"Wyoming melted you, and Utah is melting me."

"Walking wounded," I say.

Aisha nods, hard. "Right?" she says, turning toward me now. "I'm so mad, because. These people. They're like my family was." The tears are beginning to fall now. "My dad was always good to me, great to me. And then this thing. He couldn't hack it. He saw it as his failure, and he's not so good with failure. The religion thing, that made it easy for him not to deal with it. The church told him I needed fixing, so instead of working on accepting me as I've always been, he gives me an ultimatum. Be someone else, or be gone.

"So I'm sitting there looking at the smiling Baileys, and it hurts. I woke up one night at the zoo and it was raining, and I was alone out there. My dad decided it was better for me to sleep out in the fucking rain than to love me as I was. That hurts, Carson. It hurts bad."

I don't say anything. I just hug her. She hugs me back, and we lie down and look at each other. Her head is turned to the side, and her tears zip across her cheeks like they're climbing a mountain and then falling off a ledge.

"It's the hypocrisy. They preach love, but they're selling fear. I hate that so much."

"I hate it too," I say.

"Do you? Because you don't always seem to get it."

"I hate that it hurts you."

She squeezes my arm. "Thanks."

"Thank you," I say back.

"For what?"

I say, "For saving my life."

She averts her eyes. "I didn't save your life."

"You kind of did. Before you, I never had any of this — friends, adventure. You saved my life because I never knew what life could be."

She covers her eyes with her hands. "That may be the nicest thing anyone has ever said to me."

"I mean it."

"I know."

We lie there facing each other for a little while longer, until her eyes dry and suddenly we're just two happy kids on an adventure, looking at each other. Her eyes are playful, and kind, and they love me. Even if she doesn't love me like a boyfriend, it's more than I ever could have hoped for.

"So do we go back out to those awful people?" she asks.

"They're not awful."

She whispers, "I know. Come on. I'll make nice."

We do go back to dinner. Aisha apologizes again, and Mr. Bailey surprises me by spending ten minutes explaining that they're liberal Mormons, actually, and they don't agree with every position of the church, and take his wife, for instance, her work, and Aisha nods and nods until her neck gets tired. I drift off listening to the sounds of it, happy for the moment because there's harmony, even if it's awkward turtle harmony.

When I head off to my room for the night, I read more of my grandfather's journal. I've never gotten to know anyone this way before, just from their writing. And it's weird, because it's kind of like seeing myself in the future. It's like I'm finding me in another person. I flip through pages and pages with the header "Russ's Book of

Puns," because I don't feel like reading puns tonight. I stop at one of the final pages with writing on it.

*May 14, 1982*

*If I go, I'll take me with me*
*If I stay, the tarnish remains*
*My boy, so needy, so needs me*
*My life, so without purpose, so without compass*
*Morally*
*I can sit here forever, on the fence, not living*
*I need a push, God*
*I need you to tell me what to do*
*And then I need a pass, for if and when I do it, I cannot*
*Take not knowing*
*Will you be there with me?*

It takes me several seconds to close the page. His boy, so needy? Wow. My dad is, isn't he? Like that night when he thought I was his dad. And what does Russ mean, he needs a pass? Like it'll be a sin? Does he mean leaving? Is he asking for a pass in case he leaves?

I can't wait to meet my grandfather and find out.

# 28

WHEN I WAKE up in the morning and creep into the hallway, Aisha's door is open slightly, and I peer in. She's asleep on her side, her right arm splayed above her head and her left one clutching a pillow to her chest. Her head rests on her lavender pillowcase that she brought in from her car. Her hair billows around it as if it has expanded overnight. Infinite fine little wisps of Aisha, curling into themselves.

I feel as if I'm seeing something gentle and elusive. Secretive. Aisha's sleeping hair.

The floor creaks beneath me, and Aisha wakes up and sees me. "What are you doing?" she grumbles.

I don't say anything for a few seconds. "Watching you sleep."

"Can you stop?"

"Crabby," I say. "Crab shack. Crab apples."

"Not a morning person," she says, stretching her arms up above her head. "I'm not a person of the morning."

I laugh, because she's repeating my words from a few days ago, back in Montana.

Just like at the Leffs, we leave with more stuff than we had when we arrived. Gareth gives me a couple of pairs of his old shorts, just in case we aren't heading right back to Billings after meeting Mrs. Clancy. I thank him and tell him I'll send them back, but he tells me not to worry about it. Mrs. Bailey gives Aisha another pair of shorts, which Aisha at first refuses but then gratefully accepts.

"So what's the plan for the day?" Mr. Bailey asks as Aisha loads the car. Mrs. Bailey stands next to him.

"Gonna go to Temple Square to meet this woman who knew my grandfather, I guess," I say. "Have absolutely no idea beyond that."

"Oh, you'll love Temple Square!" Mrs. Bailey says.

"And if you need to stay longer, you're welcome," Mr. Bailey says, and I think, *Really? After the dinner fiasco, you'd have us stay longer?* I smile at him, and maybe that thought comes through, because he smiles back in a way that seems to say, *Yeah. Even though.*

The Baileys hug me, and then they face Aisha. Mr. Bailey asks, "Is it okay if I hug you?" Aisha nods, and then I get to watch the world's most awkward good-bye hug.

"Stop by later, dude," Gareth says. It's seven thirty in the morning and his breath already smells like beer. This time, I really don't want one.

"Yeah, sure," I say, but I know we won't. We wave good-bye, and I can tell Aisha feels extremely relieved to be out of there. I get why she feels that way, but I don't need to feel the same way. It's nice that we don't have to agree on everything.

---

We park a block south of the Temple, and as we walk to the gate, I notice that it's painfully clean here. The buildings are made of a sparkly white stone, maybe marble. Not just the tall and imposing Temple; all the buildings surrounding it too. Fountains of white with pristine turquoise waters spill over angels and cherubs and swans. Every few minutes someone pushes a cart along, sweeping up any litter, and as a result, the sidewalks sparkle as well.

"You could probably feed all the people in Rwanda for ten years with what it cost to build this shit," Aisha mutters, and I nod.

We find the Tabernacle building, which is in the southern part of the square next to the main Temple. It's a cream-white oval almost the size of a football stadium, with velvet ropes cordoning off the entrances. It makes me remember the Porcupine of Truth and the velvet ropes that separate those who die from Des Moines. I think about saying something, but I'm not sure Aisha is in the mood. Instead I say, "It's just too clean."

She nods. "Do Mormons even pee?"

"How would you figure that out? Feed one water and keep him in captivity?"

The front entrance isn't clear to us, so we circle the building clockwise, keeping an eye out for Lois Clancy. As we get to the final part of our lap, I spot an elderly woman sitting on a bench under a tree. She's wearing a beige floppy hat and a maroon jacket, and the black handbag on her lap looks too big for her small body.

I hurry over to her. "Mrs. Clancy?" I ask.

She smiles and puts her hand up in front of her mouth as if she's shocked. "You're Russ's grandson." She speaks slowly, as if her brain works at about one-fifth the speed of mine. "I didn't get a good look at you the other night."

"Yes." I stand in front of her and let her look at me.

Her smile is warm and genuine. She shakes her head. "Well, you do look like him," she says. "Isn't that something. All these years later."

I introduce her to Aisha, then we both sit down.

"I'm so terribly sorry about the other night," she says.

I realize she doesn't know that we heard her husband say that thing about black lesbians through the door. I look at Aisha, but she seems fine. "It's okay," I say, wanting to get past the awkward stuff and on to any information. "I hear you might have something for me?"

She nods and clutches her purse, and I get the sense that maybe I'm going too fast for her. "Your grandfather and I came here once and sat for hours. Such a pretty spot. We both loved choir music. Such a good man, that Russ."

"What can you tell me about him? I found a letter he sent my dad last year, and I have no idea where he is. My dad is sick, and I'm trying to reunite them before —"

"Oh dear," she says.

"So do you know where he is?"

"I don't, dear. I must say I'm surprised —"

"What? What are you surprised about?"

She tightens her lips and looks down at her purse, which she slowly opens. She pulls out a slate-gray hardcover book. The title reads *Alcoholics Anonymous*.

"This is really all I have. I wanted to keep Russ's anonymity," she says, "but maybe in this case, it's okay to break it."

My heart pounds. "What? Please, tell me."

"Your grandfather was in Alcoholics Anonymous."

"Okay. I know about AA," I say.

"He stayed with us for two weeks. I took him to his first meeting. I've been in the program now fifty-five years. We had a lot of good talks. Your grandfather was such a kind man."

My throat catches. "Was?"

She waves it away. "Oh, I don't mean that. I have no idea where he is. I lost touch with Russ about eighteen months after he stayed here. He didn't answer three letters in a row, so I stopped writing."

"Do you still have his address?"

She slowly shakes her head. "I'm sorry. That was many years ago."

"That's too bad," I say.

"We wrote back and forth all the time. He was a good friend for the year I knew him."

"Can you tell me about him?"

She is quiet for a long moment. "Hard life."

"Could you say more about that?"

Again, it's like we're having an interview on TV and there's a tape delay.

"I'm sorry, dear. I'm old-fashioned, maybe. I feel like there are things friends say to each other that shouldn't ever get repeated." She closes her eyes and bows her head. "Proverbs twenty-six twenty: 'Without wood a fire goes out; without gossip a quarrel dies down.'"

She opens her eyes and smiles at us. I glance at Aisha and we share a look that could kill an old lady.

"But you might know something that could help us find him," I say.

"The book is all I have for you. I can tell you that he was a good man, and he was never anything other than kind to me. Or my husband, who was not always kind to him." She motions toward the book. "He sent me this a year after we met. Go on. Open it."

On the inside front cover, there's an inscription. I recognize the shaky handwriting.

*To my savior, Lois. With love, Russ.*

She says, "It's the AA Big Book. Russ sent it to me from San Francisco on his first AA birthday. That's the anniversary of his first year in the program."

San Francisco! Now we're getting somewhere. "Okay," I say, waiting for the next thing. The big thing that's going to tell us what to do, where to go next. San Francisco, I guess. But that's a pretty big place.

"So he got help for his problem," Lois says.

I nod again. That's cool. I'm glad my grandfather got help. But then she doesn't say anything else. "So that's it?"

Lois looks meek. She shrugs her shoulders. "I thought you'd want the book. I thought you'd want to know that he joined the fellowship of Alcoholics Anonymous. It's life-changing, you know."

"Sorry," I say. "I'm glad. It's just, I need to find him. I feel like you know something and you're not telling me, and . . . I mean, it's still a dead end. You really won't tell me about his struggles?"

"That's not for me to tell."

I sigh, thinking about the stupid Bible quote. Maybe it's true that gossip is bad, but I'm not asking for gossip. I'm asking for information about an actual family member so I can find him and save my dad's life. But Lois doesn't seem like the kind of old lady who's going to change her mind. "You sure you don't know anything else that could help me find him?"

"I've found many answers in the book," she says slowly, and I have no idea what the hell that means, but to her it means something, I guess, because she stands up.

"Bless you both," she says. "God can, and God will. If you let him." And then she toddles off.

We sit there, watching her leave, and the only thing she's told us that's new is that my grandfather went to San Francisco. But did he stay there? What happened after he stopped writing her? Without any more information, that's just about nothing.

"Done. Over," I say. "We're heading back to Billings."

Aisha leans back on the bench. "Looks that way."

I thumb through the book absentmindedly. Two pages after my grandfather's inscription, on the bottom of the copyright page, is more writing. The writing is circled in a different color of ink.

For Russ. Keep coming back.
Turk B. 223-7849

"Huh," I say, pointing it out to Aisha.

She looks. "Keep coming back. Turk B."

"She circled it. That's a new circle."

Aisha grabs the book and studies the circle. "Yeah," she says. "That's new."

"I guess she thinks it's *not* gossip to just circle something?" Lois is out of sight now, and I have no idea where she went.

"That's so weird. Religious people can be so weird," Aisha says.

"What do you suppose the 'Keep coming back' part means?"

"I have no clue. Looks like someone gave the book to him before he sent it to Lois."

"There's a number," I say. "No area code."

Aisha pulls out her phone. "You said he went to San Francisco, right?"

"Yep."

She Googles it. "The San Francisco area code is four-one-five," she says. "Give it a try. I mean, it's from nineteen eighty-something, but —"

"This Turk B. guy could still have a landline. He's an old person," I say. My heart is in my throat. I take out my phone and punch in the number. The ring sounds old, which gives me hope. It just rings and rings. I stay on for a full minute, wishing someone would answer.

Finally I hang up. "No dice," I say to Aisha.

She says, "Wait. Say the number again."

I repeat it.

"And his name?"

"Turk B. Funny last name."

"I think they just use initials in AA," Aisha says as she types in the number. She stares at her screen and then she stands, all her attention on her phone. "Got something."

"What?" I stand too.

"Turk Braverman. Thirty-six Prosper Street, San Francisco, California, nine-four-one-one-four. Reverse lookup."

"Turk Braverman," I repeat. "Okay."

But then we just stand there, because the number is from thirty-plus years ago. It could easily be an old number. An old address. I mean, I looked up my mom once on whitepages.com, and she was still listed as living in the apartment she grew up in near Columbia University. The guy may not have known my grandfather that well, and he is probably ancient by now. He could be dead, for all I know.

"Google him," I say, and Aisha does so. The only thing that comes up is an ad for criminal background checks, and that's for Turk B., not Turk Braverman. Google asks if we mean Tzuriel Braverman, which we definitely don't.

We map the address. It's right in the center of San Francisco, near Market Street, which I think is probably a famous street since even I've heard of it. Aisha tries to pull up the satellite image on her phone. The webpage spins and spins.

"Maybe Turk Braverman will be, like, standing out in front of his house waving," I say, and Aisha laughs.

"And underneath it'll say, 'Hi, Carson and Aisha, you found me!'"

Finally the picture comes up. It's a block of thin row houses that look like they come from a hundred years ago, with intricate awnings and rickety staircases. There's an orange one, a light-blue one, and a lime-green one. But what are the odds some guy who wrote "keep coming back" to my grandfather thirty-plus years ago still knows him? And is it worth a long-ass drive just to find out? Would Aisha even go for that?

I look at her, and it's like she can read my mind. She maps the route. It's 737 miles, almost eleven hours away, according to Google Maps.

I wince. "Too far?"

"Too far for what?" she asks.

"You wouldn't be up for —"

"Hell I wouldn't!"

"You mean —"

"Carson," she says. "You think I'd rather go back to Billings than drive to San Francisco? Gay mecca of the world?"

She grins. She wants to go. A slow grin crosses my face too.

"Are we going to San Francisco?" she asks.

"We can keep calling the number on the way," I say, and she nods.

It occurs to me that we have about a hundred dollars left to our name. I try to figure out if that's enough money for gas to get there. Gas is like $3.50 a gallon.

"How many miles to a gallon of gas does the Neon get?" I ask Aisha.

"About thirty."

So $3.50 buys thirty miles. Which means seventy dollars buys six hundred miles, and ninety dollars buys seven hundred and fifty miles. Yes. We have barely enough money to get to San Francisco if we don't eat, which sounds like a bad idea to me. But so does going home, when we have this one shot at finding my granddad.

So I swallow my fear, say nothing about the cash flow situation, and shout, "San Francisco, baby!"

# 29

WE STOP AT the West Salt Lake City Flying J, a gas station, because a sign along the highway alerts us that there will not be another gas station for more than a hundred miles.

"How is that even possible?" I ask. "What if you live in between the two?"

"Might be that no one does live there," Aisha says, and I realize, of course, that I still have an East Coast perspective. Out here, the empty spaces can be as big as Rhode Island. Bigger.

After we gas up and I use the restroom, I find Aisha standing by the soft-serve ice cream station. She points to the sign. Fifty cents a cone.

"On me," I say, figuring we can afford a buck for ice cream. "This way, you can never say I was a cheap bastard."

Aisha isn't listening, though. She seems to be scanning the cavernous convenience store, and she looks — angry? Sometimes it's hard to tell with her.

I pay for the ice cream and gas, and we are down to sixty-five dollars. I'm not sure why I'm not more worried about it. I'm just not.

We drive off, and on our right is the Great Salt Lake. It's as big as an ocean, and the shore is crusty white. I don't know much about salt lakes, or what makes one lake saltier than others, but it is cool to look at.

Aisha's quiet, so I say, "Whatcha thinkin' 'bout?"

She tightens her lips. "Forget about it."

A pang in my stomach. What happened? Did I do something again? "No, tell me."

She glances over at me, and I see in her eyes that she's not mad. She's sad. "Do you know the last time I saw a person who wasn't white-skinned?"

I laugh, because that wasn't what I expected her to say. But then I think back. Wyoming? No, definitely not. Here in Utah? I scan my brain. No. Not that I can remember.

"Jesus," I say.

"I don't think about that stuff a lot, but I was looking around the gas station and it was white folks for days, and then I realized — story of my life. Not that there's anything wrong with white folks. It's just, sometimes it's nice to not feel like the only one."

I think about what that would be like. To be on this trip and not see another white person for three states. I can't imagine. Not that I somehow, like, identify with all white people and not with black people, but there's something to be said for . . . likeness?

"Wow," I say.

"I mean, Billings. What was my dad thinking? Why did he even take us out of Lincoln? Not like that was so great either. I mean, why couldn't we live anywhere where there were other people like me? Why can't I ever be around my people?" She taps the dashboard for emphasis.

"Aisha," I say, reaching over for her hand. "I'm your people."

She looks over at me and smiles. She takes my hand. "Yes. And no."

Her hand feels warm, familiar. It hadn't really occurred to me that our skin colors make us so different. I mean, I don't really think like that. But maybe I should?

"That has to be really hard," I say.

"Sometimes it is," she says. "Sometimes not."

We watch the world spin by as we speed west. My phone rings, and I see it's my dad. I feel my body tighten. For several days now, I haven't had to think about him. Should I pick up? I decide not to.

"Who was that?" Aisha asks.

"My dad," I say.

She nods but doesn't say anything. I'm glad. I don't want to talk about it.

My phone rings again. It's him again.

"Shit," I say. The man is dying. I should answer it.

I take a deep breath and pick up.

"Hello," I say, monotone.

"You left me," a weak voice says.

I hear the alcohol in his voice. "You're drunk," I say, very clearly, my blood sizzling in my veins. I feel it in my feet, my knees, my skull. "You're drunk, aren't you?"

"A little."

"I won't talk to you when you're drunk. And by the way, I didn't leave you. Mom did. I was three. I didn't do anything to you. You were a drunk. You did it to me."

He is quiet for a moment. I listen closely, and I can hear the sound of sniffling.

"I mean now," he says, sounding like a lost boy. "You left me now."

I'm not used to this. My dad drunk dialing me, my dad sounding this vulnerable. The sizzle in my bloodstream simmers down a little, like someone threw water onto a hot frying pan.

"I didn't leave you," I say, softer. "I'm coming back. Soon. There's something I need to do. Something I need to find out, okay? I'll be back. I promise."

He sniffles. "People don't come back."

The line between me and my father feels like a thin wisp of hair being pulled tight. I don't want it to break. He's dying, and as much as I hate him sometimes, I cannot allow it to break. "I'll be back," I say, in a heavy accent like Arnold Schwarzenegger, and my dad laughs, so I laugh. But then I listen more closely and he isn't laughing.

He's sobbing. For the second time in my life, and the second time in a week, I hear my dad weep. He sounds like a wounded animal.

I bite down on my lip, hard. Harder. I keep pressing until it breaks and I taste the salt flow of my own blood seep into my mouth. I run my tongue over the open cut, over and over.

"I screwed it all up," he says through his tears. "I screwed up."

"You didn't," I say, but I can't finish the sentence.

Deep sobs seep through the phone. "I'm sorry," he says. "My boy. My boy. I'm sorry. My boy."

I lose it. I lose my shit. The tears don't just dribble out of my eyes, they cascade. They soak my cheeks. I am suddenly three in his arms on the couch watching cartoons, and I am six and sitting alone on the radiator in my New York bedroom, and I am twelve and standing in right field alone, and I am fourteen and wanting to tell someone, anyone, about my first wet dream. I am fifteen and wondering how to shave and my grandfather teaches me and it's not the same. My dad. Who has always been missing. My dad, like a hole in my heart.

"Dad," I whisper. "Daddy."

Aisha pulls over, turns off the ignition, and leaps out of the car like there's a bomb about to go off. I am alone in a Dodge Neon, on the side of the road in western Utah, and my dad and I are having The Conversation. The one I've wanted my whole entire life. The one I've dreaded my whole entire life.

"I ruined it all. Is it too late now?"

"No," I say. "Never."

"I want to do better," he says. "I want to be a dad. Will you let me try?"

"Yes. Of course."

"I don't have that long, but I want to try. Will you please get back here so I can try?"

"I will, I promise," I say. I wipe my eyes and in the silence I picture him doing the same. In my mind, I see the line between us becoming thicker, fuller, just by a little bit, but still, it's changed.

"So where are you?" he asks after a while.

I tell him the truth.

"Western Utah?" he asks. "What the hell's in western Utah?"

"Absolutely nothing. Heading west. Don't tell Mom. She is going to kill me."

"She said you were visiting friends in Wyoming," he says, and that surprises me. "What are you doing out there?"

"Long story." Knowing the way he feels about his dad, I don't want to upset him further right now. "I promise I'll tell you everything when I get back."

"Okay. Don't wait too long, all right?"

As my mother might say, I *hear* what he's saying, even if he's not saying it. "I won't."

"Promise? I'm not doing too good, you know. Not guiltin' you. Just true."

"I promise. You promise to hold on?"

"I promise," he says. "I will."

"Mom driving you crazy?"

This makes him laugh. "I'm an asshole," he says. "Your mother is a saint."

"Sure," I say.

"Your mom's the love of my life, Carson. Always was, always will be."

I so want to ask again, *Why? If she was the love of your life, why didn't you stop drinking and come with us all those years ago and avoid this?* I don't get it. But I don't want to hurt him and he's tender right now and we're talking, so I don't say anything like that.

"Wow," I say. "Do you think she feels that way too?"

"I aim to find out," he says.

"You have to stop drinking."

"I know. I am. I will."

I close my eyes and imagine my family as a puzzle. There's always been a missing piece in the center, and now the piece is loosely in place, not quite clicked in yet, but it's flickering. And I know that I can't just assume my mom feels the same way as he does and she'll take him back or that he'll ever really stop drinking, plus there's the dying thing, so it's very, very complicated. But just knowing that the piece is there soothes me like a warm, heavy blanket. It feels like the midafternoon heat from the sun through the windshield.

"If you want to call me tomorrow, or you want me to call you, that would be okay," I say.

"Good," he says. "I will."

I smile. Warm blanket. "I gotta let Aisha back in the car. She's probably frying."

"Sure," he says.

"And will you maybe not drink before you call?"

"I'll try, Carson," he says. "Every second is hard. You get that?"

"Kind of. Not really," I say. "But I'll try."

"I love you, my boy," he says, and the words are hard to squeeze out of my mouth in return. I love him and I hate him and I have so much hope now and it's totally futile and if we get close, unless he miraculously recovers, we're doing it just in time for me to miss him the rest of my life.

"Love you too, Dad," I spit out, meaning it and not meaning it. Because it's what you say.

I hang up and look out the window. Aisha is on the side of the road, ahead of me and to the right, plugging away on her phone, texting God knows who. I knock on the window.

She doesn't hear.

I knock again.

She waves me off. She is intently typing away, and since she let me have my time, I give her all the time she needs. I close my eyes and recline in the passenger seat, allowing the hot sun to bake me, to be my warm blanket.

I wake up when she opens the door and settles into the driver's seat. She turns the ignition on and blasts the A/C. The car is really hot, but I was deeply asleep and it was a good sleep, hot or not. I felt at peace in a way that I have never felt before. The hole, the home-less feeling in my heart: Its throb is missing.

She turns toward me. "So you want to hear what I wrote my dad?"

I had a feeling. I nod.

She smiles, a scared, grief-stricken smile that trembles at the corners. She reads: "Dad, I know you raised me to be your baby girl. You raised me good and you raised me right, and you raised me never to raise my voice to you, which is the right thing for a father to teach a child. But I am afraid if I don't raise my voice this one time, I'm gonna lose my daddy, and my daddy is gonna lose his baby girl. So here goes."

The next part she says really loud, her voice filling every inch of the Neon.

"YOU'VE KNOWN WHO I WAS FOR A LONG TIME, DAD. I DIDN'T JUST GROW UP AND ONE DAY DECIDE I WAS GONNA BE A DYKE. I WAS LIKE THIS WHEN I WAS LITTLE, AND YOU KNOW THAT. YOU KNOW IT.

"I'M YOUR BABY GIRL AISHA, AND I CAN'T BE ANYBODY OTHER THAN YOUR BABY GIRL AISHA. YOUR BABY GIRL AISHA LIKES OTHER GIRLS, ALWAYS HAS, ALWAYS WILL. YOU REALLY THINK I'M THE DEVIL, DADDY? THIS IS HOW I WAS BORN, AND IT'S OKAY, DADDY. IT IS. IT'S NOT YOUR FAULT, AND IF IT IS YOUR FAULT, I THANK YOU BECAUSE I LIKE ME. MAYBE NOT IN BILLINGS,

BUT THERE'S OTHER PEOPLE LIKE ME IN THE WORLD, AND I'M GONNA FIND THEM, I KNOW IT. I WILL FIND OTHER PEOPLE WHO LOOK ME IN THE EYE AND KNOW ME.

"SO THIS IS WHAT'S GONNA HAPPEN, DADDY. YOU'RE GOING TO WRITE ME OR CALL ME. WE ARE GONNA FIGURE THIS OUT SO THAT WE CAN BE IN EACH OTHER'S LIVES. SO THAT WHEN I HAVE A BABY GIRL OR A BABY BOY, THEY CAN HAVE A GRANDDADDY WHO IS THE GREATEST MAN IN THE UNIVERSE, BECAUSE THAT'S WHAT I ALWAYS THOUGHT YOU WERE. ARE. I THINK YOU ARE THAT, AND THE ONLY THING YOU EVER DID WRONG, DADDY, WAS MAKE ME GO. I CAN FORGIVE YOU, BUT ONLY IF YOU CALL ME AND TALK TO ME ABOUT ALL THIS."

Her voice gets more calm now.

"One last thing, Daddy. And as you see, I've lowered my voice now, because I'm tired of yelling, and it's not right to yell at your daddy anyway. I just need to ask you this one thing. You really think God wants you to never see your daughter again? Didn't Jesus hang out with the sinners? Even if I am a sinner, and I don't think I am, I think I deserve that much from a man who follows Jesus. I believe he would want that.

"Love always, your baby girl, Aisha."

She looks up at me, and I reach over and hug her tight and bury my face in her frizzy hair. It smells like olives.

"That's awesome," I say, inhaling the scent. "You're awesome."

"Thanks," she says in my ear. "So I should hit Send?"

I pull back and look her in the eye and nod. "Hit it," I say.

She takes a deep breath, and then she taps a button and puts the phone in her pocket.

We drive in silence. My heart feels new. It doesn't feel good, because it hurts still. For Aisha and what she's going through. For my dad and what he's going through. But it feels new.

"Walking wounded no more," she says, and all I can do is grab her hand and hope that's true. For both of us.

We sail through western Utah. There are no exits, no homes, no nothing. The Great Salt Lake seems to go on for hundreds of miles to our right, and to our left is a sandy wasteland. We don't talk much. I think I fall asleep again.

When I wake up, we are driving into water. The road ahead is covered in shimmering blue. We're going to skid into it and die, and Aisha doesn't seem to see it. "Look out!" I scream, closing my eyes and putting my hands in front of my face.

She doesn't stop driving or slow down, but we don't skid into water either. I lower my hands. The water in front of us recedes. As we drive, it keeps receding. It is always twenty feet ahead.

"Is that a . . . ?"

She smiles. "A mirage. Cool, huh?"

I study it. "Can you stop the car?"

Aisha decelerates, pulls over, and stops the car. We get out. The same water we've been seeing ahead of us is to our right, and I'm not sure if it's the lake or more of the mirage. We step toward it, onto the sparkly white salt flats. They give a little under our feet, like damp sand might, and it appears there's a lake about twenty feet ahead. But there are also track marks, like someone drove across the flats and right into the water.

"You see what I see?" I ask.

"Yep."

We slowly walk out. The salt continues to give, and ten feet in, I exhale dramatically. The water keeps receding.

"It really is a mirage," I say.

"Yup."

"I could have sworn — I could have sworn that was actually water."

"Me too," she says.

"Maybe we can't trust our senses all the time?"

"I don't know."

I take a deep breath. "I always have felt like, if I can sense it, it exists. And if I can't, it doesn't. But what if my senses, like, don't give me all the information? And what if that means that there actually could be, you know, something? Like —" I can't even say it.

"So now God exists?" she asks me, her voice funny.

I don't respond. It's just . . . I don't know.

We get back in the car and drive farther, and my attention stays on the side of the road. Even though I know it's a mirage, it feels impossible for me to believe it's not actually water. But it isn't. My mind spins with new possibilities.

"Stop!" I say again. It looks real, but it's not. I need to take a picture.

We get out and walk on the salt flats again. This time, my sneakers come away wet.

So the mirage is real? Sometimes? I can't even figure out what that means. And the salt. So mesmerizing in its shimmering whiteness.

"I wonder what it tastes like," I say.

"Try some."

"It's probably the world's most poisonous salt."

"Only one way to know," Aisha says, teasing.

I bend down and scrape my finger across the ground. When I stand up again, we study the salt crystals.

"You're like Willy Wonka," I say. "Tempting me to eat something, and I'll probably turn into a saltshaker and roll away, and the Oompa Loompas will come out and sing about my personality flaws."

We stand there, both lost in thought. And then it comes to us at the same exact moment.

"Veruca Salt!" we yell, and then we point at each other and laugh.

Back in the car, Nevada can't come quickly enough. And then, at Exit 4, as if they know Utah won't last for much longer, the salt flats end. Four miles later, we cross the state line, and we woo-hoo and high-five.

We immediately notice that the drivers go faster and veer into the wrong lane far more often than they did in Utah. "Pick a lane," Aisha yells to the cars in front of us.

"Nevada: We take the second 'M' out of Mormon," I say, and Aisha laughs.

WE'RE BOTH FAMISHED when we get to the Reno city limits, as we've eaten only ice cream since breakfast at the Baileys'. We choose fast food based on our existential budget. Aisha pulls off the highway at a gas station with a Subway, and we each get five-dollar footlongs.

It's not great when a fast-food dinner costs, drinks included, one-fifth of your entire net worth. As I fill up the tank again, I try to decide whether I should tell Aisha just how low we are on cash. After paying for gas, we're down to sixteen bucks.

Google tells us we have 219 miles, or three hours and thirty-two minutes, left on our trip. It's seven fifteen at night, and eleven p.m. seems late to show up at a stranger's house. But we have no other way of finding Turk Braverman; I've called the number I have for him five times now with no answer. As we get back in the car, I'm all buzzy inside, imagining ringing the doorbell on his colorful Victorian in the heart of San Francisco. I have to hope we'll have better luck than with the Clancys. That maybe, just maybe, Turk will answer, and know my grandfather, and where he is, and why he left.

Aisha starts up the car.

And then she starts up the car.

And again.

"Shit," she says.

"What?" I ask. "Not . . ."

"Yeah," she says. "This is not great."

"Oh, come on," I say to the universe.

She keeps turning the key, and it makes that wheezing engine sound, like it's trying to find some momentum, but it never catches. The gauge on the left struggles to rise, and then the noise stops, the gauge collapses to zero, and the engine turns off.

"Has this ever happened before?" I ask.

She shakes her head.

"Come on," I repeat, thinking that if there is a God, he obviously thinks he's hilarious.

"Well, I guess we can forget San Fran for the night," Aisha sighs. "I might have triple A. I might not. I have no idea if my dad canceled it. I guess we're about to find out."

She gets out of the car and makes a call, and I get out too and listen, having no clue what it would mean if she does have it, and what it would mean if she doesn't.

"Well, there's good news and there's bad news," Aisha says once she's off the phone.

"Just tell me," I say.

"I'm still a member, so that's good. They'll tow us for free to the nearest repair place. Also, I get a discount on parts and labor, like ten percent off."

"Okay," I say.

"If it's just the battery, they'll give us a jump for free and we should be fine. The bad news is that if there's actually something wrong with the car, we'll need to pay to have it fixed."

"Ah," I say.

"Yeah. How much money do you have left?"

"Honestly?"

"No, lie to me. Yes, honestly."

I squint. "Sixteen dollars?"

She laughs. I laugh.

"No, really," she says.

"Um," I say, looking far to my left and then far to my right.

She shakes her head. "I thought your mom wired you money?"

"A hundred bucks," I say.

"Can she give us more?"

I shrug. "She ordered me to come home, so, um . . ."

Aisha stares at me, mouth open. "And you didn't tell me this because?"

I shrug again. "I'm an idiot."

She sits on the blacktop of the gas station parking lot, leaning against the door of the Neon. "Carson. Dude."

I hate when girls call me dude. "Yeah, I know. I'm sorry."

Three hours, a tow truck ride, and a plea on the surfingsofas .com bulletin board later, we are homeless and carless on the streets of Reno, the Biggest Little City in the World, whatever that means. We need a new ignition coil, which is a thing. Apparently it's what fires the spark plug, and hers is busted. It'll cost $140, and they don't have the part in stock. They won't be able to fix it until the morning. And even then, we don't have the money for it.

We are sitting at a bus stop along a boulevard with a lot of car traffic but hardly any people traffic. I have the canvas bag with our toiletries and my grandfather's journal, Aisha has her satin pillow under her armpit, and I'm carrying the Porcupine of Truth, which will not be as good a pillow as Aisha's satin one. I'm an idiot.

"Well, I guess there's some comfort in knowing you're totally screwed."

"I guess," I say.

Aisha takes out her phone and checks to see if our SOS on the surfingsofas.com board has garnered a response. Nothing. Nada.

I think about calling my mother. Nope. Not calling. It's just me and Aisha.

We sit and wait for someone from surfingsofas.com to text or call. Then we wait some more. Then we wait some more. Soon it's midnight, and we've been sitting at a bus stop for two hours.

"Maybe we can find a park," she says. "We'll take turns sleeping."

Using Google Maps, she finds us a place about half a mile away. It's a small, mostly empty park, with some grassy areas intersected by a lit path lined with benches and streetlights. The lights are so bright along the path that the pavement glimmers, unnaturally silver. We see a couple of homeless men sleeping on the benches. One wears only his underwear and a blackened sweatshirt. His legs are covered in sores.

"It's too bright here." I point to a hilly area to our left. "Maybe try the grass?"

Aisha shakes her head. "Too dark. Let's do the benches."

We find a couple of benches across from each other, right under a pair of streetlights, far away from the homeless guys. I lean back on my bench and watch Aisha curl up across from me. She tries her side for a while, which looks uncomfortable. She rolls onto her back and looks up at the sky. She laughs.

"What?" I say, laughing back.

"The car, a zoo, the car again, a park in Reno."

"You're naming places you've slept recently?"

"I'm just sensing, you know, a trajectory," she says.

"People who use the word 'trajectory' generally don't sleep in parks, do they?"

"Classist. And apparently we do," she says. "Good night, Carson."

"Sorry, by the way."

"Hey, it wasn't your car that broke down."

"Good night."

"Night."

*So this is what it feels like to be homeless*, I think. I look up at the streetlight above my bench and wish I could see stars like in Wyoming. I think about how we all share the stars. My grandfather must have his thoughts when he looks up at the sky, and so does Laurelei, and so do I, and we can never really know what other people are thinking, even when we all see the exact same thing. Sometimes I just want to be able to know what the stars look like from another set of eyes. From Aisha's eyes. I'd love to be inside her head for just one day. To know what it is to be truly beautiful, and also to know what it would take to make her be exactly her but in love with me.

Because still. There's a part of me that wishes.

Before going to bed, I text my mom. As I don't want her head to explode, I don't mention that I'm writing her from a park bench in Reno.

> I know you're pissed. Sorry. We're okay. I promise when we come back we will have a long, long talk

> about a lot of things. I love you, Mom.
>
> I'm sorry I'm a pain in the ass.

It's the middle of the night, so I don't expect a text back. I get one anyway.

> **Yes, we will talk. I feel a real resentment**
> **about your behavior, and I know that we'll**
> **need to chat about future boundaries.**
>
> I know. Love you.

She doesn't respond to that one. And I guess I can't blame her. But part of me really wishes she would respond with a "Love you too."

I put my phone away and pick up my grandfather's journal. I decide to read the final page.

*June 30, 1982*

*Well, God.*

*I asked for a push. This is not the push I was hoping for, but you know best. Or do you?*

*I don't know about you sometimes. If you're love. If you're hate. If you're love, but you just hate me. I know that this is now too big. I can-not rely only on you, or my family will suffer. Maybe my family will suffer anyway.*

*How the hell did I get here?*

*Is this some sort of punishment?*

*I know what John would say. God doesn't always give us the answer we want to hear. That's for DAMN sure!*

*I have no idea what happens now. I am out of jokes. When you run out of jokes, you're stranded.*

*I feel stranded.*

*I feel terrified.*

*If this is what you wanted for me, you got your wish.*


I hug the book close to me and quiver. My grandfather and I. We're two peas in a pod. How is it that I can be so in the dark about what was going on with him, but still feel like the words came from my own pen? He felt stranded and terrified. I'm lying on a park bench in a strange city, and I feel the same way.

His life changed so fast, it seems like. Whatever it was that made him leave, it all happened quickly. We're the same. My life has changed so much in nine days.

Would I change it back now if I could? I'm sleeping in a park. And yet, I don't think I would. I wonder if my grandfather found something that made it all better for him too.

I try to figure out what we're going to do in the morning. I don't want to call my mom and ask for a bailout. I really don't. I won't. We got ourselves here, and it's up to us to get us out of it.

My attention is drawn to a rustling near my feet. I look down. In the dim glow of the streetlights above us, I see it. A rat, about the size of a football. It sniffs the ground around my sneaker, its straight-as-an-arrow tail wiggling back and forth.

I yank my foot up onto the bench, stifling the scream that seems to originate in the pit of my belly. What the hell kind of rat gets so close to a person? A rabid one? Rats can be rabid, right? I begin to tremble.

All those times in my room, sitting on the radiator, fantasizing about leaving and the utter freedom of being on my own, rats never came to mind. I think of all the things that make me feel unsafe, like, right at this very moment. The guy with the sores on his legs, about fifty feet away from us. Not having shelter. Not being able to afford food. Losing all my stuff. Losing people. Being entirely alone.

The reality of Aisha's life smashes me in the face. She was sleeping in the zoo. She was alone out there, no safety net. I knew it, but I didn't know it.

The rat saunters across the path to Aisha's bench. He sniffs around its legs. Her left leg is actually on the ground, about ten inches away from the nasty rodent.

The rat stands on its hind legs and begins to sniff up the leg of the bench near her feet. I emit a noise I've never made before, sort of an *unhg* sound. If I wake Aisha, she'll move her leg right into the rat.

I sit up quietly, my heart pulsing in my neck. I cannot — will not — allow Aisha to get bitten by a possibly rabid rat. I stand, barely breathing. By the way Aisha snores, I know she's sound asleep.

I pound the glistening pavement with my right foot, hoping to scare it off. The rat seems not to care. I stand up and take a step toward the rat. Nothing. It disregards me completely.

I keep my eye on the rat and feel behind me for the prickly porcupine that I put by my feet on the bench. A bristle jabs my finger. I pick it up and cradle it like a football. I slowly walk around until I'm behind Aisha. The last thing I want to do is scare the rat onto her bench.

I set my feet, lift my arm, hold my breath, and hurl the porcupine down at the rat. It glances off the bench and ricochets into the rat's side. The rat squeaks, and then it scurries away, off into the darkness of the bushes behind me.

Aisha stirs. I see the whites of her eyes as she opens them. I'm looming above her, and she looks up at me and frowns. "What are you doing?"

"Sorry," I say. "Go back to sleep."

She sighs, closes her eyes, and turns over onto her side, pulling her foot off the ground.

When I feel safe enough to go back to my bench, I walk over and sit down, picking up the porcupine on the way. I take a deep breath. I hear no rats. I turn on my smartphone flashlight app and flash it into the bushes. I see no rats.

It's pretty clear I won't be closing my eyes tonight. Not gonna happen.

When my heartbeat calms, I go back to figuring out how we're going to get the money we need. This . . . this isn't suitable.

*Oh, what the hell,* I think. I close my eyes for a moment.

*God, if you exist: Please give me an idea. If you're so great, let's see you do something for us to get us out of this shitstorm I created.*

*Amen.*

# 31

I CAN'T BRING myself to wake Aisha for her turn at keeping watch. When the sun begins to rise, I haven't slept a wink, yet I feel remarkably good for someone who just spent a night in the park and narrowly avoided a possibly rabid rat attack.

"Why'd you let me sleep?" Aisha sits up and stretches her arms above her head.

"I actually fell asleep," I lie, and she gives me an admonishing look.

"Well, we survived, so that's good," she says. "We need about a hundred and fifty bucks to get my car, or we have about sixteen hours to figure out how to avoid sleeping in the park again."

I shoot her a thumbs-up. Got it covered. Overnight, I came up with a plan. It may work, it may not, but we have at least a chance to make some of the money we need to get out of this mess.

I share my idea with Aisha. At first, she balks. When she can't come up with a better idea, she decides to give it a try.

"Remember," I say, as we take a bus to our destination. "The first rule is never deny my reality. And whatever you say, I won't deny yours either."

She raises one eyebrow. "We're in Reno. We're on a bus. Hard to deny that reality."

We head for the Truckee River corridor — a shiny, recently renovated promenade overlooking the Truckee River. This is the best location for my plan, according to a site I found online. The sun is not fully up yet when we arrive, and the air is slightly chilly right off the river. To our right, a woman missing her right ear sells Native American jewelry off a red-and-blue blanket. To our left, a guy with a shaved head and huge cartoon sunglasses has set up an easel and starts hanging up caricatures he's drawn in the past. We mark our space with the canvas bag, the Porcupine of Truth, and the satin pillow, and I find an aluminum tin lying behind a garbage can to use as a tip jar. I look over to show Aisha, but she's fiddling with her phone. She must be looking for a response from her dad.

"Nothing?" I ask.

She shakes her head.

"Sorry," I say.

"Yup."

I wish there was something I could do to make Aisha's life as awesome as it should be. If I could, I would. I give her a moment, and then I ask, "You ready for this?"

"No."

"Me neither," I say.

The temperature warms up, and a bunch of people come strolling down the street. I get myself ready. I wait for a couple of people to be near our area, and I start.

"Okay, okay," I shout. "We are the improv comedy duo *Cars-Isha*. Can anyone please call out two professions?"

The two people who had been standing closest slip away.

"Tough crowd," I mumble. "Two professions," I repeat, louder.

People just walk by, ignoring me.

"Anyone? This is not rocket science. Just need two professions."

"Shut up, fool," someone yells, and when a few people laugh, my throat gets tight.

I shrug. "Something about your mom," I yell back, and Aisha laughs behind me.

"Something about how she's like a washing machine," Aisha yells. "Except when I drop a load in a washing machine, it don't follow me around for two weeks."

I look back at her in amazement. Someone in the crowd whistles in appreciation. Some people have stopped in front of our little area.

"Something about how your mom is like a Putt-Putt course," I say, and then I realize I have no punch line. So I play that up. "Um . . . something something driver?"

More whistles, and Aisha grabs my hand and lifts it over our heads. "Yes, ladies and gentlemen, we are *Cars-Isha*," she calls. "Half of our made-up-on-the-spot insults are great. Half not so much."

I see that something's happening. People are wandering over. I clap my hands together and jump out toward the front of our little area.

"Okay, so as I said before I was called a fool by the gentleman whose mom is a something of a whore, I need two jobs, please."

"Prostitute," says this caramel-skinned girl, college-aged, who has stopped to watch. Her accent sounds Latina. "Zombie killer."

"Blow job," some idiot guy in a suit yells out.

I riff back. "Now why is a blow job considered a job? A hand job — why is that considered work? Why is there no fuck job?" People are laughing now, and I feel the adrenaline pump into the backs of my knees.

"I know that's work you ain't ever gonna get," Aisha says.

"Don't I know it?" I say back. "Let's just say I'm underemployed, ladies. Way underemployed."

The Latina girl is smiling at me in this flirtatious way, and I have to look away so as to avoid boner town, population one.

"Okay, okay," I say, feeling like a game show host. "I need a possible title of a book."

"*Hunger Games*," the Latina girl's friend says.

"Oh-kay . . ." I say. "That's like an actual book title. But I guess we can work with that. Can I get a genre? Like a movie genre?"

"Documentary," a guy straddling a bicycle yells out. We're beginning to attract a crowd.

I nod a few times, letting it sink in. For a moment I worry that Aisha won't be able to do this. Then I realize I shouldn't underestimate my friend. "All right," I say. "Without further ado, I present to you a staged reading of the new movie, *The Hunger Games: The Documentary*. Performed by . . ." and I look at Aisha.

"Aisha Stinson, zombie killer," she says, her voice deep and foreboding.

"Oh, come on," I say, putting my hands on my hips and looking at her. "Isn't it enough that I am completely undersexed in real life? Now I have to play a male hooker too?" Some of the audience laughs. I exaggeratedly roll my eyes. "Fine. Hi, my name is Carson, and I'm a male prostitute."

We dive in, like we've done this a million times, even though we've never done it even once. Aisha sets up something about hungry zombies whose car breaks down in Reno, and they are desperate for human brains, and they need to figure out how to pay for a good

226

brain meal before they starve to death. I dramatize the role of a naive male prostitute who happens to work the corner near where the zombies' car broke down, and Aisha explains how the prostitute teams up with a zombie killer, because some of the prostitute's clients have in the past turned out to be zombies. The story tosses and turns and soon it's like a good song we're creating, and I'm barely aware of the audience except that they're there. We start by dramatizing the two roles, and soon we're just telling a story with more characters and slipping in and out of our roles. We both choose the same funny parts for repetition as if it's a chorus, and somehow Aisha circles back to the car breakdown. In the end, Aisha the zombie killer hides under the car at a service station and culls the zombies, using me the prostitute as bait. She cuts off a zombie's head while he's busy getting ready to chow down on me.

"Mmm . . . zombie brain," Aisha says while chewing, turning her zombie killer into an actual zombie cannibal by using a deep, funny voice, and it's as good a time as any.

"And scene!" I yell from the ground where I'm lying. I leap up, and we turn and bow. There are about fifty people watching. Some of them applaud. A lot of them don't. Many just walk away. A few of the applauders approach the tin can and throw in change. A few even give dollar bills. We thank everyone and soon everyone is done giving.

We count our money. $22.74. We worked our asses off for $22.74. That's not even close to enough to pay for the car repair.

"Shit," I say.

Aisha has a better attitude. "Hey. We do that eight times today, we have ourselves a car and a little bit of money for food."

She's right. Yeah. We can make this work.

We go again, and we start to fine-tune our skills. Aisha finds certain characters she can do really well — a domineering, hypocritical man of God who keeps making up stuff in the Bible, for one — and I work on a falsetto I use for a baby character who believes everything that is said to him. The baby accepts all the made-up stuff, and then adds insane details to the man of God's crazy claims, saying, "It's in the Bible."

The money starts to roll in, and each show we do better than the last one. About the fourth time we do the scene, I remember we have the Porcupine of Truth just sitting there. I grab her and we start this improv where Aisha goes up to heaven and I'm the gatekeeper — the Porcupine of Truth. I make the porcupine male and give him a game show host's voice, and I ask Aisha embarrassing questions. Then we riff on the audience, who we pretend are former child stars who are now dead. I point at random people and call them Michael Jackson and River Phoenix and things like that. People just eat it up, and after that show, we change our name to *The Porcupines of Truth*.

I keep a count of our cash, and by the time we've done our fifth show, we have enough money to get the Neon. But it's only noon, and we can make more. And truly, we could use more money. So I ask Aisha if it's okay if we keep going, and she's game.

We're both on an adrenaline high when we finish up our fifteenth and final performance of the day around six p.m. We count up our money.

Holy crap balls, Reno. We've made $467. I count it several times because I am so amazed. I take two hundred and put it in my pocket, and I give Aisha the rest, knowing she'll have to pay for the car. She fans her face with the cash.

We find out how to get to the auto repair shop by bus, and when we get there, our car is ready. As Aisha pays the man, I'm glowing. I feel like a new person. From the extra bounce in Aisha's step, I can tell she feels the same.

# PART III
## Yet Farther West of Not New York, i.e., Civilization

# 32

IT'S A THREE-AND-A-HALF-HOUR drive to San Francisco, so we spend the night in a trailer at the end of a goat path, thanks to Javy Sanchez and his girlfriend, Jenny Yang — twentysomethings who take us in through surfingsofas.com. They're cool, but we're exhausted, so we go to bed early.

The next morning, we're back in the car, and we know we're officially in California when we see actual trees. A smattering of pines are a welcome sight after so much brown in Nevada, and soon the hills are illuminated, golden. I think, *Golden State. Yes.*

There's this palpable feeling of victory in the car. I think some of it is because we're almost at our destination, and some of it is because we figured out how to solve a major problem and pay for car repairs on our own. It's like I've just found out that I can take care of me, after seventeen years of wishing someone else would. And some of it is because, let's face it: After barren Nevada, California looks so insanely beautiful.

Aisha must be enjoying the beauty too, because she says, "There's a line in *The Color Purple* by Alice Walker that says, 'I think it pisses God off if you walk past the color purple in a field somewhere without noticing it.' "

I snort. "Far be it for me to want to piss the Big Man in the Sky off."

Aisha shrugs, and we go back to listening to Haley Reinhart on the stereo.

"You think it's possible that there actually is a God?" she asks.

I laugh. "I think agnostic dyslexics lie awake at night, wondering if there is a dog."

She laughs a little. Something about the way she asked the question makes me think about how far we've come since Montana. Because that isn't even a possibility one of us would have considered four states ago. It takes me awhile to come up with a real answer rather than a snarky one.

"I don't know, but if there is, I don't think it's a man in the sky or anything," I say finally. "That doesn't make sense. And it doesn't make sense that he knows all. I mean, how could God or whatever know all the data about each one of us, all seven billion humans on the planet?"

"True," Aisha says. "But . . . I mean, I know I get pissed about religion and all. But it's hard to imagine that everything comes down to chance. Like, if I didn't meet you in the zoo that day — and how random was that — I wouldn't be here."

"So God decreed it? That we meet at the zoo?"

"I'm just saying," she says. "Can you imagine your life if we didn't meet?"

I pull my leg hair, hard. "No," I say. "I can't."

We're cruising through California toward the coast, possibly about to find my long-lost grandfather, who was barely on my radar two weeks ago. There's no way I'm here if my mom didn't take me to the zoo, if I didn't say just the right thing to get Aisha's attention. My mom had never, ever taken me to the zoo in New York. Why that day? I had never, ever managed to say an intelligent thing to a beautiful girl before. So what are the odds of all that?

And if I'm not here? Where would I be if I was not here? I shiver. It's unimaginable. Being here with Aisha is everything.

"So? You think it's possible? There actually is a God? Not like the judgmental one from the Bible. But — something?"

"I don't know," I say. "I mean. I really, really don't know."

"Maybe people can't know," Aisha says after a lengthy silence.

I have to stop thinking about this, because it makes my brain hurt. "I guess I'd say it's hard to know what's true," I say. "It's complicated. But I still put my faith in the Porcupine of Truth."

Aisha accelerates around a truck that is in the right lane, its blinkers on. "I'm no longer feeling the porcupine," she says.

I say, "That sentence has never been said before, ever."

Sacramento whizzes by, and soon we're surrounded by more cars than we've seen in the entirety of our road trip. We stop for a pee break in Richmond, and I call my dad. It takes everything I have not to tell him where I am, and how close I am to finding his dad. And then it gets harder, because without me even bringing the topic up, for the first time ever he starts talking about his father.

"I hate the fucker so much, but I miss him too, you know?" he says.

"Uh, yeah. I get that," I reply, but Dad misses the irony. Shocker.

"It's like you're missing a part of your body, and you get used to it until you don't even notice not having it. I tell you what. I notice it now. It sucks something terrible," he says.

"I can't even imagine what that would have been like," I deadpan.

"Nope. You can't. That's why I got all crazy on you, bud," he says, still not getting me. "Sorry about that. That day you came up and told me about whatever that letter thing was. . . . I just . . . It's like, I wanted to know but I didn't want to know."

"Sure."

"He was my dad. You know?"

"Yeah."

"I just wish, like, one time, you know . . . Before I, you know. I wish I could see him again."

*God, I hope so.* "Yeah."

He is quiet for a while. "Would you tell me?"

My heart pounds. "Tell you what?"

His voice gets soft and weak. "The letter you showed me. Is there more? You said there was more."

I want to tell him everything. But I'm afraid I'll say the wrong thing. I feel like a part of my body was missing too, and now I have it back and I want it to stay. Also, I don't want to lead him on. If I give my dad hope and then we never find his dad, I'd never be able to forgive myself.

"There were more letters, but they were unreadable. What do you want to know?"

He is quiet again. "Why didn't Mom tell me?" he asks, almost to himself.

At first I think he means my mom, but then I realize he means his. "I have no idea."

"And they got divorced."

"Yup."

"Jesus. You think it's possible that he's still —"

234

"I don't know," I say. "I really don't."

"Come home soon, okay? I can't talk to your mom about this shit. I can talk to you."

"I will. I promise."

"Don't wait too long. Really."

A chill passes through me. "Okay."

"Promise?"

"Yeah."

"Okay. Love you, son."

"Love you, Dad."

The conversation makes it all the more clear to me: I have to find Grandpa in California. Before it's too late. I have to. If I don't, I don't know what I'll do.

We get back on the road, we scoot through Berkeley, and finally, majestic San Francisco appears before us.

The finish line. We've made it to the finish line.

The skyline shimmers ahead of us and to the right as we cross the Bay Bridge. A crisp cityscape of confident high-rises stares at us from the horizon, and off in the distance, the Golden Gate Bridge sparkles like a fancy red earring on the city's left ear.

As we enter the city, I struggle not to reveal the surprise I have for Aisha. Something I looked up on my phone. I tell her I'll lead her where we're going, and she seems dubious but finally relents and follows my directions. We park a block from Dolores Park, which is not that far from Turk's place. Aisha says, "Where the hell are you taking me?" as we enter the park.

"A treat for the lady," I say.

"Woman," she says.

The game won't start until four and it's about three when we arrive. We quickly come across a group of adults practicing Tai Chi in unison. We watch from the back, and I'm amazed at the beauty of the scene, the San Francisco skyline in the distance, a row of pastel-colored Victorians behind the park, and right in front of us a slow, choreographed dance of Tai Chi done by many different kinds of bodies, people of infinite different colors and shapes.

"This, by the way, is not the treat. Not yet," I say.

Aisha and I step into the back of the line and start doing what everyone else is doing. The moves look like slow-motion karate, with lots of chops and poses.

We lie down in the grass after Tai Chi. It's a little chilly out, which surprises me. I figured since we were in California, it would be really warm, but when the wind picks up, I wish I was wearing more than a T-shirt.

Soon, I see a volleyball net being set up in the distance, and I ask Aisha to follow me. We approach a bunch of kids, all different skin tones, stretching and shaking out their legs and arms and greeting one another with hugs.

Aisha looks at me, raising an eyebrow. "Is this the treat?"

I nod. I found an LGBTQ youth pickup volleyball game on meetup.com. I figured it would make Aisha smile as widely as I've ever seen. But as we stand there, I feel a little bit like a father on the first day of kindergarten with my very shy daughter.

"Go on," I say when I realize that she's struggling to find the courage to go up to the other kids. I could play too, but this kind of feels like her thing, not mine. Finally she does go, and basically every pair of eyes in the area — girl, boy, trans — falls on her and follows her. I watch as she begins to notice it, and I see her begin to like it.

Another really gorgeous girl arrives. She isn't as crazy hot as Aisha, but she's muscular and tall, with spiked black hair and light brown skin, maybe a couple of years older than us. She hugs a few kids, and then she turns to Aisha and gives her a welcome fist bump. It's like watching two goddesses connect. Like you expect lightning will strike or a band will start playing.

All the attention seems to loosen Aisha up; I see it in the way she holds her head high, the way she allows the other kids to circle her and how her face animates as she talks to them. She starts looking taller, and when I hear her melodic laughter, I know I've done a really good thing.

The game starts, and I recline on my elbows in the grass and watch as Aisha sets and spikes and even dives to save a point. She's on the same team as the tall girl, and that's clearly not fair. They are easily the two best players, and they team up on a couple of points that look almost professional. A few times her smile goes wide like I'd hoped. Aisha is finding her people.

After the first game — Aisha's team wins, of course — the tall girl hugs Aisha. She actually lifts Aisha off the ground and spins her in a circle. Aisha hoots, and when the girl puts her down, the tall girl throws her arms around Aisha's shoulders and looks into her eyes.

Then they kiss. On the mouth. Aisha tilts her face, and the other girl leans in and puts her hand on the back of Aisha's head. Aisha doesn't pull away. I swallow hard and look away. I pull up a tuft of grass and grind it between my thumb and forefinger until grass juice coats my hand.

The kiss ends and Aisha whispers something in the girl's ear and jogs toward me. A dull ache pulses into my spine. Aisha gives me an exaggerated grin. She sneaks a look over her shoulder at her new friend, and then looks at me, her face lit up.

"What the what?" she whispers.

"You know you're sexy," I say. "You see how everyone had their eyes on you?"

She covers her mouth with her hand, like she's demure, maybe. I snort.

Aisha waves her friend over and introduces me. Her name's Brianna.

"Do you come here a lot?" I say, then wince because it sounds like I'm trying to pick her up.

She says, "Sometimes. It's fun," and I realize she's nice but not interesting enough for Aisha, who would never say something as boring as that as an opener. Where are the bears dancing through a field of daisies? Where are the wolf psychopaths?

"Looks fun," I say, feeling a bit more confident that this is not someone who Aisha will choose to replace me. She may be hot, but she's not exactly a brain surgeon. When the silence gets awkward, I ask, "So are you in school?"

"University of San Francisco," she says. "Pre-med."

Great. She is a brain surgeon. Or will be. "Awesome," I say. I tell her it's nice to meet her, she agrees, and then they gallop back to the court for another game, holding and swinging their hands along the way.

A bubble forms in the back of my throat, and I grind up another tuft of grass between my thumb and forefinger. *Time to go find Turk*

*Braverman*, I think. I'll admit that part of my reason for this detour was that I'm nervous. What if we knock on the door at 36 Prosper Street, and Turk no longer lives there? Or he doesn't know Russ Smith? To come all this way, and to fail right away. I'm not sure I could handle that.

But as I sit there, I begin to overcome that fear. I'm ready to find my grandfather, or not find him.

My attention is drawn back to Aisha and Brianna when I hear a series of catcalls. They are making out again. Aisha takes a smooch break, looks over and waves, and then she rolls her eyes like, *Can you believe this?* I force a smile and shake my head and stick out my tongue at her. She sticks her tongue out at me, and I hold the smile like someone's taking a really long time to take my picture. My jaw is tight, and I can't breathe.

I look down at the grass and carve into the dirt with my finger. I sketch a heart absentmindedly, and when I realize that's what I'm doing, I cross it out.

After the third and final game, Aisha runs back over, sweat streaking down her forehead.

"Too much fun," she says. "I hope you weren't too bored, but I gotta figure that was entertaining to watch. Let's be real here. I kicked ass. You should have played."

"Yeah," I say, trying to figure out a polite way to hurry her up. It's getting dark, and I don't want to be rude, but it's Turk time. "Would've been fun."

"So Brianna and a bunch of them are going out for dinner. Let's join them."

"Um," I say.

"Um, what?"

"Um. How about we go do what we came here to do?"

"Carson," she says. "I just met a bunch of gay kids for the first time in my entire life. Can I have, like, an hour to enjoy that?"

"Of course," I say, shrugging. "You can do whatever you want. Obviously."

She shakes her head at me. "I know you're not bitching about me having fun. Because that would be a big-time asshole thing to do, given that you brought me here and all."

"Yeah," I say. "I'm a big-time asshole. How selfish of me to want to find my grandfather."

She puts her hands on her hips. "Carson," she says, really slowly. "I know you don't get this. But this was, like, a special deal for me."

"You're welcome," I say.

"Thank you," she says, exasperation in her tone. "Really. But can we join the first-ever group of gay friends in my life for dinner, or do you need my full attention immediately?"

My shoulders hurt. I've tensed up my whole body.

"You go do what you need to do," I say. "Seriously. I'm just fine. But yeah, I'm probably gonna skip the gay pride dinner, if that's okay."

Her mouth opens wide, and her eyes too, and I immediately feel like a jerk. But I'm still mad too. It's confusing and I don't know how to fix it. So I just walk away.

"Carson," she calls to my back, her tone filled with frustration.

"Don't worry about it," I say in the most apologetic way I can muster. "I'll go see Turk myself. I'll walk, thanks. No big deal. I'll text

240

you all about it and when you're done getting gay married or whatever, you can join me if you want. Or if you don't, that's fine too."

And I close my ears and walk away from the volleyball game, wondering if I'll ever meet a person who won't trade me in for someone or something else. Yeah, probably not.

I'M SILENTLY CURSING Aisha as I leave the park, but I'm also cursing myself, because who walks away from their only friend, without clothes or toiletries or transportation, just because they're pissed?

Carson does. Idiot Carson does.

I sit down on a bench at the far edge of the park and pull out my phone so I can see how to get to Turk's on foot. It buzzes and I see a message pop up. Aisha is texting me, but she's just chosen strangers over her so-called best friend at the most important moment of his life. I'll let her think about that one for a bit. I ignore her text.

I follow the Google map to Prosper Street, which turns out to be a side street, barely wide enough for a car and lined with picturesque Victorians. I find number 36. It's lime green and white, two stories, with a garage on the ground level and a staircase with wrought-iron fencing on either side. I stand at the bottom of the steps and count to ten. Then to twenty. This is solving nothing, so I climb the steps and ring the doorbell.

Silence, other than my pounding heart. I ring again. A barking dog, frantic. My heart speeds up.

Nothing else. Just a barking dog.

"Shoot," I mumble. The barking dog tells me that someone lives here, but, duh. Most houses have people living in them. It's still not clear if that someone is Turk Braverman, and I have no way of knowing.

I descend the steps and sit down on the second stair. I'll wait a bit. Just wait and see if someone comes by. I take a moment to check out Aisha's texts, feeling a little bad for the passive-aggressive thing I'm doing but also looking forward to her apology.

**What the hell?**

**Did you just really walk away from me after I drove you to San Fran-fucking-cisco to deal with your thing? I get a couple hours to do my thing, and suddenly I'm the bad guy?**

**Gimme a break, Carson. Text me when you get a clue.**

My stomach turns. Not the apology I was looking for. *Am I actually wrong here?* I don't feel wrong. I feel very, very right. How can I be wrong? I put my phone away.

An hour later, I'm shivering. The sun is descending, and no one told me that San Francisco in July is cold. I am underdressed in shorts and a T-shirt, and the rest of my stuff is in Aisha's car.

I look up hotels, because now I have some cash and can pay for a place overnight. There's a guesthouse down the block, but they want $159 for a room with a shared bath. Then I see a place called Beck's Motor Lodge, just a couple short blocks away. They're asking $139 for a room with a king-sized bed.

That seems insane to me. Over a hundred bucks to sleep somewhere? I have just under two hundred total. But the more I surf, the more I realize that Beck's is pretty much a bargain when it comes to San Francisco. And I'm not sleeping outside again.

When I've been sitting there for ninety minutes and my teeth are chattering from the cold, I decide to head off to Beck's for the night, and I push myself to my feet.

Even upset, I feel more at home here in San Francisco than I did in Billings. Mostly it just looks like a really hilly New York. I pass a stringy-haired woman with a shopping cart who mutters curses as she trudges up the hill. Ahead of me, a middle-aged guy wearing dark sunglasses is balancing himself against a tree, apparently drunk or high off his skull. Except when I walk by I see he is not actually leaning against the tree. Rather, his arms are pointed at the tree as if he's performing a magic spell on it. *Welcome to Freakville, Carson. We've been waiting for you.*

I finally get to Market Street and see the pink-and-blue sign for Beck's Motor Lodge. It's a bit of a rundown place, and the guy who checks me in seems particularly disinterested in my welfare. When I ask him if I can pay in cash, he looks at me like I'm an idiot and points to a sign that says CREDIT CARD REQUIRED.

I say, "I don't have one. All I have is cash."

He points at the sign again, and I hold back my urge to ask him if this is how he expected his life to turn out. Instead, I just say, as nicely as possible, "Is there anything you can do? I have no car, no place to stay. I don't know anyone here. Please?"

He rolls his eyes and throws a form on the table. I say, "Thank you, thank you" as I fill out the paperwork. When I'm done, he tosses me a key.

The room is perfectly fine inside. A little musty, maybe, but there's a big TV and a huge bed. I pull my phone out of my pants pocket and stare at it. No more texts. I feel a twinge in my chest. I'm sitting alone in a hotel room in San Francisco. Maybe this is my fault? Is there something wrong with me that I feel like Aisha is in the wrong? Part of me is like, *No way. Absolutely not.* And the other part is cringing as I think about what I said to my best friend about getting gay married. She was happy. She met a girl, and I acted like a jerk. Why is that my factory setting?

I swallow my pride and text her.

sorry.

i'm an asshole. but you knew that already.
i got jealous, ok? i have a place for us to stay. text me
and i'll give you directions. sorry again.

I wait for her response. My heart pounds.

Fifteen minutes pass, and still nothing. Shit. I really fucked up.

I'm hungry, so I head out to find something to eat. Barracuda Sushi is the closest place. When I see how fancy it is, I order a teriyaki chicken plate to go.

*On my own*, I think as I jaywalk across the street. *On my own.* Better get used to it. Apparently I'm not so good at the keeping of friends.

I pass a liquor store, and I stop. So many colorful bottles. So many different kinds of beer too. Those are the most alluring to me.

I stare for a good minute, and I calculate how much cash I have left and how many beers I could buy. I fantasize about feeling nothing.

And then I think about my food getting cold.

I hustle across the street to my room and drink a soda with my dinner. And I feel a little proud because I'm not my father. At least not right now. I have a chance never to be him, or never to become what he became.

After I wolf down dinner, and Aisha still hasn't texted back, I call my dad.

"So if I told you I was someplace that a seventeen-year-old probably shouldn't be, would you react like a father or a friend?" I ask.

He laughs uncertainly. "Maybe a little of both? Where are you?"

"I'm alone in a hotel room in San Francisco," I say.

He draws in a breath. "I thought you were coming home soon."

"I am," I say. "A couple days, three tops."

"Are you drunk? High?"

Now it's my turn to laugh. "What? No."

"So you're in a hotel room in San Francisco, where you aren't high or drunk. Do you have a girl there?"

"No, and that's the problem."

He laughs again.

"Aisha is angry at me because I'm a dickwad. I thought she was being dickwad-ish, but she isn't talking to me, so I'm guessing *I* am and I don't even know it, which kinda sucks."

He laughs some more. "Apple doesn't fall far from the tree."

"Why does everyone keep saying that?" I say.

His laugh continues. It's kind and soft. I want to memorize this feeling, this tingling in my legs that tells me I have a dad and we know each other.

"So you're having an adventure, you're crashing and burning, but you're not high, drunk, or messing around with girls?"

"Yup."

"What am I supposed to be upset about?" he asks.

"Dad," I say, a little frustrated. "Is that what you're supposed to say to your kid who is marooned in a hotel room in a strange city alone?"

"Hey. Baby steps, right?"

"Have you been drinking?"

"Nope," he says.

"Good."

"Easy for you to say. It sucks monkey cock, actually. I'm jonesing for a scotch and soda."

"You gonna be okay?"

"Could you stay on the phone with me for a while? That would help," he says, and I hear that unsureness in his voice again. So I do, and I tell him the story of what happened with Aisha, and he has no advice but does laugh at the funny parts, which is better than nothing, and actually calms me down a bit. He tells me that he and my mom are getting along real well, past fighting for the first time in so long he can't even remember. She's super pissed at me, he says. "Better get her something in San Francisco. Something good."

"I'll buy her a condo," I say. "Tell her I'm okay and I'm coming back soon." Then I ask him if he could imagine us being a family again, and he has to pause before he says anything.

"That would be real nice," he says, his voice weak.

When he gets sleepy, and he promises me he's just going to hang up and close his eyes, no drinking, I say good night and I tell him I love him. It's easier this time. Not easy, but easier.

I hang up and check in case a text came in and somehow I didn't hear it. No.

I text Aisha again.

i'm worried. Please let me know you're okay
and that you're coming back to stay with me.

It takes her only a few seconds to respond.

**Let's chill for the night. We'll talk in the morning,
okay? I'm fine. Have a place to stay.**

K, I text back.

I turn off the lights and listen to the traffic outside. It soothes
me, in a way; it sounds like New York. The shadows of cars traverse
the walls and I feel the pulse of the city just outside the window.
Maybe there are kids who would take tonight and get drunk or
go looking for girls. Maybe part of me is one of those kids, I don't
know. Mostly I just want to be alone right now, and that's a bigger
part of me.

I play the entire volleyball scene over and over in my mind. What
I said. My tone. My mood. Why did I have to be that way? If I could
go back and change the entire thing, I would. I wouldn't let my pride
take over. I would not make my friend feel bad about wanting to
enjoy herself.

Tomorrow I'll either find out what happened to my grandfather,
or I never will. There's no other way it can turn out. I'll find Turk
Braverman, or I won't. If I do, he'll know my grandfather. Or he won't.

And for the second time in a few days, I find myself doing something I don't normally do.

*Please, God. Let me find my grandfather tomorrow. Please. If
you exist, please just give me that one thing. Amen.*

248

# 34

THE NEXT MORNING, I shower, get dressed in the same dirty clothes I wore yesterday, and think about texting Aisha. But I don't want to wait for her before going to see Turk Braverman. And why should I? She can join me when she wants, if she wants. I check out of the hotel and start my walk back toward 36 Prosper Street. It's chilly again, and I wonder if it ever warms up here.

I ring the bell again. I hear the dog bark again.

My heart sinks. Nothing else. No other sounds.

Then, softly, I hear the patter of slow footsteps. My pulse accelerates.

The knob turns. The door opens.

The old man who answers has extremely thin legs, which I can see because he is wearing white shorts that reach to just below his knobby knees. His upper body is thick and muscled. He looks a bit like he might topple over at any moment because he's too top-heavy. He has a mustache that has clearly been dyed black because the rest of his hair is salt-and-pepper, mostly salt. His face is craggy and lined; he has two horizontal lines across his weathered cheeks that look like minus signs to me.

"So where's your truck?" he asks, looking around.

"Excuse me?"

He raises an eyebrow and frowns. "They said you were bringing a new cable box. And you're not holding a new cable box. I'm not feeling enthusiastic about Comcast right now."

"Oh," I say. "I'm not . . . I'm not the cable guy."

"Good," he says, sizing me up. "No offense, but you look like someone who would have trouble screwing in a light bulb."

"None taken," I say. "True story."

He grins a bit. "So . . . can I help you?"

I inhale slowly and prepare myself for rejection. "You wouldn't happen to be Turk Braverman, would you?"

"I would. Who would be asking?"

"I'm Carson. Carson Smith."

His eyes go soft and his mouth opens.

"So I'm guessing that means you do know my grandfather, then?" I say, and I feel like I could explode out of my skin. Victory. I've found him.

He nods slowly. "Come in," he says, nearly breathless. "Please."

He opens the door, and there is a black, furry dog sitting at attention, a pink tongue hanging down. His mouth is in a dog approximation of a smile. When he sees me, his thick tail beats against the floor.

"This is Gomer," he says.

"Cute," I say. "What kind?"

"Australian Labradoodle."

"Does he have an accent?"

Turk laughs. "Of course you'd say that. Just like your grandfather."

I nod, stunned. This man knows my grandfather. Not like thirty years ago, he knew him for a few minutes. He knows him well enough to know his bad sense of humor. My body feels like it's going to start shaking.

I want to hear everything all at once. But Turk is taking his time.

"You can say hi to Gomer if you want," he says. "He's very friendly."

To be polite, I tentatively get down on one knee. Gomer jumps up on his hind legs to greet me. His tongue shoots at my face. I duck and tumble backward.

"Oh!" I say. "Wasn't ready for that."

Turk laughs. "Range and accuracy, this one's tongue." He reaches a hand down to lift me up, but I decline, preferring to push myself up on my own.

"Carson Smith," he says, turning to walk down the hallway to the living room. I follow. "How on earth did you find me?"

"Long story," I say.

"Well, let me get you some water," he says, and he motions to an old, weathered leather couch. I sit and look around. His place is casual and comfortable, like there's nothing in here that doesn't have history.

"I like your house," I say. "It's cool."

"This old place? Thanks."

He brings us water and then sits to my right on a smaller version of the couch I'm on.

"So tell me this long story. How did you find me?"

I take a sip and tell him about finding the letter from Russ to Pastor John. Then I back up, realizing I should just give him the whole story. About my dad and mom splitting when I was three.

About my dad being sick with cirrhosis of the liver, about us coming to Billings for the summer, meeting Aisha. His face is very reactive to everything I say, and he just lets me spill. When I mention finding his name in the book that Lois Clancy gave me, he laughs.

"Well, now I understand the phone call."

"What phone call?"

"This past Sunday. I got a call on my old landline phone that I never use anymore. It was from a woman who asked me if I was Turk B. I said I was, and she said, 'Good, you're still alive.' And then she hung up. It freaked me out. I unplugged the phone."

Which explains why the phone just rang and rang when I tried to call him, I realize. And it confirms that Lois *was* trying to tell me something when she said that there were answers in the book! I'd just thought she was a weird old lady. I silently thank her.

"So that's how I found you. And now I'm here because maybe you can tell me where I can find my grandfather. Because my dad deserves to see him before . . . you know."

"You haven't read all the letters, have you?" he asks. His expression is hard to read, and I desperately want to know what he's thinking.

"They were waterlogged," I say. "There was a flood. Why? What don't I know?"

He blinks twice. "Are you up for a drive?"

That's not what I expect him to say, and my brain spins. My grandfather. He's taking me to see my grandfather.

I never really expected this moment. I thought I did, but as soon as Turk says those words, I realize I really didn't. I picture the apartment where my grandfather will live. I imagine him taking me in his arms, hugging me tight.

I can't share any of these words or feelings, because I cannot speak. I want Aisha to be here with me, I so want her to be here to see this, but I simply cannot wait another minute.

"Please," I say, breathless. "Please."

Turk's car is a red Mustang convertible with no backseat. I've never been in a convertible before, and I simply enjoy the straight-aways and allow the chilly breeze to sweep through my hair. We don't talk much as we drive through town. It's like we're on a roller coaster, with so much up and down that my stomach feels queasy even when we're not taking a sharp turn at a high rate of speed.

We're on a main thoroughfare, California Street, when he pulls abruptly into a parking spot. The street is on such a steep incline that I'm sure we'll career downhill, even after he sets the parking brake. He turns the wheel all the way so that it's facing the curb.

Tall apartment buildings line both sides of the street. Maybe my grandfather lives in one of them? We walk a couple of blocks up the hill in silence. It's a silence of anticipation.

I'm surprised when we cross the street in the direction of a hulking structure. It would not have been one of my first two thousand guesses of where he was taking me.

# 35

AS TURK LEADS me up the thirty or so steps to the entrance of this massive church, I figure it out. My grandfather is the music director here at Grace Cathedral.

Suddenly it all makes sense, all this stuff about religion we've been coming across. It all leads here. My grandfather, the man of God. It just fits. I've found him. I'm going to meet him. And I'm going to be able to reunite him with my dad. My heart pounds from the excitement.

Inside it's ornate. There are crazy murals and stained-glass windows all over. Blue light streams in from slats in the incredibly high ceiling, and a few parishioners sit in the front pews. It's a Monday morning, so no service is going on. People mill around, looking at an artistic display.

The display is a collection of rugs hung on the walls. Huge rugs, each with eight randomly colored panels that appear to be about six feet long and maybe half as tall, in two columns of four rows. Each panel is separate, but they're stitched together to make a tapestry of sorts. They're pretty to look at, but Turk grabs my hand and pulls me along so I can't really examine them in detail. He's walking with purpose, and I have to hurry to keep up.

We arrive at a rug at the end of the right aisle. He takes me to the left edge and points up.

"Second from the top," he says, his voice husky.

I look up. The panel is black with white edges and a silver star in the upper right corner. In the lower left corner, someone has embroidered a brown grand piano with white musical notes emanating from it. In the lower right corner is a photo of a man whom I immediately recognize as my grandfather, because he looks like a weird version of my dad. Or me. His eyes are rolling left while his tongue sticks out to the right.

Underneath it reads, "If laughter is the best medicine, why am I dead?"

And in the center, embroidered in elegant script, it says,

*Russell P. Smith (12-4-41/9-2-84)*

Turk puts a hand on my shoulder and whispers, "Let it out, dear. Let it out."

My grandfather is dead.

My grandfather, who was so much like me, who was supposed to have all the answers for me, whom I was sure I was about to meet. I'll never get to look in his eyes. I'll never get to make him laugh. He won't come back to Billings with me, and reunite with my father.

Dead.

I howl. I just howl. I close my eyes and double over, and I scream the feelings onto the floor of the church until there's no more air in me. My hands are on my knees like I've just been punched in the stomach. I stay down there for a while.

He died in some way that made it noteworthy enough to memorialize, and as soon as I think that thought, I know what he died of. I open my eyes, and I stand up. All the other panels in his tapestry have men's names. The dates of birth are mostly the 1950s and 1960s. The dates of death are all in the 1980s and early 1990s.

My grandfather died of AIDS.

*My grandfather was gay.*

I close my eyes again and feel my brain spin. My grandfather, who must have felt he had to keep a secret all his life. Suddenly the pain in his journals makes perfect sense to me. He lived his life ashamed of who he was.

My grandmother, who must have felt so much agony when he told her. Who learned, more than twenty years into their relationship, that her husband wasn't who she thought he was. Who was living in a lie and didn't even know it.

My father, who has no clue why his dad left, and who must have felt his dad's pain and shame all his life. And who passed that on to me in his own way.

And for what?

Then I cry for my father, who is also dying. One day soon he will cease to be alive and I will run out of time with him and we will never throw a ball around and we will never go to the movies or watch a football game, and my father, my poor, poor father, whose father left him. Who missed out on these same things and never knew why, who doesn't know his father had AIDS, who all this time thought — I don't even know what he thought, but it wasn't good for him. Not knowing wasn't good.

My focus widens from Grandpa's panel to all the panels around his. Next to my grandfather is a panel for a man named Gordon Todd Jenkins, who was born on May 3, 1955. There's a palm tree and the sun shining down on it. He must have loved the beach. He died on January 15, 1987. He was thirty-one.

Next to Gordon is Liam Holmes, who must have liked fishing and his country, based on the fishing pole and American flag. He was born on August 17, 1966. He died on December 25, 1989. Christmas Day of his twenty-third year.

All these people. I look farther and see panels for women too. Little babies. All their lights, snuffed out. All their families, like mine. Broken up too soon. It's a tapestry of lives lost. It's hundreds upon hundreds of souls expressed in fabric.

I cry for generations of pain. Not just for my family, but for all the families. I'm like a faucet, dry for years, and in the last week it's been turned on slowly, and now it's gushing. It's ugly and snotty and loud and totally not embarrassing at all. I don't care who sees me.

This is the most intense thing I've ever witnessed, and my legs start to shake. Turk seems to understand. He grasps my shoulder and holds me upright. I keep looking at panel after panel. Eugenia Lopez and her horn-rimmed glasses. Micah "Brandy" Washington and his hammer and wrench. Trina Goodman, age six, with tiny pajamas and a teddy bear. When I look down because I can't see even one more memorial, he takes me by the shoulder and leads me toward the exit.

I turn back one last time to say good-bye to my grandfather.

# 36

TURK HANDS ME a wad of Kleenexes.

"How much do you know about AIDS?" he asks as we stand in the entrance hall. I look up at the sign above the door to the room we were in. The exhibit we've just seen is called "The NAMES Project."

"Not much," I say, embarrassed. AIDS has never felt real to me, pertinent to my life as a dorky heterosexual virgin. "I know it's a disease, and I know people used to die of it and that now there's medicine for it. That's about all."

"Do you want to hear a story?" Turk asks.

I nod, and we walk in silence out of the cathedral. It's nice to be outside. The exhibit was beautiful and awful, and it took all the air from my lungs. I need to just breathe a little.

Turk takes me across the street to a place called Huntington Park, which is sunny but windy. There's a huge fountain in the middle — angels dancing on the heads of gargoyles who spit streams of water into stone seashells. We find a bench, and it takes him awhile to maneuver his wiry-thick frame down next to me.

Once he's seated and comfortable, he turns to me.

"So once upon a time, there was a village," he says. "It was hilly and sun-filled and all the interesting kids went there when they came of age. Through a confluence of many events — the Vietnam War, the sexual revolution — it just so happened that in the 1970s, these kids started to create a real community. A neighborhood formed called the Castro. In every way possible, they let their hair hang down. Men lived with men and women lived with women. They loved and danced and screwed and laughed and sang. It wasn't just sex and drugs either. It was softball and square dancing and gardening and fixing up houses. They did it in ones or twos or sometimes even threes and fours. Never before in modern history had this been done, so there were no rules.

"And they were free — mostly — from the judgment of the outside world. The people who would have told them that they were going to hell for loving the wrong person were shut out of this party. They thrived on the outskirts, but they were not allowed in. The Castro was beautiful because it was pure. All these people, who had been alone in Iowa City and Spokane, here they were not alone. They celebrated their newfound freedom, and it was a joyous place."

He turns away and I take in his profile. The weathered skin on his face looks like it's been through a war.

"Then, one nippy day in the center of the neighborhood where they lived, a bunch of men stood in front of the pharmacy window, looking at photographs of a young man. These photos showed the purple blotches he had inside his mouth and on his chest. In Magic Marker he had written, 'Careful, guys, there's something out there.'

"Nobody thought much about it. Nobody knew what to think. Besides, only a few people were sick.

"But then, more young men began to come down with incredibly rare maladies. The florist took ill with a bird parasite in his brain that no medicine could touch. The first baseman for a softball team couldn't keep food down and was told he had a cow parasite that normally would have required just a small course of antibiotics, but now was untreatable. The chef for a popular upscale eatery came down with a rare pneumonia that killed him within a week. A well-loved community theater actor contracted a typically benign cancer that invaded his organs. Soon, purple splotches covered his entire face. Then he died.

"Panic spread throughout the city where once there had been so much joy. How was it possible that so many healthy, beautiful men could age in appearance fifty years in two months, and die looking like concentration camp victims?"

I look at Turk's face, and I realize he has it too. Something about his sunken cheekbones and those minus signs under his eyes. I saw it right away, but I didn't know what it was. He's probably had it a long time.

"Some people moved away, hoping to escape it. Some of those people died anyway. Others dug in and took care of the ill. The women, some of whom were friends with the men and others who felt excluded by them, came together and nursed their brothers.

"At first some of us decided it was only the most promiscuous who got it. That was just denial. A banker moved in with a painter in 1980, not knowing that one random night in 1978, the painter had enjoyed a perfectly delightful evening with an accountant and came home with a silent virus in his blood. The banker and the painter, monogamous and faithful, would perish within months of each other in 1986, and no one could make it stop.

"It tore us apart. The disease. The way people reacted to it. Nationally, there was no reaction. Only fear that it would cross over and start killing straights. Otherwise, it was barely mentioned in the media, and the president didn't mention it at all. Six years went by and twenty thousand died before he said the word *AIDS*.

"Some claimed that AIDS was God's punishment for being gay. That was particularly harsh, because many of the dying had been told all their lives that they were evil. They finally got past that only to be told, on their deathbeds, that God had decreed their deaths. Very cruel."

"That's horrible," I say.

"Of course, other religious people came through and cared for the dying. It seems like the disease brought out the best and worst in people, and I sometimes wonder if that would be the case today, or if the world has changed. Do you think it would be different today?"

"Probably," I say.

He smiles weakly. "Well, good. Progress. Can you handle another story?"

I nod.

"This one is about a man from Billings, Montana."

"Right," I say, looking back at the cathedral as if he's still in there.

"His name was Russ Smith, and he was a tall, goofy man. Looked a lot like you, actually."

I blush.

He smiles. "Russ was a religious man. He was also a man of music. He could hear a melody, and an hour later he would still be able to remember it and could create four or five different harmonies to it. And he knew scripture. Tons of scripture.

"But ever since he was a kid, he felt like a freak. Because it was the fifties, and he knew that other boys, not girls, interested him.

And he lived in Montana, where those things were definitely not discussed.

"So he got married to a woman named Phyllis, and he had a son, and like many, many other men at the time, he coped with living the wrong life by drinking. A lot. Living the right life was impossible."

I close my eyes and try to imagine a world in which I'm made to marry a guy. The idea is hard to fathom. I don't think of guys the way I think of girls. Their bodies are just — not what I want to touch. What if I had to? Could I do it?

"So mostly he drank himself to sleep, and as the drinking got worse, he got mean. He yelled at his wife. He loved his son, but sometimes he ignored him. And because he was basically good inside, this tore him up further, and he thought about ending it all.

"One day in the mid-seventies, he heard about a choir director's conference in San Francisco, and he convinced the pastor at his church to let him go. It was the first of several consecutive years in which he flew to San Francisco for a week.

"Those weeks were what he looked forward to through all the cold winters. The second week of April. A chance to be somewhere else. To be someone else. To follow his heart. And during those weeks, I feel strange saying this to you, but he —"

"I get it," I say.

He nods and smiles. "You get it. Let's just say he made many friends, friends he'd spend time with once a year.

"Sometime in the late spring of 1982, he was getting dressed and looked down and saw a purple spot on his shoulder. He rubbed it. It looked mostly like a pimple that had popped, but a little different than that. Over the course of the next few weeks, several more formed on his chest and one on his neck. He went to the doctor in Billings. The doctor had no idea what it was. He went for tests. They were worried he had skin cancer. The news came back good, in a way. It was a rare form of benign cancer called Kaposi's sarcoma. The only thing strange about it was that he wasn't a sixty-year-old Mediterranean man. That's who usually got the condition, and they'd put up with the unsightly lesions and die of something else, years later.

"Russ went to the library to do some research. He couldn't find anything, until one day, a search turned up an article about Kaposi's sarcoma cases in gay men. His heart flipped in his chest. He cried, because he knew that was him. He knew these things were related.

"Information was scarce, but he learned what he could about what was at the time called gay-related immune deficiency. He learned that it was fatal. He learned that it might be possible to pass it to sex partners, and even though he and Phyllis were no longer physical, he thought about how he'd kissed her on the cheek a few times, and he sobbed in the library. He stole the medical journal he was reading, and he played hooky from work for a week, wondering what he was supposed to do. No doctors in Montana would know anything about what was then called GRID."

"GRID!" I yell. "That was in the letter. 'The world's most dangerous and expensive grid'! What's KSREF?"

"Oh!" Turk blurts, like he's been goosed. "Blast from the past! The . . . Kaposi's Sarcoma Research and Education . . . Foundation, I suppose?"

"Wow," I say. "So not a Kansas referee?"

He smiles. It's a sad smile, but it makes me feel closer to him.

"So anyway, Montana doctors had no idea what was going on, since it was happening in Los Angeles, San Francisco, and New York. And even if they did, this was Billings, Montana. Russ knew if anyone found out, he'd bring shame to his family.

"Finally he gathered up the courage to tell his boss."

"Pastor John," I interrupt him.

"Yes, you mentioned him earlier. A name I had enjoyed not thinking about for a long time. So he told this Pastor John fellow, his best friend, and the man was good to him. To some degree, anyway. Your grandfather didn't have much money saved up, and he knew he had to get to San Francisco for treatment. The pastor helped him get here. He used church funds to pay for Russ's trip, and he created something of an underground railroad of religious friends for him to stay with. It was quite a journey."

"I know my granddad joined AA along the way."

Turk smiles. "A good thing too. Because when Russ got to San Francisco, he called his friend Graham. Graham, God rest his soul, had one friend who was in AA, and that friend was me. So when Russ arrived in town, guess who got to take him to his first meeting here?"

Turk looks out into the distance. A serene expression passes over his face.

"We fell in love almost right away. He was such a big, goofy guy. I get that when he was an active drunk, he was awful to be around, and there were moments when it was awful here too. Not easy, giving up the booze. But mostly he was sweet and incredibly creative.

"One morning in bed, I asked him for some orange juice. He went to the kitchen and didn't return, and I started to wonder if he'd heard me. Ten minutes later, he came back and handed me a piece of paper. He'd drawn three rabbis wearing orange coats in Magic Marker. At the bottom, he wrote, 'Orange Jews.'"

I shiver. "Oh my God. I would do that," I say.

"You poor kid," he says.

"I know."

"The thing is, his health got better. Thanks to AA, he certainly got happier. His face got brighter and you could see that he was shining through, because for the first time in his life, he was himself, totally.

"We set up house, and, well, I was sick too. A few times, he had to nurse me through stuff. Pneumonia, mostly. And I had to nurse him through some ugly stuff as well. But we persevered. We went to AA meetings five times a week, and we talked about life and I learned to understand his faith, and by the end, it became a much kinder faith. He was a lovely, lovely man.

"In the late summer of 1984, he came down with a cold. A simple cold. But it stayed. One night, he woke me up gasping for breath, and I just knew. I rushed him to the hospital. It was pneumocystis, which was the pneumonia that killed so many people early on in the epidemic. And like he had a 'Kick me' sign on him, as they were treating him for that, the spots activated. The KS. They attacked his mouth and then his lungs and then, well, then. He just . . ."

Turk wipes a tear out of his right eye.

"It was so fast. He was my life. When he died, my heart died. Somehow I survived long enough to get the cocktail of drugs that's kept me alive, but that's a part of me that didn't make it. I've dated since, but never once have I allowed anyone to move in, because they couldn't possibly take his place. He's that one-of-a-kind person we all search for. He'd serenade me in the evening, making up non-sense songs that were so, so strange and so, so funny."

"I just read his song 'Three Sightless Rodents,'" I say.

He looks up at me, and I sing it to Turk.

"Three sightless rodents, three sightless rodents. See how they perambulate, see how they perambulate. They all perambulated after the agriculturist's spouse. She cut off their lower extremities with a utensil designed for the dissection of meat. Have you ever seen such a spectacle in all your existence, as three sightless rodents, three sightless rodents."

This makes him laugh, and the laugh soon turns to sobs, and he puts his head in his hands and his thick back heaves up and down. I don't know what to do, so I put my hand on his neck. It feels interesting. Like I'm touching family, in a way. And I am.

He finally wipes away the wetness from his face and wipes his nose a few times too. I reach into my pocket and pull out one of the unused Kleenexes he handed me back in the church. He takes it and thanks me.

"His biggest regret was that he never made peace with your father," he says. "Pastor Logan asked him not to tell anyone, even his wife. The help was conditional. The money came from the church, and the pastor was petrified of a scandal. What if his congregants found out that their money was going to someone with gay cancer?"

"Whoa," I say.

"Yes, well. Anyhow, Russ disobeyed that and did tell Phyllis, and she was so angry and ashamed. She demanded that he not tell your father. And it tore him up that he couldn't, but he promised her. . . . They got divorced by mail. Afterward, it plagued Russ, knowing that his son didn't know where he was. And many times, he woke me up crying. He knew he'd hurt Phyllis, but he couldn't understand why she'd punish Matthew. He wrote him a letter, telling him the truth. But he just couldn't mail it, and that was a failing on his part. I still have trouble forgiving him for that, for leaving it untended and for leaving it on me."

"What about all the letters we found?"

"The unreadable ones?"

"Yeah."

"Well, if they hadn't been unreadable, you'd know that they were all birthday cards. The first two were from Russ. He decided that he'd keep it light and avoid any mention of what was going on, in the hopes that Phyllis would have a change of heart and let Matthew see them. A couple months after he died, I took over the practice and sent your father a birthday card. Mine was not so tame, as I hadn't made any agreement with Phyllis, and I felt Matthew had the right to know. So in that first card, I explained to him what had happened. I hoped that by leaving off the return address, it might get past your grandmother, and for the first decade or so I included an address inside the notes, in case he wanted to write back. I so wanted to know your father, but he never responded. I was never sure if that was his choice or Phyllis's. How long ago did she die?"

"Seven years ago."

"Hmm," Turk says. "Where did you find the letters?"

"In a box with all of his stuff, at the pastor's place."

"So if your grandmother was intercepting my notes before she died, apparently Pastor Logan took it on himself to keep up the practice."

I think back to something weird my dad told me the first time I saw him back in Billings.

"My dad said the pastor always brought in my dad's mail. He must have been funneling the letters out for years. Why would he do that?"

Turk looks angry. He shakes his head. "Beats the hell out of me. Did you know I went to Billings? Did you know I met your father and grandmother?"

"You did?"

"I did. Spring of '85. It was torture, not knowing whether your father had even seen the notes, and at a certain point I figured I'd take a trip and meet Russ's people. I found the house and rang the doorbell, and your grandmother answered. The moment I saw her face, I realized I couldn't follow through. I pretended to ask for directions, and we spoke for maybe thirty seconds. When I lingered after, hoping to catch a glimpse of your father, I saw the pastor peek out through his blinds. I nodded at him, and he was very strange, kept looking out his blinds at me. One of them called the police on me, and I remember seeing your father come outside when the police car arrived. I had to tell them I had the wrong address and was sorry to have bothered anyone. Your father, he was maybe twenty by then, handsome beyond belief. I always felt, well — I always felt that in some way he knew who I was. I'm sure that's crazy. It's just a feeling I had and never got rid of. The way he looked at me."

"He didn't, I'm sure," I say. "I'm pretty sure this will be news to him."

"So we're going to tell him?"

I put my hand on his back in a way that feels normal, now that I understand that he's my blood. He is me, and I am him, and I am my grandfather. We're the same. It's freaky to think that someone who is just like me died of AIDS. That someday, I might get a disease because I'm a human and all humans get diseases and die. It's part of life, I guess, and that makes me feel surprisingly alive.

"So can I call you Grandpa?" I ask.

The smile starts at his ears and lengthens the minus signs to full dashes, and I see his teeth, so small and a little browned out, and I love them.

"You must," he says.

MY NEW GRANDPA and I have lunch at a pasta place in his neighborhood, and even though the news he just gave me is sad, I feel a little giddy. Maybe I haven't found my grandfather, but I have found someone I like, who seems to understand me pretty darn well. I especially like telling Turk funny things, because of his reactions. I explain to him, for instance, how my mother says things like, "I need to own this feeling," and then add, "I think it would be cool if there was some sort of business out there that bought and sold feelings, leased them, or allowed people to buy aftermarket feelings at reduced rates." He looks at me with kind eyes and says, "Oh, Russ."

It could be creepy. But it isn't creepy. It makes me feel connected to my granddad.

When he goes to the restroom, I look at my phone. I have a bunch of text messages from Aisha. The most recent is all question marks. I know I should answer, but I just want to focus on Turk.

I write: **Call you in a bit. All good.**

Toward the end of lunch, I see someone with a beer walk by. I look at Turk and say, "Would it surprise you if I told you I'm a little too curious about alcohol?

"No," he says. "It wouldn't surprise me. Alcoholism can run in families, you know."

"How would I know if I'm an alcoholic? If I should be going to meetings?"

"How much do you drink?"

"I had my first beers in Salt Lake City. Three of them. Pissed Aisha off big-time."

He nods. "I think if you're worried, you shouldn't drink. It gets bad, Carson. And it happens fast. Once that train starts rolling, you can't stop it. I promise."

In that moment, I make a vow to myself. I may have a million other problems. I may make all sorts of mistakes in my life. But I will not become an alcoholic. I will not cross that line, and I'll do it by never drinking, ever. It's the only way I can be sure.

"Thanks. You may have just saved my life."

"Don't mention it," he says, smiling.

He sees the waiter and asks for the check, and when the check comes, he motions for the waiter to bend down so he can whisper in the guy's ear. The waiter looks confused, and then he smiles. And I'm like, *Is he propositioning the waiter?*

When the waiter walks away, I say, "What was that all about?"

Turk waves me off. The check comes, and Turk gives the guy his credit card.

We sit in awkward silence. "You're really not going to tell me what that was?"

"Don't you worry about it," he says, giving me a quizzical look.

The guy brings back two credit card slips. Um, what's happening here? Is he paying the guy? Is this like a prostitution thing? A drug thing? My stomach sinks.

"Now you really have to tell me," I say.

"Carson," my new grandfather says. "For God's sake. Drop it."

As we leave the restaurant, the waiter gives Turk a hug. Once outside, I stop walking. "No. You one hundred percent have to tell me what's going on. I am freaking out here."

He shakes his head at me. "Good God, you're a drama queen. You really need to know?"

"Yes."

"You're very nosy," he says.

"Just tell me," I say.

He runs his craggy left hand through what's left of his hair. "I just *attempted* to do a random act of kindness, if you must know. I paid the restaurant an extra sum of money, *none of your business how much*, so that the next few people could eat for free. But since it was supposed to be an *anonymous* random act of kindness, I suppose the *anonymous* part is null and void now."

He walks on and I just stand there, feeling dirt low about what I suspected. "Sorry," I mumble.

He waits for me to catch up, and we walk on together. "Don't worry about it," he says.

"No, really," I say. "I'm sorry. I trust you. I won't do that again."

"You're a sweet kid," he says. "Like your grandpa."

"He was, like, forty, right?"

"That's a kid," he says.

By the time we get back to his place, I feel like I've known Turk forever. I curl up on the couch, and Gomer sits next to me and rests his muzzle on my feet, which is cool. Maybe I'm beginning to get dogs.

"So what's the average price of a present you would have given me, say, every birthday and Christmas?" I ask, patting Gomer's head, which makes him turn around and pant, his mouth open wide, his tongue sticking out.

Turk laughs. "Is this a shakedown? On the very first day of my grandfatherhood?"

I nod. "Yep. Total shakedown."

"What the hell do I care?" he says, throwing his hands in the air. "I got all the funds I'll ever need, and a severe lack of family. Seems like a good trade. What do you need?"

When I explain to him the first thing I really want, he isn't so sure he can do it.

"You sure? How about a nice sweater? I would happily improve your wardrobe. Because this," he says, pointing up and down at my ratty T-shirt and Gareth's baggy shorts. "This is unbecoming."

"This is unbecoming because we left for a day trip a week ago and all I've had since then is what I was wearing that day, plus what a Wyoming oldster and a Salt Lake City boozer-in-training was willing to give me. And, of course, most of what I have is currently in Aisha's car."

He wrinkles his nose. Then he sits down and relents. "Fine. Dial for me."

"Thanks," I say. "I owe you on this one. And since this has no monetary value, we'll start on the birthday and Christmas presents after, okay?"

He grins and mutters, "The kids these days."

Turk takes the phone from me. He nods slightly when the call is picked up.

"Hi," he says. "Would this be Aisha Stinson? I'm calling on behalf of a misguided child named Carson Smith. This is Turk Braverman, Carson's late grandfather's ex-lover."

I can't hear the words, but I can actually hear a happy shriek through the phone, and I realize how much I miss Aisha.

"Well, get on over here. I'll catch you all up. And yes, you have a place to stay tonight."

He listens more.

"I'm well aware you're angry at him. As Carson's newly minted grandfather and as someone who knows his bloodline a wee bit, I feel it's my place to tell you he comes by his stubbornness honestly."

"Hey!" I yell.

He ignores me. "And his selfishness, and his moodiness. Now, young lady, what part of this is on you?"

This I want to hear, but all I can do is watch and listen.

"Fair enough. Come on over and we'll work things out. You have directions?"

She does, so they say good-bye. He hangs up and gives me an impish look, which is funny on an old guy. "All settled. She's willing to consider forgiving you for being a jackass — her words — if you're willing to consider forgiving her for being a janeass — my word."

I laugh. I have liked a lot of people on this trip, but none of them so much as I like Turk right away.

While we wait for Aisha, we talk about what needs to happen next, and Turk is generous to a fault about it. No problem is too big. Everything has a solution. So when it's all settled, I call my mom.

"So I'm coming home," I say, by way of hello. Gomer sits up and licks my cheek. I wipe his slobber off my face. Gross.

"Good," Mom says, her voice icy.

"Yeah," I say. "Are you going to ask where I am or what I'm doing? Because it's pretty big. I have big news."

"Carson," she says, "I just want you to come home. I really don't care to hear any more stories. Your dad is doing very poorly today."

"Tell him to hold on, please. Tell him I'm coming home and I have something for him. Tell him that exactly, okay?"

She exhales. "Just tell me when you'll be here, please."

"I'll be back tomorrow evening. We're flying in. As I said, we have a surprise. Okay?"

She hangs up on me.

I look at Turk. I don't know what he sees, but he puts his arms around me.

"Well, that hurt," I say.

He nods and nods. "Your mom is a tough one?"

"Yep."

"I'll work my Turk magic on her," he says, and that makes me smile.

I call my dad, and my mom is right; he sounds rough. I keep it nice and short.

"I'm gonna be back tomorrow night."

"Good," he says. "Good."

"I love you. Did you know that?"

"Wow," he says. "That's . . . nice, Carson."

"I love you and I'm just sorry for everything that's happened to you in your life." I feel myself getting emotional, and Turk gives me a supportive nod.

"Thanks," my dad says, sounding bewildered.

"When I come back tomorrow, I'm gonna have . . . some answers for you. It's gonna be good. You're gonna hear some things that you need to hear. It's gonna be all right, okay?"

Long pause. "Okay."

Nothing more.

"I'm scared," he says.

"Don't be scared. I'm done being scared. Just know I love you. You're loved, Dad."

"You're freakin' me out," he says.

"I'm a little freaked out too. But good freaked out. Well. Yeah, good. Trust me. All will be revealed."

And then I'm off the phone, and then everything hits me all at once, and I'm exhausted. I feel like I've climbed a mountain. Turk sets up the guest room, puts me to bed, and closes the door. Within seconds I'm deeply asleep.

The craziest thing happens while I'm sleeping. I open my eyes and focus on the ceiling, and I swear I see my grandfather's face there. Hovering over me. Staring down at me. Calm, serene. Just there.

I don't freak out. I don't yell out to see if Turk can come in and see what I see. I just look. The more I look, the more I'm sure of it, that it's the outline of his face. Once in a while, it's like the face of the Burger King dude, and then it morphs back to my grandfather.

I think about mirages. I realize I don't know. I want it to be him.

So it is him. Like Laurelei said. It's true for me.

We smile at each other, me and my grandfather. And I decide that I will never share this with anyone. This secret I'll carry with me the rest of my life.

When Grandpa fades, I close my eyes and sleep some more, and it's a calm sleep. When I wake up, there are voices in the other room, amiable voices. I hear Aisha laughing, and then Turk laughing, and I wrap the blanket around me and feel this content feeling in my chest. It's how I used to feel on days when I pretended to be sick and stayed home from school, and my grandparents would be in the living room and I'd be all cozy in bed. I would stare at a spot above the window, just stare at it, until the room became distorted and the window would lose all proportion and the spot would suddenly be so big, and me so small. I'd feel a buzz in my head as I breathed and stared, and I felt — safe. There was safety in being small. I knew in those moments it was all going to be okay, and it was delicious, that strange, distorted little place of my own, with the comfort of my grandparents just beyond the door.

I savor it for a while, and when I'm ready, I get up and walk out to the living room.

Aisha is sitting in my spot on the couch, sprawled out with her arms above her head and her feet on the floor. Gomer is lying on her stomach. When she sees me, she shoos Gomer away and looks at the floor in front of her. She says, "Hey."

"Hey."

"Hey," she says again, creating an imbalance of heys, two against one.

I study the floor too.

"Oh my God," Turk says. "Do you have any idea how over the bickering children thing I am? I've had you both here for, what, three minutes? No wonder I didn't have any kids. Exhausting."

I steal a glance at Aisha just in time to see her stealing one at me.

Turk points to the door. "Out," he says. "And no, I'm not abandoning you, because heaven knows there are enough abandonment issues here to sink the *Titanic*. You're going out into the world to say what you need to say to each other. And then you're coming back here, and I'm making dinner, and we'll eat it like one big happy family, which we will be, because you'll have your shit together. Understood? Understood."

We tentatively walk toward the door.

"Go, go," he says, waving his hand. "I'll be eagerly awaiting the new and improved and made-up Carson and Aisha. God, do I hate conflict."

I walk down the stairs behind her, a little bewildered by whatever that was. It's funny getting to know a grandfather when you're already seventeen. It's like you should already know his quirks, but you just don't.

"You okay?" she asks when we're at the bottom of the stairs. She sits down, so I do too.

"I guess so," I say, looking down at the ground. "I'm exhausted thinking about it, but I'm glad I know. We're flying home —"

"He told me," Aisha says.

"I'm well aware that I'm an asshole. The volleyball game was not my finest hour. I'm sorry."

She shrugs. "Me too. And just so you know, Brianna's over. She wanted a one-time thing. So I guess I probably overreacted about how exciting it all was."

"I'm sorry," I say, but in truth I feel relieved. Does that make me a bad person?

"I do that again and again. I get all excited about someone new, and it's too much, too soon. I did it with Kayla and I did it again here."

I don't have a whole lot of relationship wisdom to share, so again I just say, "Sorry."

"I've never been looked at like that before," she says.

I cock my head at her. "You're looked at everywhere you go, actually."

"Maybe. But this was different. It was, like, people liked what they saw, instead of me just standing out as different. I loved it."

I take a look at my friend, my beautiful friend. She is even better on the inside than the outside, and people don't know that. They don't see it. I wish people could see what I see. "I get that," I say.

"I'm not your sidekick," Aisha blurts out.

"What?"

She turns toward me. "All this trip, it's like, Carson's stuff. We're in my car, but this is Carson's journey. To find your grandfather. Did it ever occur to you, even once, that I might be doing this for me too?"

I bite my lip. I'm learning to not say the first thing that comes to my mind, I guess, because I don't say, *This wasn't just some trip. This is my life we're talking about here. My grandfather. My dad.* And then I'm so glad I don't say it, because I hear it, and for the first time it occurs to me: Me. My life. Aisha. Her life. Shit. How come I'm so selfish and stupid and dense sometimes? She has her own life, and all this time I was treating her thing with her dad like it was some side issue, when for her it's *the* issue.

I close my eyes, afraid to look at her. Finally I get up the courage to speak. "You're right. I didn't get that. I'm sorry. I get a little in my head, I guess."

She nods, and then she smiles a bit, and I think, *Say something! Say you're cool with it! Say a joke! Anything!*

But she doesn't say anything. Just keeps that little, content smile on her face.

As an old lady pushing a shopping cart saunters by, Aisha says, "I'm okay if you want to be the sidekick in my life."

"I'd be lucky to be that," I say. "And by the way, you can kiss girls. I'll learn not to want to stab them in the eye."

"So can you. And I'd be jealous if you started kissing some girl too, by the way."

I blush, for the first time ever with Aisha.

"Thanks for that," I say.

EARLY THE NEXT morning, we take a nice stroll with Gomer through the Castro, Turk's neighborhood. He explains that when he moved there, back in 1975, it was pretty much all gay. It's become a lot more mixed, he says, his expression sour.

"So diversity is a bad thing?" I say.

Aisha and Turk share a look. "I forgot we have a breeder in our midst," he says. He pats my shoulder condescendingly as we keep walking. "No, sweet child. Diversity is not a bad thing. But neither was having one neighborhood in all of America — back then, anyway — where it was considered normal to be gay. In fact, that would still be a nice thing."

I say, "So you want to be normal? That sounds boring."

They share another look. This has been happening a lot, this two against one thing. In the last fifteen hours, Aisha and Turk have become this team, and for once I'm not jealous. I get it. They have something in common. I'm just happy to see Aisha smiling and joking.

Scratch that. Aisha, Turk, and Gomer are a team. I'm not sure if Gomer is gay, but he did sleep with Aisha last night — the lucky dog. He hasn't left her side since, possibly because she gives him these epic belly rubs. He stretches out on his back and she scratches his belly with both hands. In response, Gomer's eyes and mouth open as wide as they can.

Yeah, I can see why people love dogs.

Gomer is trotting, prancing, really, his tail up like he's proud to be taking a walk. Every person we meet needs to stop and fawn all over him, and Gomer greets them by standing up on his hind legs and attempting to lick their faces when they bend down. We wind through tree-lined streets chock-full of Victorian houses scrunched together. When we pass a nondescript cream-colored building with purple doors pushed up against a row of skinny Victorians, Turk stops.

"This is my church."

Aisha and I laugh. I've known the man for a day, and the one thing he isn't is religious. Last night at dinner, he started over-sharing about his lack of a sex life in the last two decades. I'd never heard a seventy-year-old person talk about sex before, and frankly I'll be okay if I don't again for a while. But Turk doesn't change expression.

"You serious?" Aisha says, an eyebrow raised.

"As a heart attack. Why wouldn't I be?"

"You're, like, Christian and a fag?"

"Whoa," I say, but Turk doesn't seem quite as taken aback.

"There are literally millions of us Christian fags, dear."

"But don't Christians basically think we're going to hell?"

" 'Christian' is a rather wide range. To group all Christians together is rather like grouping all homosexuals together, wouldn't you say?"

I think back to Mr. Bailey saying the same thing, and I savor the irony of Turk and Mr. Bailey agreeing on something. Gomer pulls on his leash as a big dog trots by. Turk reins him in.

"All I know is my dad threw me out based on his beliefs, and he's a Christian," Aisha says.

Turk pulls her toward him, firmly but gently. "What your dad did," he says directly into her ear, "that's not Christlike, okay? That's not Christian. Do you hear me? Do you understand?"

"Oh, he's a real Christian all right," Aisha says, and I feel my shoulders rise and tense.

"He may think that," Turk says. "But true followers of Jesus Christ would never turn their back on a child who was suffering. That's not conscionable. He's living in fear."

"Okay," Aisha says.

We're all more comfortable when Turk lets go of Aisha and we start walking again.

"Forgive me," he says, chewing on his mustache. "I get so sick of assholes hijacking organized religion. Seriously. Somebody told your father, in the name of Christ, to kick you out of the house? Totally unacceptable. Sitting in a church makes you no more of a Christ follower than sitting in a Ford dealership makes you a Mustang owner."

I say, "So you believe that Jesus Christ is the Son of God? That he was born without his mom having sex? That he was crucified and resurrected? That he died for our sins? Really?"

"Actually, I was born Jewish."

I raise an eyebrow, as best I can, anyway. "Turk? What kind of Jewish name is that?"

"It's a nickname. My given name is Tzuriel. It means 'Rock of God' in Hebrew."

"I think Tzuriel Braverman came up when we Googled Turk

Braverman back in wherever," I say. "We didn't pursue it, as we didn't think it was a thing."

He laughs. "Tzuriel is my given name, and my professional name. I'm an author. I tend to write about religion and sexuality."

"You write books about God?" Aisha asks.

He nods.

"Cool," she says, and I'm like, *Yeah. It is kinda cool.*

"So you're Jewish?" she asks.

"Well, I was born Jewish. I love the Jewish religion, what it stands for. In essence, Judaism is about being the best person you can be. I love that. As I've gotten older, though, I've dabbled here and there. I mean, how can you be Jewish or Christian when the Dalai Lama exists? How can you be Buddhist or Muslim when there's Christ's teachings? There are so many wise people who have taught us so many wise lessons. How can a person choose to follow only some of the wisdom of the world?"

I ask, "So you're not Christian, but you go to church?"

"This is the Metropolitan Community Church. There are tons of open and affirming churches. To me, a church that isn't open and affirming isn't really a church at all. This one is run by and for LGBTQ people."

I look at Aisha. She's just staring at the building. "I wish I could go to a service here," she says, and we go back to walking.

"Well, you'll need to fly back and get your car, won't you?"

Aisha nods. I've been so focused on our flight back to Billings later today and introducing Turk to my dad that I'd forgotten we'll return here in a few days.

"Well then, it's a date. You'll love it. There's so much love in there, so much kindness. I sometimes feel as though the walls can't hold it all in."

We walk for a while. I try to digest what he's told me. He's a Jew who goes to a church and loves the Dalai Lama. He talks about sex and he's a recovering alcoholic with forty years in AA and he writes books about God and he drives his convertible too fast.

*God, Grandpa,* I think to myself. *Why'd you have to marry such a stereotype?*

Turk is a local celebrity. Every block, he runs into someone he knows and stops to hug. He introduces me to some people as his new grandson, and to others as "Russ's grandson." The first garners puzzled looks; the second gets me hugged tight the few times it comes up.

As we get back to Market Street, I say, "So you believe in heaven and hell?"

Turk pulls on Gomer's leash to stop him from sniffing a big pile of poop. "To me, hell is on earth. We've all been to hell. Heaven too. Living well takes us there."

I snort. It sounds like a slogan you'd see on some late-night infomercial by some quack with a bad toupee selling CDs for $59.99, money-back guarantee if not completely sent to heaven for eternity, some restrictions apply.

Turk gives me an admonishing look. "Look. I get that there are assholes out there. They were out in full force when my friends were dying. I just refuse to let them rule me. I think Christianity is mostly good. I think religion is mostly good, even if it's been the cause of most of our wars. That comes from a lack of flexibility, from not allowing others to disagree. Rigidity is dangerous. When someone tells you they know exactly what God is, run from that person."

"For you," I say, thinking of what Laurelei said.

"Huh?" Turk says, as Gomer does a little lamb leap toward a dog that's obviously familiar to him, since the other dog makes a similar leap in Gomer's direction. That owner waves and the two dogs sniff each other's snouts and begin to circle each other.

"Laurelei in Wyoming said that to me. She said whatever people believe about God is undeniably true, so long as it's followed by the words, *for me*."

"I like that," Turk says. "And I'll add a resounding 'fuck you' for anytime someone else tries to put their 'for me' *on me*."

"Ain't that the truth," Aisha says.

"The Porcupine of Truth," I say.

Aisha rolls her eyes. "Inside joke," she says to Turk. "Carson has no joke filter. When he's uncomfortable, he goes for the laugh."

"Oh, I'm familiar," Turk says, as we turn onto a side street. "If I had a nickel for every time Russ would say some nonsense when things got real. It was utterly adorable and truly obnoxious."

Aisha puts her finger on her nose and points at Turk, who laughs.

"I'm standing right here," I say. "Am I invisible?"

Turk ruffles my hair. "What's the Porcupine of Truth?" he asks.

Aisha explains it to him. He takes it all in and slowly nods. "That's definitely something Russ would have invented," he says, his eyes a little sad.

We walk together in silence, our steps in a comfortable rhythm. When we get back to his street, Aisha says, "And you really believe in heaven?"

"Oh, most definitely," Turk says. "You want to see what heaven is like? To my way of thinking?"

We nod.

He hands me Gomer's leash and then waves us off. "Take Gomer to the dog park. I'll tell you where it is. That, my young friends, is heaven on earth."

---

There are two gates to the dog park. We open up a huge wrought-iron doorway and enter what I guess is a vestibule before we reach the second gate. As we do so, a bunch of dogs run up to the second gate to see who is coming in. Gomer eagerly looks out at the expectant pack of dogs, his black tail wagging back and forth like a metronome.

We remove his leash as Turk told us to do and open the second gate, and Gomer rockets into a world unlike any I've seen before.

It's a beautiful morning and the sun is coming up over the bright green, grassy field. Dozens of dogs of all types congregate in small groups or jump and run and play in pairs and packs. There are huge dogs with pointy snouts, low-to-the-ground dogs waddling around with big bellies, miniature dogs yipping and chasing the tails of larger dogs that look like they could eat the mini ones for breakfast. A diverse cluster of dogs tromps around the perimeter of the park in pack formation. Two dogs, one black and small, the other reddish and slightly bigger, wrestle, the smaller one standing on his hind legs trying to gain an advantage.

Dozens of people of all types stand around, some talking and laughing. Others lounge on benches, watching the scene in solitude. Fat white men in sweat suits chat with skinny black ladies in skirts who look like they must be on their way to the office after this. Hipster chicks wearing librarian glasses cavort with dudes in skullcaps.

I watch Gomer saunter up to a big German shepherd. They sniff each other's snouts for a moment, and then the German shepherd walks around to the back of Gomer and sniffs his butt.

"Oh my," I say.

"That's how they check each other out," Aisha says. "We used to have a mini schnauzer."

"I did not know that," I say. "Either of those pieces of information, actually."

Gomer allows the bigger dog to sniff him. And then, just as quickly, the German shepherd gallops off, and Gomer, his tail waving like a fan, takes off after him. The bigger dog runs in a wide circle, and Gomer, lower and more compact, has to move his legs twice as fast to keep up. Then the bigger dog turns and starts chasing Gomer, and a medium-sized white dog with a funny-looking snout joins in.

A bulldog, wheezing like he's out of shape, scampers by my feet. A tiny, fluffy white dog follows him. I look around. No dogs are left out. They're all playing with each other.

Gomer runs past a poodle sitting expectantly, looking at its owner. He's a wiry-looking guy in a trucker hat. Gomer barks at the poodle, and both dogs' tails start wagging. The poodle takes off, chasing Gomer. "Hazel! Girl, get back here," he yells, and the dogs stop running. Hazel the poodle trots back over to her owner, who turns his attention to Gomer. "Get away from her, you stupid mutt," he says.

I run over. "Sorry," I say.

He ignores me, and I feel my shoulders droop. This trip has allowed me to forget how it feels to be invisible. Now I remember: I don't like it.

"C'mon, Gomer," I say, monotone, and he trots away from the poodles. He doesn't seem to care that he was just yelled at; he has the same smile on his adorable face that he almost always has. He races off to join a group of smaller dogs who are running in circles. He puts his nose right up against a large, furry white dog's behind. He goes up to all the dogs and does it. Doesn't matter if they're bigger or smaller. Gomer sniffs the boys, the girls, the white-furred ones, the red-furred ones, the black-furred ones. The nearly shaved, the puffy.

"What do you think the sniffing is all about?" I ask.

"They're curious. Like why they come running to the door when another dog comes in. They want to know about him or her."

"Wouldn't that be cool if we could be like that?"

"Sniffing butts?" she asks, sniffing my shoulder.

"Not afraid of what other people think. Not embarrassed to be interested in someone else. That kind of thing. Do you think that's why Turk thinks it's heaven? Why can't humans be like that? What are we afraid of?"

She doesn't have time to answer my litany of questions, because suddenly there is a commotion. Hazel the poodle is on her back and a large gray dog stands over her, growling.

"Hey!" the nasty guy says, kicking at the gray dog.

The dog eludes his kick and saunters away. The owner of the gray dog, a large, nondescript man whose belly spills over his brown jeans, hurries over.

"You control your dog or next time I'll punt it," the wiry guy spits at him.

The man in the brown jeans says, "He was just playing. I'm sorry."

"You bet you're sorry," the wiry guy says. "Control him, or next time I'll punt *you*."

Aisha and I look at each other. Everyone in the park is watching the altercation. Meanwhile, a pack of German shepherds has cordoned off the gray dog from the rest. After a little bit of roughhousing, they let the gray dog go. He trots off in search of other playmates.

"That's how the dogs take care of each other," Aisha says to me. "They set him straight."

The guy in the trucker hat stands rigid, his arms crossed tight across his chest. Turk said this was heaven, and for a while I could totally see that. Then trucker hat guy yelled at Gomer, and then at the other guy. Suddenly we're not in heaven anymore.

Trucker hat guy is motioning with his arms in front of Hazel, who is just sitting there, not playing with the other dogs. I feel bad for her. All these dogs are out having a good time, and poor Hazel is like a prisoner to that jerk.

"The problem with this place is the entrance," I tell Aisha. "Replace that double gate with a velvet rope, get the Porcupine out there to choose who gets in, and then this place really would be Des Moines."

Aisha laughs. "Get rid of these gates and add a velvet rope, and what you really have is chaos."

I get that she's kidding, that she means that a velvet rope would not be an ideal way to fence in dogs. But I'm being serious. The thing that keeps this place from truly being heaven, in my opinion, is who is let in.

The dogs run and fetch and play, and the people do their thing too. On the other side of the park, the brown jeans guy is standing by himself with his head down. It's like I can feel his shame.

I tug on Aisha's shirt and walk toward the guy. She follows, keeping an eye on Gomer, who is being petted by a muscular black dude with a blond buzz cut.

"Hey," I say as we approach. "What's your name?"

The brown jeans guy looks surprised that someone is talking to him. "Larry."

"Hey, Larry. I'm Carson and this is Aisha."

"Hi," he says.

"Which dog is yours?" I ask, pretending not to have seen the altercation.

He points tentatively at his gray dog, which is currently sniffing a woman's feet.

"So cute. What kind is he?" Aisha asks.

"He's an Australian shepherd."

I scan the park for Gomer. "Ours is the Labradoodle currently on his back with his legs in the air. Can't take him anywhere."

Larry laughs. "Yep. He looks like a nice dog."

"He is."

"Shit," he mutters under his breath. His Australian shepherd is now peeing on a tennis ball a guy had been using to play fetch with his dog. The guy goes off in search of another ball. "Matty!" Larry yells, but the dog ignores him and begins to growl at a skinny, hairless dog about a quarter of his size. He shakes his head. "My dog is a fucking asshole."

I laugh, but Aisha doesn't. "You have him since he was a pup?" she asks.

The guy nods. "Got him at a pet store. He lives in our garage 'cause he kept peeing all over the place and chewing up the furniture."

I don't know a lot about dogs, but I can tell there's something not great about this story. I mean, don't dogs need training? Maybe not as much as poor Hazel, but.

I'm about to say something else when a woman who is walking past us with her German shepherd points across the way. "Oh! I think Brent's about to have Hazel do Russian Bear," she says. "Have you seen this?"

I turn and watch. She's pointing at trucker hat guy. He is kneeling in front of Hazel like they're having an intense conversation. Then he pats her on the head, stands, and puts his arms out wide. "Russian bear," he says.

Hazel stands on her hind legs and slowly lifts her paws high above her head. She does look kind of like a bear, I realize, and begrudgingly I grin.

Aisha gasps. "I've never seen a dog do that!"

"Isn't that great?" the woman says. She and her German shepherd have stopped walking.

When Hazel gets down from her pose, the trucker guy holds up a treat, which Hazel gobbles down while he affectionately rubs her head.

The woman who told us to watch smiles. "Brent is so good with her. Ever since his wife left him last year, training Hazel has become his one passion."

"That was pretty amazing," Aisha says.

Larry isn't listening. "Fuck. Matty!" he yells, running over to him. Matty has taken down another dog, this one small and apricot with floppy ears. He is growling over it.

Larry grabs Matty by the collar and drags him a good fifteen feet. He then smacks Matty in the snout and says, "Stupid, fucking, useless mutt."

"And some people, less amazing," the woman says, matter-of-fact, and she continues her perimeter walk.

Larry puts Matty on his leash and heads toward the exit.

"You ever have an initial reaction to something and it turns out totally wrong?" I ask Aisha.

She tosses a ball high in the air, and Gomer leaps for it and catches it in his mouth. Then he drops it at Aisha's feet and looks up at her. "All the time," she says.

I'm about to tell her all the thoughts I had about Brent after he yelled at Gomer, and then I realize maybe there's a better way to deal with this.

"Follow me," I say to Aisha, and she slaps her leg and somehow

Gomer knows to walk with us. I slowly approach Brent and Hazel, and as Aisha figures out where we're going, she puts Gomer on a leash.

I stop a few feet away from Brent, keeping my distance in case he's gonna get nasty again. "That was so cool," I say.

"Yeah?" he asks, barely glancing up at me.

"We put our dog on a leash this time," I say. "Don't worry."

"Thanks," he says, and this time he does look at me and gives me a smile.

"How'd you teach her to do that?"

Brent studies us like he's not sure what our angle is. Like we're messing with him. But we aren't.

"One day Hazel was trying to steal herself a treat that was on the kitchen counter. There was a stool in the way, so when I walked into the kitchen, there she was, looking like a big old white Russian bear." He laughs. "I figured maybe I could figure out how to turn her bad habit into a good one."

"That's awesome. She's an amazing dog," Aisha says.

"Thanks," Brent says, and that stern, nasty demeanor is gone. "Hey, listen. Sorry 'bout that before. I sometimes bark before I think. I know you didn't mean any trouble."

"I appreciate it," I say, genuinely surprised that he even knew I was the owner of the dog he yelled at. "I get that you're protective of Hazel."

He nods.

"What about that other guy?"

He shakes his head. "That guy needs to stop bringing his dog here. Seen him a hundred times, and he never gets the message."

"Fair enough," I say, and I stick out my hand for him to shake. He does. "Catch you another time."

When Gomer starts to pant and his tongue begins to hang from his mouth, we decide it's time to leave. Aisha wrangles him back onto his leash, and we head for the exit.

"So is this heaven?" I ask as we get to the exit.

We turn and look back at the park one last time.

"For me it is," Aisha says.

I take in the whole scene. Turk's heaven on earth is filled with laughter and play and barking and roughhousing and dog pee, and as many different breeds of people as there are of dogs. And there are humans who get along, and others who don't, and some who do the wrong thing, or at least the wrong thing according to *me*.

I smile. If you had told me two weeks ago in New York that I'd find heaven on earth in a grassy field soaked with dog urine, watching a fat guy smack his misbehaving dog on the snout, I would have laughed at you.

But it's not two weeks ago. I'm not in New York, and everything's different now. At least I am, because now I can stop judging everything for long enough to realize where I am.

A perfectly imperfect place.

"For me too," I say, resting my head on Aisha's shoulder. "Totally heaven."

# PART IV
## Back to
## Not New York

IT'S LATE EVENING when Turk pulls his rental car into the driveway of my dad's place. A sense of dread seizes my chest. The party is over. Now it's time for the reckoning. As much as I can't wait even another second to introduce my dad and Turk, the uncertainty of how my dad will react to learning what happened to his dad makes me want to lock us in the car and never, ever get out.

We carefully navigate the steep driveway in the dark and walk around to the front door. Something about this reunion feels inappropriate for the back door and the kitchen.

My mother answers when we knock. Her face is tense, and her lips are tighter. Part of me wants to grab her and hug her so hard that it'll wring all the anger out of her and me. Another part wants to run.

"Hi Mom," I say. "Not sure how to do this, so. Um. This is Turk Braverman. Dad's dad's . . . significant other. Turk, this is my mom, Renee Warren."

She sticks her hand out tentatively, like she's not sure if this is an appropriate response to what I've said. Thank God for Turk, who gently takes her hand and then steps forward and hugs her tense body.

Then the three of us walk in, and I squeeze her shoulder as I walk by. It's like a squeeze question: *Are we okay?* I'm pretty sure we're not. She doesn't respond in any way I notice.

"He's resting," she says, as I point to my dad's bedroom door.

Turk turns to her as if to ask permission. She nods ever so slightly.

Turk and I walk to the door. He knocks, and it takes Dad a long, long time to answer.

He looks at least a year older than when I left. His unshaven face sags, sallow. I think, *No. This is not the person I've been talking to on the phone.*

I hug him as tightly as I feel I can without hurting him. He smells stale, unshowered.

"You came back," he says, his words labored as he squeezes me. "Yay."

"Dad," I say, pulling back from the hug. "This is Turk Braverman. He knew your dad."

My dad just stands there, like he doesn't know how to react. Turk sticks out his hand. My dad barely shakes it.

"Would you mind if I came in and talked with you for a bit?" Turk asks.

My dad looks scared. He looks at me. I nod. He looks at my mom, who nods too.

Even with his frailties, I am used to Turk being decisive in every action, every movement. So watching the way he reacts to my father is stunning to me. I can feel his uncertainty. I see it in his tentative glances, and the way he avoids looking at my dad. *How weird this must be for him*, I think.

My dad steps aside and allows Turk into his room. Turk closes the door.

I look at my mom, whose eyes plead for more information.

"I'm gonna hang out downstairs," Aisha says, and she slips into the kitchen, heading toward the basement stairs.

When my mother and I are alone in the living room, neither of us speaks for a long time. I sit down on the couch, and she sits down in the love seat. I simply don't know what to say. I don't know what her excuse is.

Finally, she takes a deep breath, crosses her legs, and says, "I recognize that what you've done here is significant, Carson. I thank you for that. But that doesn't change the fact that I feel like we need to have a real conversation about boundaries. I feel as though I allow you a lot of leeway, but I am your parent. It's important for me to locate it when I feel as though my boundaries as a parent have been crossed."

My face heats up. It gets hot, and then hotter. I feel like a tea-kettle with the heat turned way up, like if I don't let something out right now, my head's gonna start to whistle.

"MORE, PLEASE! ANYTHING, PLEASE! JUST . . . MORE!"

My mother reacts as if I've just socked her in the gut.

"I need more than that kind of talk. I mean it. You can't do this to me anymore. I'm your kid. Who says that to their kid?"

"Who says what?"

"All this 'locate,' 'own,' 'allow' . . . You're so clinical, so cold, Mom. You freeze me out."

"You think I'm cold?" She sucks in her lips.

I don't say anything. Her eyes redden and moisten. She swallows. A first tear falls.

This. This is what I've been afraid of all my life. This is why I count. So I don't say something that melts my mom. I have melted my mother. I have made my mother cry.

"I don't think —" I say, and then I stop. We're here already. No going back. "I just think you sometimes play psychologist with me instead of, you know. Being my mom. You don't show emotion. You don't seem to care enough to get angry most of the time. You never hug me."

This just makes the tears fall more, and she doesn't wipe them away. It's like she's thawing. Liquid streams down her face as she speaks.

"Do you think I don't know I'm not cut out for this? Do you think I haven't told myself, every day since I had you, that I can't do this? Every day, Carson. I hear the voice every day. *Renee, you're doing it wrong. You're a terrible mother.* I try to keep it together, and that only makes it worse."

"I didn't say you were a terrible mother," I say. I look at her face, and she's grimacing. "Mom —"

"You think you're the only person with a mother who disappoints you? You think my parents were any better? My mother disapproved of every single choice I ever made. Driving around the country alone made me seem like a . . . prostitute. Getting pregnant before I was married? Do you have any idea? She wore black to my wedding, Carson. She told me your father was a huge mistake, that I was wasting my life away. When I came back to New York after the divorce, she told me I'd gone and ruined two lives. All I wanted to be was the kind of mother who didn't do that to her child."

I can't imagine my grandma, my sweet, lovable grandma, doing these things. Saying these things. Is nobody pure? Is everybody fucked up? Is that life? Is that okay? Is it acceptable?

"Do you have any idea how much energy I spend trying to keep it together? Do you get that when I measure my words, I'm trying to protect you from me losing my . . . do you get that?"

"Maybe we should stop," I say.

"Stop?"

"Trying to keep it together. Trying to protect each other from each other."

Mom slides down from the love seat until she is sitting against it on the floor. I do the same off the couch. Our outstretched legs touch, and I'm waiting for her to pull her legs away. But she doesn't. She doesn't do or say anything.

I study her face. It's tired. Discontent. She has a pimple on her forehead. She raises her head just slightly, and there's just a bit of a booger visible at the end of her left nostril.

This horrible, stinky, sad idea strikes me and takes all the air from my body. *My mom is just a person.* A fucked-up person, like me, like Dad, like everyone.

It occurs to me for the first time in my life that it's truly possible to know something and not know it at the same time. Because how could I not know that my mother is a flawed person? That she's just me with slightly more experience? That she dropped me off at the zoo the first day we were here, not because her normal, brilliant understanding of the world had momentarily warped, but because she had no idea what else to do?

I crawl over to her and wrap my arms around her. She slowly gives in to the hug, uncoiling her tense body almost one vertebra at a time. I feel her letting go, and soon she turns toward me and hugs me back.

She leans her head against mine. I don't pull away. "Thanks," I say, marveling at the warm feeling of her skull against mine. "That was a treat. This is."

She sniffles and wipes her nose with the back of her hand. "It shouldn't be."

We keep our heads connected, and we talk. For basically the first time in our lives, we talk for real. I like feeling the vibration of her words inside my ears. I tell her about how Grandpa died, and she shuts her eyes and nods as she takes this information in. For the first time in my life, I can feel my mom's love for my dad. I feel it in my scalp, this palpable love, despite everything, that she has for him.

That feeling is confirmed when she tells me it's been hard to be back here, but she's realized that she still cares for Dad, all this time later. Part of me lights up when she tells me this, because it's the missing puzzle piece, and it flickers brighter.

I tell her about all the people we met on our trip, and all the adventures. She pulls away a bit, and I remember that while Aisha and I were doing all that, I was actively ignoring her.

"Mom," I say. "It's okay, really. "

"What's okay?"

"That you're pissed at me. I'd be pissed at me too."

I feel her nod. "I am . . . pissed."

I lift my head off hers and look her in the eye.

"If you have to, like, yell at me, you should yell at me," I say.

"You want me to yell at you?" she asks, like she's not sure if I mean it.

302

"I want you to yell sometimes. When I screw up."

"You sure?"

"Yeah."

She mock-screams, "No! I won't yell at you!"

For the first time, I realize my dad is not my only parent with a weird sense of humor. This makes me smile. She smiles just a bit too.

"You're grounded, by the way," she says. "Incredibly, outrageously grounded. Possibly for eternity. And if you ever, for any reason, even a very good one, leave the state you're supposed to be in without telling me, I will come find you and make you sorry you ever lived."

"Maybe pull back on the yelling a tad," I say.

She smiles again, and my whole body relaxes. My mom.

When Aisha comes back upstairs, my mom and I are still hanging out, chatting. I can see Aisha take in that something has happened here, and then she just goes with it, pretends that it's not unusual for Mom and me to talk like we're actually inhabiting the same world. Turk and my dad are still in the bedroom, and I am anxious for them to come out so I can see how Dad is doing with all this.

Aisha and Mom talk for really the first time ever too, and I get to see a different side of my mom. She's still her psychologist self; I mean, I guess I'd be surprised if she ever lost that therapist tone. But she also opens up a bit about how scared she felt when she didn't know where I was, and at the same time how glad she was to know I had Aisha there with me.

"You're more than welcome to stay here as long as we're here," my mother says. "I know how important you are to Carson, and that's meaningful to me."

I roll my eyes and say to Aisha, "We want you to locate yourself here."

My mom narrows her eyes at me.

"Too soon?" I ask.

"Much too soon," my mother says.

"Be nice to your mom," Aisha says.

"Sorry."

I crawl over and kiss my mom on the cheek, and she cups my chin in her hands.

"Apology accepted," she says.

I hear the door to my father's bedroom creak open. Dad and Turk emerge slowly. My mom and I stand up. Dad looks small. He stares at the ground, emotionless.

"It's chilly in here," he says, and no one responds. No one says anything and no one moves. We're all just waiting for something we can work with, I guess.

When she gets tired of waiting, my mom goes over to my dad. She clasps his hand in hers. The she leans in to him, and he puts his head on her shoulder. She envelops him in a hug, and he hangs there in her arms, his own arms splayed out and not around her, and someone who didn't know my dad might think he didn't want the hug. But I know him a bit, and I know he does want it, that he desperately needs it. He just doesn't know how to react because he's sad and he's broken, and that's a tough combination.

Watching my mom hold my dad is like the time I went to the planetarium and watched this show about the stars and the planets. There's this place where the planets shift, or maybe the sun covers the moon completely or vice versa, I don't remember exactly what. I just remember feeling like the earth was shifting and my balance was gone and even though I was sitting and looking up at the ceiling, I felt like I could just fall over.

Turk comes and stands on my right, and Aisha stands on my left. I lean on both of them. They hold me up, and I've never felt this way before, supported like a building needs support beams. They keep me upright as the planets of my parents collide and stay collided.

Eventually we all sit down, my mom and dad on the love seat and the three of us on the big couch. No one says much of anything.

My dad finally says, "He was alone and sick, and I couldn't help him."

Turk shakes his head slowly. "He wasn't alone."

My dad nods vacantly.

"He loved you very much and he knew you loved him and that's the truth," Turk says.

"Why did this have to happen to me?" Dad asks. "Us, I mean."

No one has an answer for that one.

"All this wasted time. . . ." he says.

Turk tells a few funny stories about the things my granddad did in San Francisco, like the time he dressed up for Halloween in a blond wig, pantsuit, and poofy hat, and around his midsection was a bulky felt square, with six round white dots on the back side, one round white dot on the front.

"He was Princess Die," Turk says, and my mother, of all people, laughs. My dad hangs his head, and I realize it's not that easy taking this all in, hearing about what your dad was doing when he wasn't with you, for whatever reason. Like if your dad can't be with you, he should be miserable the whole time. I definitely know that feeling.

I guess Turk gets it too, because he says, "At least once a week, Matthew, I'd wake up to your dad's sobs. He was an utter mess, not being able to be with you."

My dad chews his bottom lip. My mom squeezes his hand, and after a while, I see him squeeze hers back.

It's after midnight when we finish talking, and my mother tries to figure out where everyone can sleep. Turk will get the living room couch, she says, and she brings out fresh linen for him.

"Would you be happier on a nice, working air mattress?" I ask.

He moves his head from side to side, considering this. "You have an extra one?"

"Nope. We don't have any. We have one that leaks air, and Aisha's been sleeping on that one. I've been sleeping on the rug with a blanket. But on the positive side, I now have a wealthy grandfather who owes me presents."

"Carson," my mother says, but Turk laughs.

"He's right, you know. I'm a single guy in my seventies with money and no one to spend it on. Until now, that is. Let's go shopping in the morning."

"That meeting," my dad says softly.

"Of course," Turk says. He looks at all of us and says, "Your father has asked me to take him to an AA meeting. Aisha, would you take a look online and find one tomorrow morning?"

She nods, and the room seems to soften. I close my eyes and it's almost like I can feel my grandfather's spirit expand and sigh and relax. And I know that whether or not that's really happening, wherever my grandfather is or isn't, he's happy about this.

# 40

THE NEXT MORNING, I jump out of bed as soon as I'm awake, kiss the still-sleeping Aisha on the forehead, and speed upstairs. It feels like Christmas morning to me. Like there are presents under the tree.

Turk is snoring on the living room couch, and even though I don't hear any other creatures stirring, I go into my dad's room. He's sleeping. I stand and watch, and then I find myself looking for glasses and bottles, which is kind of terrible. I know he's going to a meeting today, but part of me is worried that the conversation with Turk was too much for him, and he must have snuck a drink.

"What are you doing?" he groans when he opens his eyes and sees me on all fours, peering under his bed.

"Nothing," I say, standing up. "Sorry."

"I guess I can't blame you," he says. "But no. No booze. I promise."

I sit on his bed next to him. The sheets are a bit sweaty, and he feels warm.

He yawns audibly. "Everything okay?"

"Everything's fine. I just . . ."

My brain and my heart are full. It feels like I could open my mouth and everything I ever held in there could come out, jokes or yells or tears or who knows what. I don't know what's first and what's last, and I'm tired of trying to control it.

"I miss you," I blurt. "Goddamn . . . Not like a week's worth. Freakin' . . . Like years' worth. Can I just sit here with you for a bit? We don't have to talk. I just want to be with you."

A smile pours over his face. "Sure, kiddo. Yeah. That'd be all right."

I smile back, then I put his hand in mine and I squeeze. I try to squeeze life into it.

"I told you I'd come back," I say.

"Yup."

"It was a long trip," I say. I'm fishing for a compliment, so I stop.

"Thanks," he says. "If I didn't say that yet. Thanks."

"It was nothing."

"Yeah." He tickles my palm with his fingers. "Sounds like a whole lot of nothing."

I want to ask him everything at once. I want to know how he's feeling, and what's going through his mind. But he's staring off into the distance, and sometimes it's okay to not say anything. No jokes, just being together in the silence.

He finally says, "Thanks for not listening to me and doing what you did. You're a good son."

I look at him. His eyes are young like a child's, and they're weary like an old man's, and then he smiles, and his teeth are yellowed in places. I don't know if he'll make it to fall, and that's not something I can deal with. He has to be okay. He just has to. You can't come back into someone's life and then die. It's just not right.

"You're a . . . dad," I say, leaving the "good" part out.

He laughs. It's good to have someone who shares your blood, who gets your jokes and you don't have to explain. I've missed that in my life. And now, at least for this moment, I don't have to.

After breakfast, Aisha asks me if I'll take a ride with her. I know where we're going. She sits rigid as she drives us up Rimrock Road about a mile and then turns north, up toward the actual rim.

"Here goes everything," she says.

The house she's lived in all through high school is tall, thin, and built up into the rocks. It's elevated a good twenty feet, and we have to climb some stone steps to get to the entrance. There are huge floor-to-ceiling windows on the first and second floors. We stand at the top of the steps and look up at it. The house looms over us, judgmental and stern. I feel really small standing there, and Aisha's fear radiates off her skin as she tries to catch her breath.

Finally we march up to the bright-red front door.

Her mom answers. She's a smallish, dark-skinned woman with Aisha's cheekbones, and she wraps her arms around Aisha and squeezes with all her might. Aisha stands there, arms at her sides, and it's like the air around us swirls with unsaid stuff.

"This is my friend, Carson," Aisha says, pulling away, and her mother eyes me. "He's been putting me up."

Her mother gulps. "Thank you," she whispers to me.

"Who is it?" a loud voice booms from above us.

Aisha's mother jumps a bit. "No one."

"Mommy!" It's the youngest I've ever heard Aisha sound.

Her mom shakes her head. She puts her finger on Aisha's lips, and she steps outside and closes the door behind her. "He's not ready. You know how he is," she says.

"Well, he needs to get over himself. Or else you're not gonna be seeing me again."

"You have to be patient with him. You know your daddy."

"But —"

Her mother raises a finger, telling us to wait. She scurries inside and returns with a slip of paper, which she hands to Aisha. "I got a second cell. He doesn't know about this number. You stay in touch with me, hear?"

"Mommy, you gotta —"

"He's on a rampage," she says. "Football stuff. This is not the right time."

And her mother is closing the door on us.

Aisha screams, "Dad!"

Nothing.

"Dad! Get down here, Dad." Her voice echoes in the canyon beneath the Rim. I hear it reverberate off the rock.

More nothing.

"I know you can hear me. You have to come down. You have to stop this. You don't come down and that's it. Hear me? . . . You're gonna lose me. Forever. Dad?"

We stand in front of the door for a bit. Then we sit down on the steps, and Aisha puts her head in her hands, and she cries. I hug her and she cries some more, and then I cry too, because Aisha deserves to be celebrated by her dad. She doesn't deserve to lose her father.

No one deserves that.

When the tears subside, we stand up, and Aisha stares at the door like she's trying to memorize it, like she's trying to memorialize the moment. I let her do her thing, and then she clasps my hand and we walk back down the stairs in silence.

When we get down to the bottom, she glances back at the house. We both look up, and there, standing against the floor-to-ceiling window on the second floor, is a huge, bald black man with his large arms crossed against his chest.

Aisha raises her hand to him.

He doesn't move. I feel my heart crack.

Then he slowly uncrosses his arms, and he raises a hand back to her and places it against the glass window, and Aisha makes a noise I've never heard before, like a squeaky bleat, and she bounds up the stairs. Her dad disappears from the window. From a distance, I watch as the door opens, and he grabs her in his arms and lifts and hugs her, and he swings her around.

I can't hear the words. Standing there, I realize that I may never get to know what the words are. I'm the sidekick, and this is her moment. They talk for a bit, and Aisha's dad crosses his huge arms again and Aisha motions wildly with hers while she says whatever she says. Then she leans in and listens to him as he says whatever.

She rises onto her tiptoes to kiss his cheek, and he puts his face in his hands and his body begins to convulse. He turns away from her, shaking, and Aisha watches, her hands on her hips.

He turns back and gently kisses her on the cheek, then he hides his face again and walks inside. Aisha is left standing alone, in front of the red door.

Just as I'm deciding to go to her, she comes walking down the stairs. I see her eyes are wet and glassy. I give her a big hug, and then we get in the car and drive off.

"Well, I suppose it's better to know" is all she says.

---

Aisha takes a grief nap when we get back, and I tell my mom what happened. She listens with her hands holding her head like a vice, like she's trying to keep her skull from exploding.

"Where will Aisha stay when we go back to New York?" my mother asks.

I shake my head. I can't even think about that. If we go back, does that mean Dad is dead? Could he come with us? Too many variables, too many things I don't want to imagine.

"Is she done with high school?"

"Just graduated. Was going to Rocky Mountain College here, but her dad withdrew her."

"Maybe I can chat with her about her options," she says, and I stand up and kiss my mom on the cheek.

"Thank you," I say.

---

Dad and Turk return after going to two AA meetings back-to-back, and Dad looks glassy-eyed and wasted. I notice his legs as he sits on the couch. They are so skinny. It makes me think of my grandfather, and how thin and frail he probably was at the end of his life.

"I don't think this is going to work for me," he says.

"You don't need to think," Turk tells him. He's sitting on the other couch. I'm in the doorway, just listening. "Not right now. Just go in with an open mind and listen."

"It won't work. Not if we get to the point where I have to pray."

"God wants you to be quiet."

Dad squeezes his eyes shut. "Did you just tell me to shut up? Did you just tell me *God* wants me to shut up?"

"No," Turk says. "Be quiet. There's a difference."

---

That night we have dinner as a family. Mom grills chicken breasts and Turk helps out in the kitchen, boiling corn on the cob and slicing tomatoes for everyone.

Mom sits next to Dad at the table and cuts up his food for him. The look in his eyes as he watches her care for him tells me he still loves her completely. And when I see how tender she is as she tucks a napkin into the lapel of his shirt, I see that she loves him too.

"Delicious," my dad says.

"Thanks," says my mother. "I'm glad you like it."

"So when we head back to New York, where are Aisha and Dad going to stay?" I say, half kidding and half not kidding at all. I expect my mom to stare daggers at me for saying this, because obviously we don't have the room. Unless Aisha sleeps with me and Dad sleeps with her. . . . Well, come to think of it.

"We'll see," Mom says.

"For the record," I note, "that's not a no."

"Let's be here now," she says, and I don't snort but I want to.

I savor the tart of the tomato against the roof of my mouth. "Can we get a dog when we go back to New York?"

"I would say that's down the list of priorities quite a ways," she says.

"Ours is a family that could use a dog. That would help."

As Dad talks a bit about the drunks at the meeting and the things they said, and Turk keeps shaking his head and saying, "Anonymity, Matthew, anonymity," I think about how amazing it is that we're having dinner together as a family. Before Aisha arrived, Dad ate in his room, and Mom and I were like two ships passing in the night. Even after, we were this weird, fractured household. How did this happen?

I love it. I love sharing food with all these crazy-ass, totally imperfect people like me.

My mom stabs another piece of corn and puts it on my dad's plate. "How are you doing?" she asks Aisha.

Aisha says, "Scrambled."

I reach over and squeeze her arm. "Scrambled how?" I ask.

"I'm sad, but also I'm done," she says. "Like truly done with them. And I'm done letting them own God. Nobody gets to use God as a weapon against me anymore. I just fucking reject that stuff. Nobody owns my God."

I know my mom wants to say, "Language," but she doesn't. Turk smiles. "Good. Good for you."

"You should trademark God," my dad says.

Mom exhales. "I love you, Matthew. I do. But shut up, please. Really."

My dad smiles and zips his lips closed.

Apple, meet tree, I guess. Because the sad truth is that the trademark comment came into my head too. So I zip my lips shut too, and my dad laughs.

Aisha says, "I think that's the worst thing you can do to a person. Make them believe that whatever you think about them, that's what God thinks too."

That makes me remember Pastor Logan, because the one thing that has not happened today is the thing I most want to see. I want to know what in the world he was thinking, keeping what he knew a secret from my dad for so long, all while continuing to pretend to be this close, caring friend of the family.

"The pastor," I say to Turk. "Let's ambush him. I'll go with you. Go over there and just watch his eyes pop out of his skull when he sees you. I want him to burn."

Turk shakes his head. "I get it, but no. I don't think so."

I'm shocked. Outspoken religious rebel Turk? He's not going to confront the pastor? I look over at Aisha for support, and she seems game.

Turk takes a drink of water. "Explain this to me. How did you find me? How did all this get started?"

I describe going over to ask the pastor a few questions, and Aisha seeing one of Grandma's boxes. I tell him what it took to get the box, and how Pastor Logan came so close to catching me in his attic that he nearly sat on my head. My mom looks like she's going to have a heart attack. My dad laughs.

"So do you want the twelve-step reaction to all this?" Turk asks.

This shuts my dad's laughing up, and I shake my head. "No thank you, please," I say, and I cut off a piece of chicken breast and stuff it in my mouth with my fingers.

When no one else says anything, I relent. "Fine, go ahead," I say.

"We talk about cleaning up our own side of the street. We ask the question, 'What's my part in this?' I cannot change someone else. It isn't my job, actually, to tell the pastor what he did wrong. I'm happiest if I do the best I can do, and leave the rest to God."

I stick my finger down my throat dramatically and look at Aisha.

She isn't laughing. "That's like me and my dad," she says. "I can't make him do the right thing. I just have to take care of me."

"You got it, dear," Turk says, putting his arm around her. "That's it exactly."

Aisha gives me a gloating look and sticks her tongue out at me.

"Teacher's pet," I say. "So I'm supposed to just let God punish him, as if God sits around punishing people for their ways?"

Turk shakes his head. "What business is it of yours whether he's punished?"

"Well, he should be."

"So you're God now?"

I shrug. "I'd be a good one."

"No doubt," Turk says. "But maybe for now, you can figure that the pastor is punishing himself. You don't think he feels a little bit guilty about his role in all this?"

I think about it. The pastor has been taking care of my dad for years. Of course there must be some guilt in there. I'd never thought about that before.

So after dinner, I go over to the pastor's by myself.

He answers the door in his red-and-white striped pajamas. "Carson," he says.

"I'm just here to say sorry for stealing that box."

He sucks in his lips. "I had a feeling you might be responsible for that."

"It was wrong of me to steal it, and I'm sorry. But the stuff in it belongs to my family, so we're going to keep it."

He lowers his gaze to the ground. "Do you know?"

I nod. "My granddad's lover is next door." I want the word *lover* to scald him.

"I've prayed about this," he says. "I've prayed and prayed."

I have so many things I want to yell. The rage is heating my chest from the inside. But Turk said not to. So I don't.

"I promised your grandmother. It was her dying wish. She did not want your father to have to deal with who his father was."

It's like an apology without the apology. Instead of just saying sorry, which I would actually like to hear, all I'm getting is a rationalization.

So I put my trembling hand up. "Nope. Not interested. None of my business."

I walk away with the pastor still standing there at the open door.

# 41

WHEN I WAKE up in the morning, I find my nose being tickled by a bunch of rubbery strands. I sit up, and Aisha is standing there, a proud look on her face.

"Behold, the new, improved, softer Porcupine of Truth!"

I look down. Aisha has replaced the broom bristles with rubber bands that appear to have been cut in half.

I shake my head. "And you did this because —"

"Hey. Porcupine two point oh is a great improvement. Far fewer God-related injuries. Puncture wounds and the like."

"I do prefer the softer version," I admit, picking her up and turning her over and over in my hands. "I mean, who likes being attacked by a truth porcupine, after all?"

We take her upstairs to show Turk, who is breakfasting and thrilled with the change, since he had been one of the first to mention his discomfort with our bristly deity, on the plane.

"I like a God that is more approachable. Less prickly," he says.

"True dat," Aisha says.

He picks it up and admires her handiwork. "Finally, the rubber meets the God," he says, and we look at him funny. "It was supposed to be a play on 'the rubber meets the road.' Sorry."

"My grandpa would have had a better one," I say, and Turk nods.

---

The Billings Zoo has some animals. Not like a ton, but some.

It also has some damn beautiful paths to walk down, and probably the biggest change, when I go back for the second time, exactly two weeks after the first, is that I notice this.

That, and I have my family around me.

Some of my family can't be here. My dad, because it would just be too much for him. My mom, because she'd rather be with my dad. But Aisha and Turk are definitely my family now, and I certainly don't feel close to alone anymore.

"You know how the sika deer got their name?" I say.

"I'm truly afraid to ask," Turk replies.

Aisha hijacks it. "It was this one deer. A doe. Got totally tired of being around only other deer. Where were the walruses? The goats? She whined and whined until the other deer shunned her, and then she started her own breed: 'sick-a deer.'"

Turk puts his arm around her. "Are you sure you don't have a little Smith blood in you?"

"If only," Aisha says, and she half rolls her eyes at me to show me she's basically kidding, that my people aren't so great either.

I elbow her in the ribs. "Hey. Anytime you want to decide that you're straight and take my name, you know where to find me."

Sometimes we make up stories about the animals as we walk, and sometimes we just look at them. I hate that they're locked up; I really do. But I am also really glad I get to look at animals, because they make me think about what it means to be an animal. I am one. Sometimes I'm all up in my head, which is a very human place to be. Other times, I'm ruled by my body, and that's okay too, I guess. I stare at the Siberian tiger and think about how powerful he is, and also how powerful I am. I never knew. I always thought I had zero power in this world. But look where I am, and who I'm with. I have to have at least a little power to change things if I got here with these awesome people.

It's not like my life is perfect. I mean, my dad. That's not perfect, obviously. Mom still talks like I'm her patient about 50 percent of the time. This morning she told me that it was important to feel my grief about my dad even now, that there's grief even now. She's right, but you know? I'd really rather have a hug. The difference is, this time I said that, and she looked a little annoyed, but she did give me a hug. Progress.

Our path diverges, with one sign pointing toward the bighorn sheep to the right and another toward the Canada lynx to the left. We follow Aisha to the left.

"It's hard with my dad, because I'm just getting to know him, and what if he dies?" I say. "I don't know if anyone can quite understand what that's like."

Turk stops walking. I turn around and realize that of course he knows what that feels like.

"I'm sorry," I say.

"It's okay," he says. "Your grandfather was an idiot sometimes too."

We walk in silence some more. I think about my grandfather. Who might have been an idiot, but Turk loved him anyway. So did my dad. So did my grandmother. That makes me feel happy and relieved, because apparently I have idiot tendencies too. It's a Smith thing, I guess. And it's okay. More and more these days, I'm realizing that I might be crazy, but I'm loved too. I don't think I ever really knew that before, but I do now.

---

We stop for ice cream at this outdoor stand on Broadwater Avenue that Aisha recommends. I get a chocolate peanut butter cone that starts dripping immediately.

"So when should I break it to my mother that I'm flying back to San Francisco with you?" I say to Aisha between frantic Gomer-like licks. "That you and I will drive back?"

Aisha looks at Turk. Turk looks at Aisha. My stomach drops below my shoes.

"So here's the deal," Aisha says. "Can I tell him?"

Turk nods.

"So I'm actually going to stay in San Francisco," she says.

"You are?"

She smiles, a beautiful, warm, happy smile. "I mean, I have no place to live here. And you're going to go back to New York at some point."

"But maybe you can come. With me. With us," I say. "My mom said —"

She shakes her head. "This makes more sense. I can take care of Turk, and then maybe enroll in community college in the fall. Next year, if my grades are good, who knows?"

I feel like my body is going to cave into itself. I don't want to feel these feelings.

"No, no," Aisha says, seeing my expression. "It's a good thing,

Carson. We're family now. Don't you get it? I'm staying with your grandfather. We already told your folks. Your mom agrees. You can come visit any time you want. Turk will pay. And when you're done with high school, if you wanna, you can move to San Francisco too. But for now, you have to be with your dad and your mom. Because you have a dad and a mom. Understand?"

I nod slowly. What two seconds ago felt like a kick in the gut is beginning to feel different. Like I can see how Aisha's life will unfold, and it's better, so much better than it was.

"Not to mention I could use the help," Turk says. "My days of grocery shopping need to be over. If Aisha doesn't show up, I'm about six months from a nursing home. Seriously."

I simply can't speak, because I'm so overcome with the emotion of all that's happened in less than three weeks. Aisha's life. Totally changed. My life. Totally changed. My parents. Turk. All the lives impacted, and maybe it's not perfect. Maybe my dad will die soon. Maybe my mom is not the perfect mom. But despite all that, there's change. Surprising, messy, wonderful change.

"I'll call you every day," Aisha says. "This isn't good-bye, Carson. I mean, it will be, in a few days. But you will never be without me. I'm gonna be there on your phone and on your Skype 'til you're sick of my ass."

"Never," I say. It's ironic. I could not have been closer to people physically than I was in New York. Sometimes on the train, you're pushed up against them. And yet I never really felt connected to people until I came West, where there are so many fewer people to connect with.

I guess in some ways, my grandfather and I took the same trip.

Neither of us felt connected at the start, and by the end, we did. To me, that's a huge thing. Because now that my heart is full, I just want my heart to stay full always. Even if it means losing my dad, I'd rather have him in my heart and then miss him than not ever have him in my heart.

Turk has to run to the bathroom. As we sit there, licking our cones, I try to imagine Billings without Aisha. It's impossible.

"I'm gonna miss the shit out of you," I say.

Aisha holds her cone away from her, then leans over and hugs me tight with her other arm. I bury my face in her neck, making sure not to douse her with my own cone.

"I'm gonna miss the shit out of you too," she says.

I keep on hugging her for what feels like a long time, and what's funny is that it doesn't feel like a long time, really. It feels just about right. A long, right hug.

"I've never had a friend like you," I say, finally pulling back.

"Black?" she says, raising an eyebrow, and I laugh.

"Exactly. That's exactly what I meant."

She smiles that Aisha smile, the one where her whole face gets involved. "I've never had a friend like you either. And we're family now."

"Yeah. We're family."

"In fact," she says, rubbing her chin, "now that I'm kind of like your grandfather's husband's sort of daughter, I guess I'm like, I don't know, your mom."

I crack up, and I feel so much joy when she laughs too. Seeing Aisha laugh is like seeing something you only get to see a couple of times in your life. A waterfall or a meteor shower. Except you get to see it all the time if you're lucky enough to be with her.

"I'm calling you Mommy from now on," I say.

"Awesome. Imma hold you to that."

---

That night, lying on a brand-new air mattress (thanks, Grandpa Turk!), I stare up at the ceiling that I cannot see and think about things.

I think about God. Is there a God? I prayed for help when we were sleeping in the park in Reno, and help came, in the form of an idea to do improv. But who's to say I wouldn't have gotten that idea without praying?

But is it possible that all this just happened randomly in the last few weeks, that I randomly met this girl, and we randomly came across this stuff, and we randomly set out on a quest, and by doing so, all our lives were forever changed?

I really don't know. I don't know what to think about God. Part of me wants to believe. Part of me has to believe. Part of me cannot believe.

Maybe that's God, right there. The thing that lets us believe three different things all at once, three ideas in conflict, and yet it feels rational and normal and okay. Maybe that's not God. Maybe that's just my brain.

I remember what the meditation lady said in Wyoming. How prayer is like talking to God, and meditation is like listening.

So I listen. I listen for the thoughts-tripping-over-thoughts that is and always has been me. My brain that never shuts up.

And for once, that noise in my head is gone. I am lying in a basement in Billings, Montana, with my best friend asleep near me. My parents upstairs. My new grandfather too. I can hear my thoughts. They have slowed not to a crawl, but to a mere jog, and they aren't tripping all over each other.

For once, I am quiet. Actually quiet. Which is different than not saying anything.

I remember something Aisha said to me on our never-ending drive across Utah. She said that during meditation, the leader said that when she started to pray for the first time, she was told that the basic prayer is one word: *Thanks.*

So I close my eyes and I say it. Not out loud, because I don't want to get into a whole big thing about it. Just in my head. I'm not sure who I'm saying it to. I'm not 100 percent sure it matters.

*Thanks,* I say. *Thanks.*

# Author's Note

SOME OF THE material used in Russ's journals, most notably the puns found on pages 94–95 and 166, come courtesy of my father, Bob Konigsberg, who has been a professional punster for more than seventy years. His version of "Three Sightless Rodents" was sung to me as a child, and he is not sure if he made it up as a child, or if he heard it elsewhere. It is my great joy that these puns will be forever commemorated in this novel. Love you, Dad.

# Acknowledgments

AS ALWAYS, I want to thank first and foremost my husband, Chuck Cahoy, who puts up with my frequent bouts of writer's brain. I am the luckiest. Thanks also to my family: my mother, Shelley Doctors; my father, Bob Konigsberg; my sister, Pam Yoss; and my brother, Dan Konigsberg. You love me as I am, and I love you back as you are. To my editor, Cheryl Klein, whose reserved Midwestern sense matches perfectly with my New York "I never met an emotion I didn't need to express" sensibility. This book would be in tatters without you. To Arthur Levine, for his support, kindness, and wisdom; the amazing team at Scholastic, especially Sheila Marie Everett, Antonio Gonzalez, Lizette Serrano, Bess Braswell, Annette Hughes, Emily Heddleson, and Tracy van Straaten. You are a dream team and I deeply appreciate your hard work and support. To my agent, Linda Epstein, who believed in me when I was faltering in that belief; Jennifer DiChiara, whose expertise is priceless to me; my dear friend

Debbie Schenk, who played Aisha to my Carson on an epic research road trip; Richard Fitzgerald and Jeff Haliczer, my couchsurfing hosts, who put us up and helped me understand what it means to surf couches; Michael Abracham, my friend and San Francisco connection; the Piper Center for Creative Writing at Arizona State University; the writer friends who have been so helpful during this process, especially Brent Hartinger, Lisa McMann, Kriste Peoples, Lou Ceci, and Joey Avalos. Thank you all for your honest feedback. To early readers of *Porcupine* who gave me so much to think about, especially Kameron Martinez, Annika Browne, Alexis Redden, Adam Huss, Brandi Stewart, Evan Walsh, Emily Lesnick, Cathy Bonnell, and Alex Corey. You guys all changed this book for the better. To the authors/friends who amaze me with their words and inspire me to be a better writer, David Levithan, Alex London, Aaron Hartzler, A. S. King, Laurie Halse Anderson, Benjamin Alire Saenz, Jewell Parker-Rhodes, Tom Leveen, Andrew Smith, Daphne Benedis-Grab, Elizabeth Eulberg, and Martin Wilson, among others; Jeff Baranczyk for his hipster café suggestion; Eric Gaspar for his car repair expertise; and never least, to my fans, young and old, who interact with these characters I create and bring them to life. I love you and I appreciate you. Without you, these books would not exist.